Getting Over Mr Right

Also by Chrissie Manby

Flatmates
Second Prize
Deep Heat
Lizzie Jordan's Secret Life
Running Away From Richard
Getting Personal
Seven Sunny Days
Girl Meets Ape
Ready Or Not?
The Matchbreaker
Marrying for Money
Spa Wars
Crazy in Love

Chrissie Manby

Getting Over Mr Right

HODDER &
STOUGHTON

First published in Great Britain in 2010 by Hodder & Stoughton
An Hachette UK company

1

A CIP catalogue record for this title is available from the British Library

Hardback ISBN 978 0 340 99277 7
Trade paperback ISBN 978 0 340 99278 4

Typeset in Sabon MT by Palimpsest Book Production Limited,
Grangemouth, Stirlingshire

Printed and bound by Clays Ltd, St Ives plc

Hodder & Stoughton policy is to use papers that are natural, renewable
and recyclable products and made from wood grown in sustainable forests.
The logging and manufacturing processes are expected to conform to
the environmental regulations of the country of origin.

Hodder & Stoughton Ltd
338 Euston Road
London NW1 3BH

www.hodder.co.uk

To Mark Carroll

Prologue

It goes without saying that there is no nice way to be dumped, but there are definitely some ways that cause less toe-curling anguish than others. A face-to-face conversation or a phone call if you're dating long-distance seem to be the best of a bad bunch. A handwritten letter would show some respect, but since eighties pop star and very unlikely heart-throb Phil Collins dumped his first wife by fax, standards of ending etiquette have been dropping dramatically. From Phil's fax to the horror of email to Britney dumping K-Fed by SMS. Oh, how I wish my ex had had the old-fashioned decency to dump me by text message! You see, I, Ashleigh Prince, found out that I had been dumped via *Facebook*.

I

My love life was and always had been a disaster. It started badly and it went downhill from there.

I had my first kiss aged eight, during a game of 'kiss chase' in my primary-school playground. When it was my turn to do the chasing, I knew exactly which hapless lad I was going for and poor Justin Ashford didn't stand a chance. When someone shouted, 'Go,' Justin was in the middle of tying a shoelace (he was eleven before he cracked bows), but I showed no mercy. While he was still on the ground, I pounced on him like a vampire bat on a squirrel and my passionate lips squashed the words 'not fair' right back into his gorgeous pouting mouth. Later that day he pinned me against a wall by the school gym and stuck chewing gum in my hair. I had to have both my pigtails cut off.

The next three years flew by in a haze of similarly rebuffed advances and Chinese burns. When I was nine, Justin Ashford sent me a Valentine's card with the charming message 'Drop dead' written rather neatly inside. For my eleventh birthday he gave me three de-winged bluebottles in a matchbox. You have to admit that shows imagination, but it's not exactly Tiffany . . . Things didn't pick up when I went to secondary school. It was an all-girls school and the only opportunity for mixing with the opposite sex during term-time came via doing handstands at the far edge of the playing field to incite the local flasher.

At the age of fourteen I did manage to get my second

3

kiss from a boy called Malcolm who lived at the top of my street, and that sort of blossomed into my first 'relation-ship'. Certainly, we spent every moment we could together. But while our parents assumed we were up to no good and I received lectures on the perils of teenage motherhood at least twice a week, our romance was much more chaste than that. It was largely based on a mutual appreciation of horror comics. And when I say 'mutual appreciation', what I actu-ally mean is that Malcolm was obsessed with horror comics and I pretended to be interested so that I could tell Lucy Jones, the hardest girl in my class, that I had a boyfriend and therefore she had no need to scratch 'lezzer' on the lid of my brand-new metal pencil case.

Alas, Malcolm and I parted ways as soon as hormones reared their ugly heads. One Saturday afternoon, when my parents were at Sainsbury's and we had the house to ourselves, I asked him if he'd like to take my virginity. We were both seventeen, after all. He went quite pale and said, 'No.' He wouldn't. And he didn't. Our romance had reached its end.

Instead I lost the virginity that seemed to weigh so heavily to the first chap I dated at uni. His name was Steve. He was a chemistry student. We shared almost three years of jacket potatoes and the missionary position. Steve was a big fan of Depeche Mode. I still can't hear 'Just Can't Get Enough' without remembering those lost afternoons when Steve ground away like the Duracell bunny and I worried he might be wearing a hole in the condom.

My relationship with Steve was fairly unremarkable, but it was the first real indication of the more serious trouble I would have with love later in my life. Looking back, I can't honestly say I even liked him that much. Steve had the looks of Shrek without the personality, and the lack of feeling was mutual. When he broke up with me, though, I dedicated my entire life to getting back together. I spent hours and hours, when I should have been studying for my finals, writing poems and letters in an attempt to convince him that ours was a star-crossed love. Steve was not moved and I had to resit my final exams, while he got a first, a top-class consulting job and married a model less than a year after graduating. 'Sorted' was one of Steve's favourite words. When it came to love and relationships, 'hopeless' was rapidly becoming mine.

Degree belatedly in hand, I set course for London and a shared house with a bunch of the uni friends who had been so patient during the Steve years. While they worked diligently on finding a place for themselves in the world of work, I was like a girl straight out of Jane Austen, hell-bent on finding my place as somebody's missus. My first five years in London were a blur of bad dates and brief, nasty relationships, but somehow I kept my sense of optimism. After each frog I kissed that turned out to be a toad, I managed to convince myself that the very next one would be the prince. Or the next. Or the next. Or the next.

My optimism remained high as my friends started to pair off in a serious way. The year I turned twenty-six was the summer of eight weddings. I was almost bankrupted by the hen-weekends and the extravagant wedding lists at Peter Jones, but I was grateful and excited to attend each and every one of those ceremonies because I'd read in the *Evening Standard* that twenty-seven per cent of people meet their future spouse at a wedding reception. Eight weddings! Surely I had to get lucky that year.

I didn't, needless to say. At one wedding I actually found myself on the children's table. But my dance card was rarely blank. Five out of seven nights I would be on a date of some description. I believed in making an effort – turning every stone – so I went out with anyone who asked me, from the brother of a girl I'd sat next to in a lecture on Italian futurism to the chap who worked at the dry-cleaner's next to the Tube station. (After two dates at Pizza Hut he refused to pick up the phone and I had to take my cleaning elsewhere.)

If you were making a movie montage of years six to eight in London, you would definitely have to include the man who brought his own sandwiches to our lunch date in a pub garden (and didn't offer to share), and the man who asked me to wear his ex-girlfriend's T-shirt while we were in bed together, since he could only be aroused by her smell, and the man who came with me to a former workmate's party at the Pitcher and Piano and went home with the birthday girl while I sobbed into my shandy. Then there was the corporate lawyer who told me he couldn't wait to settle down and start a family. The only problem with him was that he already had a wife and three children in Dulwich. After him came the body-building champion who decided he was in love with his best friend (another champion body builder. Male). And then there was the guy who stood me up after I had dropped everything (including the best part of a grand) to meet him for dinner. In New York.

Yep, stick me in the corner of any party in any town and I would seek out and start falling for the biggest loser in the room within seconds. I attracted jerks like iron filings to a magnet. I got through pigs faster than swine flu.

'I just don't understand why you keep picking such awful men!' my mother exclaimed in despair when I called her from a phone box in Manhattan at the bitter end of my brief Ny-Lon romance.

Back then I didn't understand it either. It wasn't as though I was always going for the same type. I dated actuaries and actors, bakers and bankers. I dated Christian Scientists and cruise-liner captains. There were no obvious similarities in the worlds they inhabited or in the way that they looked. But in the way things turned out? That was a different story. No matter how promisingly things started, after two to three months I was planning a wedding and they were planning a speedy escape. Scratch any one of my princely ex-boyfriends and you would find an amphibian beneath.

So you probably won't be surprised to hear that after the Manhattan incident, in which I blew three days' holiday allowance and nearly a month's wages on a flight to the mini-break that became a mini-break-up, my confidence suffered a bit of a knock.

'That's it,' I said to my best friend, Becky. 'I am giving up on men.'

'I'll believe it when I see it,' Becky said.

'Believe it, Becks. This time I'm serious.'

The following day I went to a thirtieth birthday party at a flat over a nail bar in Balham and met my Mr Right.

2

It had to be fate. I had finally, after almost two decades spent dating for Great Britain, announced I was giving up on my man hunt. At long last, I had decided to try taking the one piece of advice I always found so hard to swallow: 'Love will only come when you're not looking for it.'

How many times had I heard that irritating maxim (usually from someone who had been every bit as desperate to pair up as me six months earlier)? And how many times had I protested that it simply wasn't true? Well, I had announced that I was no longer looking for love and just twenty-four hours later I found myself in the kitchen at that thirtieth birthday party, discussing the merits of the latest government budget with the most attractive man I had ever seen in my life!

OK, so I didn't actually find him all that attractive at first . . .

Romantic that I was, I had always imagined that when love came to me – when it was real, proper, true love – I would know the second I laid eyes on him. I had experienced so many thunderbolts that turned out to herald nothing but emotional drizzle that, surely, when real love walked into my life, the entire earth would shake with the magnitude of the moment. The heavens would open. Long-dead volcanoes would erupt. My personal choir of angels would stop filing their nails and start singing the 'Hallelujah' chorus with a guest solo from Elvis. But it wasn't like that at all.

When Michael – Michael Parker, the man who would turn my world upside down – walked into the kitchen at that party in Balham, he barely registered on my radar. I was busy looking for a clean glass among the jumble of plastic cups and dirty mugs on the draining board. To attract my attention, Michael swilled out the wine glass he had been drinking from and handed it to me.

'It's safe,' he said. 'I don't have anything contagious.'

(That was his first lie.)

I thanked him for the glass and helped myself to some wine from the bottle I had brought with me. Though it was only nine in the evening, Helen's birthday party was already shaping up to be the kind of affair where you couldn't be certain that the yellowish liquid in the bottle on the counter really was chardonnay. Glass refilled, I was planning to head back into the sitting room, where Becky and her brand-new boyfriend, Henry, had bagged a sofa, but just as I was about to sashay out of the kitchen and out of trouble, Michael attempted to strike up a conversation.

'How do you know Helen?' he asked. Not a very original opening gambit, but better than 'I bet you look good with no clothes on', which was how the Ny-Lon disaster had started.

'Helen and I were at uni together,' I explained.

'Oh. That's great. Durham, wasn't it?'

I nodded.

'We work in the same office,' said Michael. 'Me and Helen.'

Which must mean he's an accountant, I said to myself, switching off.

'Which means I'm an accountant,' he said. 'But we're not all boring!'

He took the words right out of my head.

'I don't think accountants are boring,' I lied.

At that moment Helen, the birthday girl, lurched into the kitchen. She was certainly doing her best to show her guests that accountants really can be fun. Outrageous, wacky, 'dial 999!' amounts of fun. She was wearing a pair of red crotch-less knickers to prove it.

Thank goodness she was wearing them *over* her jeans.

'Aren't these just ker-razy?' she said, pinging her knicker elastic. 'They're a present from Kevin. He said that now I'm officially over the hill I'm going to need all the help I can get to get the guys going!'

I made a mental note *not* to ask if I could be introduced to Kevin. He sounded a perfect charmer.

'Kevin is one of our workmates,' Michael explained. 'He's always playing practical jokes.'

'What a lot of fun it must be to work in your office,' I said.

'Oh, I see you've met Michael,' said Helen, throwing her arm round his shoulders. 'He's such a great guy.' She tickled him under the chin and he squirmed playfully. 'Really sexy,' she added in a stage whisper to me.

Sexy? Was she joking? I took in the way Michael was dressed that night. He was at least two inches shorter than me in my heels and was wearing the kind of clothes more commonly seen on a member of a contemporary-mime group. His faded black turtleneck sweater emphasised the soft contours of his torso, and the high waistband of his black jeans was kidding no one about the real length of his legs. I glanced down at his feet. Tasselled loafers. Brown. I was reminded of my first boyfriend, Malcolm, who had to wear his school shoes at the weekend. Michael looked about as sexy as John Sergeant.

But he was also funny. And funny is my weakness. Trapped as I was by an increasing number of Helen's workmates pouring into the kitchen in search of booze, I had no choice but to get to know Michael better. Half a bottle of wine later, I was finding him very amusing indeed. Hilarious, in fact. His take on the comings and goings at his accountancy firm was as humorous as an episode of *The Office*. Before I could say, 'I'm afraid I'm on a man-break,' I found I had given him my phone number and said that I would be very happy to have dinner with him the following week. On Monday, Tuesday or Wednesday. Or Thursday, Friday, Saturday or Sunday if the other days didn't work for him. When he joked that he would rearrange the following evening's morris dancing practice just for me, I was smitten.

I was doomed.

3

So much for my man-break. And so much for playing by *The Rules*, which was something else I had promised I would do if I ever found myself in the unlikely position of going on a date again. Having broken half a dozen commandments from that terribly useful book by acting pathetically keen to see Michael once more, I continued my amateur strategy. That's right. You've guessed it. I went to bed with Michael right after our first date.

The date took place at Bertorelli in Covent Garden. It was certainly a step up from Pizza Hut with the chap from Supa Clean. The evening went beautifully. The conversation flowed. I managed not to spill anything on my dress (Karen Millen, bought in a rush that afternoon, and afterwards, though we lived on different Tube lines, Michael insisted on accompanying me home to my Clapham flat. We were having such a lovely conversation that it seemed a shame to part, so I invited him in, I made him a coffee, and he didn't leave until the following morning.

Our physical connection was a revelation. And it pretty much sealed my fate. If you had told me that someone who had the watery eyes of a basset hound in a face like a mouldy potato would kiss like you imagine Brad Pitt once kissed Angelina, I would never have believed it possible. But it was wonderful. My whole body fizzed with excitement from the moment he laid his hand on mine and my new-found peace in celibacy was short-lived indeed. At the touch of Michael's lips I crumbled like a chocaholic locked in a room containing nothing but a box of melting KitKats. I couldn't take my hands off the man. I caught his nasty cold as a result.

But I didn't care. Kissing Michael was well worth a bout of the sniffles. When I saw Becky the following day for a first-date post-mortem, she sighed and rolled her eyes in despair. She had heard it all before. The kiss. The thunderbolt. The beginning of an obsession that could only end in disaster . . . But when, between Lemsips, I described Michael to her in more detail, she couldn't help but nod approvingly. He was an accountant, just like her boyfriend; therefore she couldn't complain that he was a flaky creative type. (I had a penchant for flaky creative types.) And he wasn't devastatingly good-looking. (Becky thought his frankly average looks a plus, since it meant that he wouldn't be as arrogant as some of the better-looking guys I had loved.) Then I let her know that Michael had told me he'd had a live-in relationship that lasted five years. That, Becky decided, was the clincher. It was proof that he wasn't afraid of commitment, but it came without the complications of a starter marriage and subsequent divorce.

'Perfect. I like the sound of him,' said Becky. 'From what you've told me, I would say he's mature. He's got a proper job. He's already tried out commitment. He sounds to me like a man about to ripen and when he does . . .' She grinned.

Ripening. This was Becky's favourite theory. Men don't look for Miss Right in the way that we girls spend our time looking for the perfect man. Instead men get 'ripe'. They reach a stage in their life when all their mates are getting married or their hair starts to fall out and they decide it's time to settle down before no one decent will have them. They marry the next girl who smiles at them in passing. All we girls have to do is be in the right place at the right time to catch a ripe one before he hits the ground and starts to go rotten.

'Yep,' said Becky, nodding wisely. 'It sounds to me as though you have finally found your one.'

Could it be true? I so wanted to believe it.

When Michael texted moments later to ask if I was free on Friday night, Becky's judgement was confirmed.

'It's only Monday and he already wants to know what you're doing on Friday night. That is an excellent sign,' she said. 'Just don't screw it up.'

Well, thank God for that, I thought. After years of dating men who were about as ripe as a 'perfectly ripe' avocado from the supermarket (those ones that go from rock-hard to rotting without passing edible), I had found my ready man. My Mr Ripe.

Though once again I had thrown strategy out of the window (who needs strategy when you've found true love?), I soon noticed that Michael did everything *The Rules* girls said a serious man ought to. I was used to guys who called at the last minute to ask if I would meet them in their part of town for a quickie after the pub closed. In contrast Michael always made an effort. He called me early in the week to make plans for the weekend. He would always make sure I got home safely. He considered my likes and dislikes when choosing activities. He was unfailingly chivalrous. He didn't seem to have anything to hide.

So, naturally, I fell for him. I fell as hard as a penny from the top of the Empire State Building that cracks the pavement for miles around. And he seemed to be falling for me too. When I cooked for him (I'm a great cook. Baking cakes is my hobby), he would sigh in ecstasy at whatever I put in front of him and tell me that I would make someone a wonderful wife. And, as Becky pointed out, men never use the word 'wife' in front of someone they consider to be fling material. They would rather boil their own testicles.

'It means he's taking you seriously,' she told me sagely.

I dared to dream of the wedding I had imagined for myself since I was four years old, when I had watched Diana marry Charles in the ultimate fairytale dress on the black-and-white TV set in my grandmother's house. Never mind how that particular marriage turned out.

4

So, months passed. Became a year. And I felt as though I was finally, truly living the dream.

On the first anniversary of our meeting, Michael took me out to dinner at J Sheekey, the famous fish restaurant in Covent Garden. He ordered a bottle of champagne. Not just the house stuff either; it was vintage. Because there was more to celebrate than our twelve months of being together. That day Michael told me that he had been made a partner at Wellington Burke, the accountancy firm where he worked. This was big news, he said. Really big news. It was the career jump he had been working towards since he first learned to add and subtract. It meant much more responsibility, he explained. And more money. It meant that he could afford to upgrade his two-bedroom flat in Stockwell for something far more befitting his new status.

I was thrilled. Something more befitting his new status! I immediately imagined the tall Victorian house on the edge of Wandsworth Common where we would raise our beautiful children. I saw myself in the kitchen with professional standard fixtures and fittings making elaborate birthday cakes for the golden-haired twins.

When Michael warned me he would have to work extra hard now, I told him I would be there to make life easier for him. Michael's promotion to partner made the fact that I had recently been refused a pay-rise somewhat easier to handle. How much longer would I have to keep my crappy job anyhow, now that Michael was starting to think about our first marital home?

Except that he wasn't.

A couple of months later Michael sold his flat in Stockwell and bought a bigger flat in a chi-chi new development by the riverside in Battersea. He was thrilled with the built-in coffee machine and the integrated sound system. I stood on the balcony that would be incredibly impractical and dangerous for a toddler and bit my lip. There was nothing about the flat that said 'family home'. But I chose not to say anything. I was comforted by an article I'd read only recently, which said that men often have a final fling before settling down, and that final fling could take the shape of an unsuitable apartment with an integrated entertainment system rather than shagging someone at the office. The magazine writer's advice was to let him get on with it. Be understanding.

'It's a great flat,' I said. 'It'll be very easy to sell on.'

'Sell on?' said Michael. 'What are you talking about? I've only just moved in.'

'Yes, but eventually . . .'

'I don't think I'll ever get tired of this view,' he said, wrapping his arms round my waist.

I decided that it was best to cut short the resale conversation and help Michael 'christen' his new bedroom.

Looking back, I can see that the riverside flat was the first red flag, but I soon rationalised the significance of it away. Michael had never really had money before. It was understandable that he wanted to spend his hard-earned cash on a few of the things he had lusted after as a student and twenty-something. As time went on, however, it became increasingly difficult to ignore the fact that Michael was ticking the boxes on a very different list to mine.

A few months after the new apartment came the new car. A two-seater sports-model BMW. Red paint, soft top and definitely no room for a baby seat. He also bought a set of golf clubs and a fancy mountain bike. Then, on the advice of his new temporary secretary – an Essex blonde ten years my junior – he booked a personal-shopping session at Harvey Nics and his wardrobe went from 'geek' to 'chic' in the space of an afternoon. He even changed his hairstyle.

'Why didn't you make me get rid of those terrible jeans?' he asked me. 'I looked like Simon Cowell.'

'I thought you liked looking like that,' I said. 'And, anyway, you know I would love you whatever you wore.'

I didn't tell him that I had hated those bloody jeans but had resisted the urge to forcibly update his wardrobe because I had read in another women's-magazine article that you should never try to change a man's appearance until you had a ring on your finger. Otherwise you will just be giving him the makeover he needs to upgrade to a better girlfriend. I wanted Michael in those awful high-waisted trousers because I didn't want any other woman to notice the prince I saw beneath the horrible turtleneck sweaters and the poo-brown suede blouson. While I still had no engagement ring, his Iranian-president style suited me just fine.

'Well, it's all going to the charity shop,' said Michael as he flicked through a copy of *GQ* (to which he'd just taken out a subscription). 'I'll drop it off on my way to the gym.'

The gym?

New flat, sports car, fancy clothes and the gym. The four self-improvements of the Apocalypse.

Michael's personal growth was now in stark contrast to the lack of forward motion in our relationship. I couldn't help comparing our timeline with that of Becky and her man, Henry. Becky had met Henry just a couple of weeks before

I met Michael. Eighteen months on, she had moved into Henry's flat. I still lived a forty-minute bus-ride away from Michael. Further away, in fact, than when he had his flat in Stockwell.

On the second anniversary of their first meeting. Henry took Becky to Paris and proposed to her at the top of the Eiffel Tower. He'd had the ring made specially. A diamond solitaire on a band engraved with the words 'Forever yours'. Meanwhile, Michael took me to the Thai restaurant just along the river from his bachelor pad and spent the entire evening checking his BlackBerry for news of some import-ant assignment. So much for a celebration. It turned out he hadn't actually remembered it was our anniversary. We were only at the restaurant because he hadn't had time to fill the fridge. He looked very surprised when I pulled out my anniversary card.

'I've also made a cake,' I said. Inside the Marks & Spencer's carrier bag beneath the table was a chocolate sponge with thick butter icing.

'Ashleigh,' said Michael, 'you know I'm trying to diet.' He was determined he would have a six-pack for the summer.

'But two years . . .'

'Is it really two years?' he said.

I couldn't help but notice the expression that crossed his face, albeit briefly. That expression said 'two years' with a sense of horror rather than wonder. I would never forget it, despite the big smile that Michael plastered on right away.

'In that case I suppose I'll have a little bit of that cake you brought. Just for you.'

We missed Becky and Henry's engagement party to go to Michael's company's Christmas party, which took place in a marquee specially erected for the party season in the middle of the City. Michael, who looked his best ever in a bespoke tuxedo (oh, yes, he was buying bespoke now), swanned around that tent like master of the universe. He left me talking to some of the dullest people on earth while he schmoozed senior partners and important clients. He spent a lot of time talking to one woman in particular. She had big hair and an even bigger chest, which was barely contained by her bright-red dress. She did a lot of giggling and hair-flicking. I couldn't imagine what she found so amusing about my man.

'She can't be an accountant,' I said to Helen, my old university friend, who was about to leave Michael's firm to give birth to her first baby (with Kevin, the chap who bought her the crotchless panties for her thirtieth).

'Oh, no,' said Helen. 'You're right. She's not. She's an interior designer. She's been redoing the reception areas. I think she's from Brazil.'

When Michael came back to my side ten minutes later, I told him that I wasn't feeling too good and wanted to go home.

'Shall I get you a car on account?' he said. He didn't offer to come with me. Seeing the woman in the red dress circling menacingly, I told him that I suddenly felt better and stayed to the bitter end.

When Michael took to the dance floor for 'Dancing Queen' – a song I hate – I followed him like a shadow. I felt as though I was dancing for my life.

5

Cut to: four months after that terrible Christmas party.

It was an ordinary Wednesday morning in the office. Back then I was working for a small advertising company called Maximal Media. It sounds more exciting than it was. I bet you're thinking innovative campaigns for mobile phones and sugar-free energy drinks that go well with vodka. In reality, we had a nice line providing services for the manufacturers of such exciting products as ironing-board covers and easy-clean juicers. The sort of thing you see advertised in the back of the *Sunday Express* magazine.

I'd been with the company pretty much ever since I left university, back when I thought that advertising was a glamorous career worth pursuing. I had jumped at the chance of a temp admin job that consisted largely of fetching coffee. I worked my way up from that job to the position of account manager with responsibility for just about everything regarding the clients I was given. And over the years I had been given some corking clients. Remember those info-mercials in which an ageing soap actress demonstrates the ease of using a stair-lift? That's some of my best work. I seemed to get assigned a lot of the OAP products.

In fact that morning I should have been working on a presentation for the clients from Effortless Bathing, whose product was not, alas, a swanky swimming pool but a walk-in bath for the elderly and infirm. You know the kind of thing. It looks like an ordinary bath but it has a little door in the side so that you don't have to clamber over and risk a fall. Instead you step in, sit down, turn on the taps and die of hypothermia while you wait for it to fill. It was a very boring product, but my boss, Barry, had promised the people from the step-in-bath company all sorts of excitement and sexy innovation in their push for sales-figure glory. Tasked with turning those promises into advertising gold, I had so far spent the best part of two hours doodling hearts on my notepad.

As soon as I was sure Barry had left the office for a 'business lunch', I risked logging on to my networking accounts. Facebook first. And that was when it happened.

The first thing I noticed was that Michael's Facebook status, which he hadn't updated in months (how could he find the time now he was a partner at Wellington Burke?), was showing something new. And somewhat cryptic. It said, 'Michael Parker is making some tough decisions.'

Tough decisions about what? I wondered. I went through the possibilities. He had mentioned a few weeks earlier that he had been head-hunted by another accountancy company. Was he still thinking of leaving the firm he had been with for so many years to take another job? I thought he'd decided against it. Or perhaps he was being facetious? When he said 'tough decisions', was he talking about the decisions he had to make regarding the new carpet he wanted for his flat? The previous weekend he had got into quite a bad mood as he examined various different swatches in search of the elusive carpet that would fit in with the chic, pale ultimate-bachelor furnishing scheme he wanted and yet not show too much dirt.

I was just about to leave a message on his wall saying, 'Go for the oatmeal berber from John Lewis,' when the live news feed on my profile page refreshed itself with some very strange and unwelcome news indeed.

It said, 'Michael Parker is no longer listed as "in a relationship".'

This devastating titbit was accompanied by a graphic of a tiny red heart in two pieces.

You can imagine my reaction. I spat tea on to my keyboard. Michael Parker is no longer in a relationship? What the hell did that mean? I quickly sent him a message via the site: 'Wot's with the relationship update?' And then I sent him a text for good measure: 'Just saw your Facebook page. No longer in a relationship? Very funny. Ha ha ha.'

It had to be a slip of the mouse or, at worst, a very bad joke, but Michael responded to neither request for an explanation. I called his mobile. He didn't pick up. I put that down to the fact that since he'd been made a partner, he'd moved to an office on the other side of the building and the mobile reception was patchy there, but when I called his direct line, he didn't pick that up either.

'He's just gone into a meeting,' said Tina, his unnecessarily gorgeous assistant.

'Will you tell him to call me as soon as he gets out?'

'Of course.'

I felt a little relieved by that exchange. There was nothing in Tina's voice that suggested anything was awry. But three hours later Michael still hadn't phoned me back and I was starting to get anxious. It began to dawn on me that Michael might be serious. I ran through all the possible reasons why Michael might be in a bad mood with me. Was he still upset about the small disagreement we'd had a couple of nights before, when I'd asked him if he wanted to go halves on renting a country cottage with Becky and Henry over the August bank holiday and he said he hadn't thought that far ahead? Or maybe he was angry because I'd questioned why he was spending so much time at the gym when I loved him just the way he was: slightly soft around the edges. In retrospect, I could see it was a mistake to have used those words.

All those little things suddenly seemed like perfectly good reasons to start a passive-aggressive fight by changing your relationship status on stupid Facebook, but things were about to get worse.

The ultimate humiliation was right upon me. When I logged back into Facebook, to send Michael a message asking if he could elaborate on what I might have done wrong, I discovered that Michael's profile was no longer on my friends list. I had been *defriended*.

6

Defriended by my own boyfriend! And still Michael refused to get in touch with me. It was time to call in forensics. I needed another girl's view. I called Becky, who was a teacher, and had her pulled out of an A-level history class to talk to me.

'What's happened? Are you hurt?'

Becky had told all her friends that she could *never* talk during work hours unless something had gone *seriously* wrong. I had always respected her request, but that day . . . Well, this was serious in my opinion.

'Michael has defriended me.'

'What?'

'Becky, I think I've been dumped.'

'Ashleigh! What are you talking about? The school secretary said it was an emergency.'

'And being dumped by the love of my life isn't?'

'When did he dump you? And how come you're not sure that he did? What on earth is going on?'

I explained exactly what had happened, hoping that Becky would tell me I had over-reacted. She would read between the lines and come up with some other explanation. Of course Michael hadn't dumped me, was the answer I was hoping for. It was clear he was just messing around. Or that Facebook had been infected by a computer virus that had wiped everyone's relationship status clean. I should check my own status for a start. But Becky had no such good news for me. She dismissed out of hand my idea of a brain tumour that had altered Michael's personality and said that the simplest explanation is usually accurate. As far as she could see, the simple explanation was that I had really been dumped.

'Though it is pretty unbelievable,' she admitted. 'I've never heard of anyone over the age of fifteen being dumped by Facebook.'

'Then there's no way that's what happened. He would have told me.'

'But he has told you. He's told all his Facebook friends. Incredible. I can't believe he's been such a shit.'

'I'm going to go to his flat to find out what he's thinking,' I said.

'Do not go to Michael's flat,' said Becky.

'But I have to. I have to know what's going on!'

'But you know what's going on. The selfish, thoughtless idiot has dumped you. On Facebook. Like a total coward. Even my year sevens show more sensitivity. You've left him messages and you've sent him texts and emails asking for an explanation. The next step is up to him. He has to get in touch with you and tell you what is happening. At the very least he needs to call you and give you an apology for being so . . . so thoughtless.'

'But I can't wait that long,' I told her.

'Sweetheart, you have to. If this is going to have any kind of happy ending, you absolutely have to remind him that the way he's behaving is not nice or right at all. If and when he rings up or comes round, you have permission to give him hell. Nothing else. You must do nothing else, do you understand?'

'But . . .' I whined.

'No buts,' said Becky. 'Stay strong. If he's going to act like a child, you have to treat him like one. You have to show him that you're not to be messed around. If you don't do what he's almost certainly expecting, if you don't go round and sit on his doorstep, howling at the moon like an abandoned dog, that just might get him wondering whether he's been so clever after all.'

'Do you think so?'

'I know so. The first time Henry started bleating about being unsure whether he was ready for a relationship, I simply told him that I was *absolutely* ready and if he wasn't up to the job, I would start looking for a new boyfriend. He soon got his act together.'

'You didn't tell me.'

'I didn't need to. Henry's wobble lasted less than two hours.'

As she said that, I heard the voice she used for the children in her class at school. It was the voice that said 'no nonsense' and got exactly that.

'Now, are you feeling any better?' Becky asked. 'Do you want me to come round and sit on you to make sure that you don't do anything silly?'

'No,' I said.

'OK. Here's what you should do. Concentrate on your work for the rest of the day. Then, when you get home, make yourself a cup of tea and sit down in front of the television. Watch *The Apprentice*. Watch your DVD boxed set of *Lost* if you have to. But do not contact Michael again. Definitely *do not* go round to Michael's flat. You have to promise me that. Because this is a waiting game now and I want you to win it.'

'Thank you,' I said in a tiny voice.

'I'm sure everything will work out. Now I have to get back to my year twelves and the Reformation. A teacher's work . . .'

'Right. Thanks. I'll do what you suggested.'

But there was no chance that I would be able to get on with my own work. I had to get out of the office.

I told Ellie, my assistant, that I thought I had food poisoning. She told me I didn't look any worse than usual but agreed I should go home at once. The positive after-effects of Becky's pep talk lasted for, oh, at least three-quarters of an hour after I got back to my flat. About as long as it took me to make a cup of tea and go through my DVD collection looking for that *Lost* boxed set. Whereupon I realised that I didn't have my *Lost* boxed set because Michael did. We had once spent a whole weekend tucked up in his bed watching the series from the very beginning. Even with Michael's learned commentary, I didn't have a clue what was going on, but I had so enjoyed being under the duvet with him for a whole forty-eight hours, getting out only to accept a pizza from the delivery boy.

The memory of that weekend assailed me like a chimpanzee with a sledge-hammer. Feeling suddenly quite weak with the shock of my Facebook dismissal, I lay on my back on the sheepskin rug from Ikea and stared at the ceiling until the tears came. And come they did, wracking my body until I was a snivelling, snot-faced shadow of the girl I had been when I set out for work that morning.

What on earth was happening? I struggled into a sitting position and wiped the snot away on the back of my shirt-sleeve. Was I really dumped? How was it possible that Michael wanted to end things? Anyone seeing us together that *Lost* weekend would surely have placed money on our being together for a very long time. For ever, in fact. I remembered how Michael had smoothed my hair from my forehead and kissed the tip of my nose, telling me that I made him feel like a shy sixth-former again. He made me feel the same way. I was giddy with the kind of love you can only feel when you've never been hurt before because, somehow, being with Michael had cleaned the slate. Being with him had magically blanked out all those years of disaster and rejection.

Those feelings can't be faked, can they? I had felt sure that when he told me that he loved me, Michael meant it. Why would he have stopped meaning it? His strange behaviour had to be due to something else. Perhaps he was suffering from an undue amount of stress at work and I just hadn't noticed. Perhaps I hadn't been supportive enough. I knew that lately I had been moody too. Things in my own office hadn't been so great and it was possible that Michael was getting fed up of me bringing home my worries when he had so many of his own. I could change that. I could buck myself up to help him. I would do whatever it took.

But I had to go round there to convince him. Becky's strategy may have been right for most relationships, but it wasn't right for Michael and me. We had something that shouldn't be sullied by game-playing and strategic withdrawals. If Michael needed me, I was going to be there beside him, regardless of whether he thought he wanted me there. I was going to make everything all right.

Becky sent me a text: 'I hope you're not at Michael's.'

I sent her a text back: 'Of course not.'

7

Seconds later I called a minicab to take me to the apartment block where Michael lived. As I sat in the back of that taxi, taking half as many breaths as normal to avoid inhaling too much toxic air-freshener, I planned my approach. I juggled my iPhone from one hand to the other. Should I call him to tell him that I was on my way? Should I text? I decided against it. Michael had yet to respond to any of that day's frantic calls and texts from me, so I had very good reason to believe that if he saw my number illuminate the screen of his phone, he would send me straight to voicemail. Even if he did pick up, if I told him I was coming over, he would almost certainly tell me not to. I couldn't risk that. I had to see him before I went insane.

As the taxi pulled up outside the block, I panicked again. If I rang Michael's doorbell, he might not let me in. What could I do? River Heights was a very exclusive development with a high level of security. According to Michael, an oligarch had bought the top two floors of the main building for his chauffeurs. The guy on the gate wasn't supposed to let anyone in without the approval of the person they were visiting. I knew that, in general, the security staff stuck to that rule rather rigidly. I'd tried to turn up with a surprise cake for Michael's birthday and they'd insisted on letting him know I was there. 'Might be a cake, might be a bomb,' the jobsworth on the gate had told me.

But right then my luck changed. Whoever was meant to

be manning the gate that evening was taking a tea break and the forbidding gatehouse was empty. And here was someone staggering towards the entrance to River Heights with armfuls of carrier bags. It was a man I recognised as one of Michael's neighbours. We had met at Michael's flat-warming party. I couldn't for the life of me remember his name, but as he came near, I said, 'The stupid intercom seems to be broken again. Can I follow you through?'

Michael's neighbour didn't question my explanation. He opened the gate with his key and ushered me inside. He probably hoped I would help him carry his shopping in return. I didn't. Once inside the complex, I was like a Royal Marine on an undercover mission. I had to get across the courtyard without Michael seeing me from his kitchen window. I stayed close to the neatly trimmed hedges that surrounded the courtyard. I took advantage of the shade and shelter of the trees. I made it to Michael's block unnoticed. But how could I get inside?

I had to wait for his neighbour again.

'Is the buzzer broken here too?' he asked curiously.

'Seems to be,' I lied. I hopped from foot to foot as I waited for him to find his key and let me through the penultimate door between me and my beloved. Leaving the neighbour with his bags, I climbed the stairs two at a time and composed myself for just a second before I pressed Michael's doorbell.

I imagined Michael getting up from his computer desk and crossing the hall, wondering who was ringing, perhaps assuming that it was one of his neighbours since he'd had no call from the gatehouse. I thought I heard his leather slippers on the polished wooden floor. I plastered on a warm and super-friendly smile. I'd decided in the minicab that my best strategy was to act as though the whole Facebook thing had been a joke but . . . nothing.

He didn't answer the door. I pressed the buzzer again.

Perhaps he hadn't heard it. Still no answer. I lay my ear against the door and listened for sounds of life beyond its blank plywood face. I could hear nothing. No loud music that might have masked my ringing. No sounds of life at all in fact. But I didn't take that to mean he wasn't in. Oh, no. I decided he must have seen me cross the courtyard. He was hiding from me, staying still and silent until I gave up and went home.

'Michael!' I put my mouth to the crack in the door. (There was no letterbox. Post was left at the porter's lodge.) 'Michael, I know you are in there.'

Still nothing.

'Michael!' This time I shouted and knocked at the same time. 'Michael! Michael! Michael! Please open the door.'

My entreaties were not met.

'Michael!' This time I shouted and hammered *and* kicked. 'Let me in! Let me in, for God's sake. Michael! We need to talk. For pity's sake. I love you. You can't do this to me. I won't let you. You can't pretend I don't exist! Open up! Open up!' I kicked so hard that I made a dent in the plywood. Two dents. A small hole. I had a sudden image of him lying on the floor of his bathroom, a bottle of pills in his hand. Perhaps he'd dumped me on Facebook as a cry for help! I kept kicking.

'I know you're in there! I know you are.'

'No, I'm not.'

It was true. He was standing behind me. I turned to face him, my fists still balled.

'Ashleigh, how did you get in here? And what on earth are you doing?'

Michael was not alone. He was carrying two of his neighbour's shopping bags. The neighbour looked almost as anxious as Michael did.

'What on earth have you *done*?' I countered. 'Have you really dumped me via Facebook?'

Michael smiled tightly. His neighbour was taking an awfully long time to let himself into his flat.

'I've been trying to get hold of you since ten o'clock this morning,' I continued. 'I've been so worried. What is happening? You have to tell me what's wrong.'

'It's not what you think,' he said. More for the neighbour's benefit than mine, I know now.

'Then what is it?' I asked. 'Tell me what's going on.'

'I suppose you had better come in.'

8

'Come on,' he said. 'Before somebody calls the police.' He took me by the upper arm, as though he were apprehending a shoplifter, and pulled me inside. We went straight to the kitchen. He kept hold of my arm until we got there. Perhaps he was scared I'd throw a punch if he let me go. When he finally did let me go, I stood opposite him with my hands on my hips and said, now that I was no longer worried that he'd suffered a sudden breakdown and killed himself, in the fiercest tone I could muster, 'So?'

My wait outside his front door had rather rattled my composure, but still I saw Michael's eyes flick appreciatively from my cleavage to my knees and back again.

'Are you going out to dinner or something?' he asked.

I shook my head. 'It's just . . . I just thought I'd wear a dress. That's all.'

I had put on my best LBD, figuring that if this break-up was for real, I needed all the help I could get.

'Oh. OK,' said Michael.

Then he said he was hungry and started to make himself a sandwich. As an afterthought he asked if he could make me one too.

'I didn't come round here for a sandwich,' I said. 'I just want to know what's going on.'

Michael looked pained. 'Let's have a glass of wine first,' he said. He motioned me towards the kitchen table and poured out a couple of glasses of pinot grigio. His smile was so sweet right then I could almost believe he was going to tell me the Facebook thing had been a big mistake and he hoped I would forgive him. 'Talk?' he'd laugh. The only thing he wanted to talk about was my day and how soon I could take a few days off to go to Venice . . .

'How did the meeting with the people from Effortless Bathing go?' he asked.

'I cancelled when I saw what you'd written on Facebook.'

Michael frowned and shook his head. 'I didn't want that to happen.'

'But what did you think would happen when you declared yourself single like that? And then defriended me? I couldn't ignore it. I tried to get through to you so you could tell me what was going on but you wouldn't take any of my calls. I was going mental. There's no way I could have given a presentation in that state.'

'I'm sorry,' he said. 'I didn't think you were allowed to access Facebook from the office. I didn't think you'd see it until you got home.'

'What? Is this a joke?'

'Look, Ashleigh.' He focused his gaze on his hands and I knew that the 'Dear Jane' speech was about to begin. 'You and I have had some good times. I consider you to be a really great friend . . .'

'Really great friend?' I squeaked.

'Yes. Really great.' He nodded. 'But lately I've been wondering if it's time for me to be on my own again. We're going in different directions you and I. I'm holding you back.'

A subtle variation on 'It's not you, it's me', as Becky would later point out.

'You're not holding me back,' I said. 'I've never said that.'

'You don't have to say anything. I just know. Look, when you and I got together, I had only recently come out of a long-term relationship. It had been difficult. That break-up turned my world upside down. I didn't know myself. I wasn't myself. Yet it felt right when I met you and we got together. You brought me back to life.'

'And that's good, isn't it?'

'It was fantastic. And I'm very grateful. But now I realise that you need something different from me. Something more than I can give you. I know that you want to get married and have children . . .'

'I don't,' I protested. 'I never said that. Never. Not once.'

It would strike me much later that I hadn't dared.

'But you don't have to. I know you're not happy with things the way they are.'

'I am,' I lied. 'I am.'

'Ashleigh,' Michael sighed. '*I'm* not happy with the way things are.'

'Then tell me what you want me to change!' I begged him.

'There's nothing I want you to change. I just can't do this any longer,' was his reply.

I tried to take his hand, but he moved it deftly out of the way on the pretence of picking up his wine glass. He smiled at me again. It was a pitiful smile of the kind you give a door-to-door salesman even as you're closing the door on him. 'We have to break-up,' he sighed. 'I just want to be on my own.'

'Look,' I said. 'I think you're being too hasty. What about all the wonderful things we have in common and the good times we've had?'

I reminded him of a few. Big nights out. Camping trips. The time we made love beneath a bush in Kew Gardens.

He couldn't disagree that had been fun. 'I'll never forget those times,' he said. 'They'll always be dear to me.'

But I wouldn't, was what he was saying.

'You've got to understand that I haven't taken this decision lightly,' he continued. 'I've been thinking about breaking things off with you for the past six months.'

'Six months!'

'Yes.' He nodded. 'Since October.'

'And all that time I thought that we were moving forward,' I said. 'I thought we were getting closer to a proper commitment and you didn't tell me otherwise.'

'It was all in your head,' he informed me. 'I never made you any promises.'

9

No promises! The arrogant swine. I should have left right then, with my head held high. That might have made him consider the sense of breaking up with me. But I couldn't. I simply couldn't get up and walk away. I couldn't say, 'Fuck you,' and see if that brought him to a different viewpoint. I had to cling on. I had to beg. I had to make a fool of myself.

'You don't have to promise me anything,' I said.

Michael let me plead my case for the best part of three hours, but though he claimed to agree with much of what I said about the good times we'd had together, he would offer me no hope whatsoever. He was adamant that his future had no room for me. Except as a friend. We could always be friends, he assured me.

'But, Michael!' I sobbed. 'I don't want to be your friend. I don't want to split up with you! I–I–I–love you!' I added, as I quickly reached hysteria. The tears ran freely down my face.

I had always been so careful not to use tears as a weapon in relationships. I thought it was a manipulative thing to do, and I really didn't believe that tears worked, in any case. But I was to be surprised that evening. To my mind, I had lost it absolutely. I could feel my carefully applied make-up melting into a Halloween mask. Each breath I took seemed to come out as a honk. At one point I'm embarrassed to say I even blew a bubble of snot from my nose. Pathetic. I could not have been a pretty sight. But after two bottles of wine and with the time drawing close to midnight my crying seemed to have an effect on Michael. And not the one I had expected.

'Hey, hey,' he crooned. 'It's not that bad.' He leaped up to get me some kitchen roll, and when he sat back down, he reached across the table for my hand. As I began to calm down, he let his fingers wander up my bare arm to the crook of my elbow. He traced little circles on the thin skin there, which made me feel ticklish, but I didn't dare ask him to stop. I just wanted him to keep on touching me. It was evidence that he cared and perhaps, perhaps that part of him still wanted me in his life.

I leaned forward over the table, hoping he might progress from stroking my arm to stroking my face, like he used to. The action of leaning forward slightly opened the neckline of my dress. Michael looked deep into my cleavage. It wasn't quite as romantic as having him look deep into my eyes, but it was something, I supposed. I shifted surreptitiously so that the lace of my bra showed quite clearly and Michael was transfixed like a chicken locking eyes with a hawk.

'It's late,' he said then. It was past midnight. He let go of my hand and stood up. I waited for him to suggest a taxi, but instead he said, 'Let's go to bed.'

I followed him mutely into the bedroom I had come to know so well. Without speaking, Michael helped me take off my dress. He undressed himself and together we slipped between the clean white sheets. There was no question as to what would come next.

That night we made love more passionately than we had done in months. Lately our sexual routine, while athletic, had become just that – routine – starting and ending in the same way with the same repertoire of positions in between. That night I felt that we were properly connected again, like we had been when we first got together. When we were face to face, he looked into my eyes. When he came, I thought he called my name. Ashleigh! Though in retrospect, he may have said, 'Ah, shit.'

Anyway, as Michael fell asleep, his breath falling into the familiar pattern that told me he was about to start snoring, I felt, at last and for the first time since I saw that awful update on Facebook, some proper relief. I was still in Michael's bed, so I was still his girlfriend, right? Sure, he hadn't whipped out a diamond engagement ring, as Becky's Henry had done, but we were sleeping together. His head was next to mine on the pillow. His arm lay across my stomach. It all seemed so perfectly natural. It had to mean I was still in the game.

When Michael let out his first snore, I gently wriggled my way out from beneath his heavy arm and searched on the floor beside the bed for my handbag. I pulled out my iPhone and texted Becky. She would want to know how the evening had gone.

'Everything is OK,' I texted. Because it was OK. Wasn't it?

10

The next morning began as had a thousand mornings of our relationship. Michael's radio alarm broke the early silence with the dulcet tones of Chris Moyles's morning show. Michael groaned and rolled over to press the snooze button. Three minutes later Moyles was back with the tail end of the story he had been telling before.

Without really opening his eyes, Michael got out of bed and walked like a zombie to the en suite bathroom. I heard him turn on the shower. He gasped as the water hit him. It was either still colder or hotter than he expected. Shock over, he began to sing tunelessly as he went about his ablutions. I took that to be a good sign. People only sing when they're happy, right?

I sat up in bed and surveyed my reflection in the mirror on his wardrobe. Surprisingly, I looked OK. Although I hadn't taken my make-up off the night before, the damage was not so bad. I didn't look as though I had been sobbing my heart out the previous evening. Instead I looked as though I'd just had a slightly heavy night on the champers and, if I said so myself, almost foxy.

Poufing up my artfully dishevelled hair, I got out of bed and skipped, naked, to the bathroom.

Michael was out of the shower and drying himself off. As I pushed open the bathroom door, he snatched his towel closely to himself as though I had surprised him.

'Sorry,' I said. 'I didn't mean to scare you.'

'It's OK,' said Michael, working a corner of his towel into his ear.

I leaned against the doorframe and arranged my body to best effect.

'Can I get in the shower?' I asked.

'Of course,' he said. He stepped to one side so I could pass him.

'Have you finished in here? I mean, are you sure you're properly clean?' I asked. He didn't take the playful hint that he should jump back into the shower with me.

'I'm clean,' he said.

For the next five minutes or so I practically performed the Dance of the Seven Veils behind that shower curtain in the hope that he might change his mind and join me for a quick rub-down, but he didn't. He didn't even glance up to see my sexy silhouette. He brushed and flossed his teeth. He shaved. Then he went back to working on his ears. This time with a cotton bud.

Eventually I had to get out of the shower. It was only then that I noticed there was no towel for me.

'Oh, have this,' he said, handing the one he had used to clean his ears. 'All the others are in the wash.'

'OK.' I tried to make the best of it. I wiggled it across my shoulders in a little shimmy. It wasn't very big and I was starting to feel cold. Meanwhile Michael combed his hair flat across his head.

'So,' I said, preparing to seal the deal. 'I was wondering what you want to do this weekend.'

'What?'

'This weekend?'

Michael stopped combing his hair and just stood there, with the comb still poised over his head. He looked at me via the mirror.

I pressed on. 'I don't have anything planned at all, though

I would like to go to John Lewis to have a look for Becky and Henry's wedding present. You can come if you like.'

'I have other plans,' said Michael.

'Like what?' I asked. 'Anything I can go along with?'

Michael paused. He cleared his throat. 'I mean I wasn't intending to spend my weekend with you.'

'But . . .'

'Ashleigh.' Michael put down his comb and gave me that sorrowful smile. Still via the mirror. He wasn't going to turn round and give me that smile in person. 'We went through this all last night. You and me. We're finished. You know we are. We can't carry on pretending. This just isn't working out.'

I suddenly felt far colder than I should have done, even if I was wet and dripping in an unheated bathroom.

'But you just slept with me!' I said eventually. 'You took me to bed!'

'I know,' said Michael. 'I shouldn't have done that. But what can I say? I'm a man . . . I'm weak.' He shrugged his shoulders and pulled a 'Tchuh! Boys!' kind of face, as though to cue a laugh.

Weak? If I hadn't felt so bloody weak right then, I might have socked him in the jaw.

'You came over and you looked so great and you got so drunk . . .'

'That you decided to take advantage of me! Michael! I thought it meant something.'

'It did,' Michael told me.

'What?' I spat. 'What did it mean to you?'

'I suppose that part of me thought it was a good way of saying goodbye.'

'First shag, last shag?'

'If you want to put it like that.' He winced. 'It does sort of complete the circle. Is that such a bad thing?'

'Yes! Yes!' I shouted. 'Yes, it bloody well is a bad thing. How could you?'

'You were the one who got into my bed naked,' Michael pointed out.

'As you said, I'd had quite a bit to drink. You could have refused to get in there with me. You could have slept in your spare room.'

'That bed's uncomfortable,' he said. 'The mattress is all lumpy.'

'You mean a lumpy mattress made it seem better for you to use me like some kind of unpaid prostitute?'

'Now, come on, Ashleigh. You know it's not like that. You know that I always had the very finest feelings for you . . .'

'And I *still* have the very finest feelings for you. And you knew that because I told you and yet, knowing that you weren't going to get back with me, you still took me to bed? You must have realised I'd get the wrong idea.'

'I didn't tell you I'd changed my mind.'

'But you acted as though you had! What was I supposed to think?'

'I'm sorry,' said Michael. He still hadn't turned round.

'Turn round and look at me when you say that!' I demanded.

He turned round, but he didn't look contrite any more. Instead he looked frankly irritated to find me still standing there, as though there had been a chance that my reflection in the mirror was some kind of mirage. 'I'm sorry,' he said again. 'But, Ashleigh, you need to put your clothes on. I've got to go to work. And so have you, I'm sure.'

'You can't go to work right now. Not while we're in the middle of talking about the most important thing in our lives!'

'I've got a breakfast meeting,' he told me.

'And you're actually going to go to it?'

'I can't miss it.'

He left me standing alone in the bathroom while he went to get dressed and make himself a coffee. Though he had looked fairly rattled as he walked out, less than two minutes later I could hear him singing again. The pig! It was no time for bloody singing. I pulled on my dress and followed him into the kitchen. I continued to tell him what I thought of him while he swallowed his vitamin tablets.

'You're an absolute c—' I said, using a word I ordinarily considered unthinkable.

Michael had the decency to choke on his cod-liver oil.

'I can't believe you called me that!'

'I can't believe you turned out to be one!'

I was still arguing as Michael shuffled me out of his front door, with my hair dripping and the buttons on my dress done up wrongly. A car was already waiting to take him to his big, important meeting. The meeting that was so much more important than our relationship!

'Take a taxi home,' he said, pressing a twenty into my hand. 'I'll call you later.'

He didn't kiss me – not even on the cheek – and there was no disguising the relief on his face as the car pulled away from the kerb with him safely in the back seat.

What was I supposed to do?

'You . . . you utter utter twat!' I called after him.

A woman walking her dog past the main gate gave me a very disapproving look. Michael lived in the kind of complex where the residents would call the police if they saw someone wearing high-street clothes passing by, let along shouting obscenities. In my walk-of-shame outfit, clutching the twenty-pound note that Michael had just pressed upon me, I must have looked very dodgy indeed. The woman crossed the road away from me, as though I might be a bad influence on her pedigree Chihuahua.

I I

So, I was down, but was I out? No way. Michael may have thought he had broken up with me for real now but I had a very different idea. Was I going to accept my dismissal? Was I hell!

I was determined that I would not let Michael's decision stand. Even before I got home, I tried to call him fifteen times to tell him so, but, surprise, surprise, he let me go to voicemail. Breathing deeply in the back of the cab, I replayed the previous evening and our horrible fight in the bathroom. It was ridiculous that Michael thought he could throw away two and a half years with just one conversation. There had to be further negotiations and there would be. I consoled myself with the fact that he obviously still found me attractive – the sex had proved that – and that he had said he would call. When he did, I needed to be ready to take full advantage of that window. As I realised that, I felt an odd calm come over me. All was not yet lost.

I called my office and told Ellie I would not be coming in again before the weekend. I claimed that the food poisoning had left me too weak and listless to do anything but lie in bed.

'People normally get over food poisoning in twenty-four hours,' said Ellie.

'I've got it really bad.'

'And it sounds like you're sitting in a taxi,' said Ellie, tuning in to the diesel engine.

46

'I'm leaning my head out of my bedroom window,' I told her. 'To get some air.'

Bloody Ellie. Her job title may have been assistant but I frequently felt as though she was the boss in our relation-ship.

'All right,' she said. 'Get better soon. We're all thinking of you.'

I accepted her platitudes, though I knew that if her dreams came true, I would not get better at all. Ellie had been after my job since the day she started at Maximal Media. Any disappointment she expressed at my absence was entirely perfunctory. I imagined she was already standing in my office, deciding where she would put her degree certificate and photos from her gap year. It was a risk, giving her the opportunity to step into my shoes for however short a period, but something bigger than my job was at stake here.

By the time I got back home, I had decided I needed a new strategy. The Internet was my first resort. I didn't even bother to change out of my little black dress before I fired up my laptop. Changing, washing, eating, drinking meant nothing to me now. I could only focus on what I could do to make Michael change his mind. I typed the words 'get boyfriend back' into the Google window. They were three little words that were the key to a world I could not have imagined.

The good news was that plenty of other people had put their minds to the problem of rescuing a relationship. The bad news was that the first twenty sites I looked at came up with twenty different methods. They didn't agree on a single strategy that made any sense. *Call him. Don't call him. Cry. Don't cry. Learn a new sexual position and try it out on his best friend . . .*

There were literally thousands of pages and chatroom

threads devoted to the subject of winning back an ex-lover and no way of knowing what really worked. Still, taking up a pencil and using all the research skills I had honed over my career, I started to make notes and gradually saw a pattern emerge. The advice wasn't so diverse after all. It actually fell broadly into two camps: ignore the lover who spurned you to reignite their interest, or, more controversially, stalk him relentlessly until he decides it would be easier to take you back than put up with you shadowing him at work. I read through sites for the broken-hearted until my eyes started crossing, not even stopping to make a cup of tea. I hadn't worked so hard since I retook my finals. All the while I had one eye on my iPhone for a call or a text from Michael. Nothing came.

By five in the afternoon I had read all the free advice I could find, so I paid $29.95 for a 'foolproof method' to get your ex back in the form of an Ebook. Unfortunately, the foolproof method required that I make no contact with Michael for at least a month. A month without Michael? No way! What's more, during that month I had to work out for an hour every single day and date at least three new guys a week. If I hadn't been totally disgusted by the idea anyway, it would have been impossible.

I continued to Google. At eleven in the evening I found another site, run by the Break-Up Babe, who promised much faster results. 'I can give you the magic formula that will have him back in your arms and ready to commit to whatever you want – living together, marriage or babies – within days.' Well, that had to be worth $69.95. I input my credit-card details and waited eagerly for the download to arrive in my in-box.

Just a week earlier I might have read that e-book with some sense of humour, but as the clock ticked past midnight, just over twenty-four hours since Michael broke up with me, I read every word the Break-Up Babe had to say in deadly earnest, nodding at every sentiment I recognised.

'Right now you're feeling lost,' she said.

Oh, boy, was I ever.

'You're probably feeling that all hope is gone.'

That was an understatement.

'But there is a method that will restore your love within minutes.'

Just give me the bloody method, I muttered, as I scrolled through three chapters of platitudes.

At last, in Chapter Eleven, the Break-Up Babe got to the point.

The Break-Up Babe explained that all relationship issues were down to poor communication and learning the right way to communicate with a man would instantly make all the difference. As I read the eleventh chapter, it became instantly and quite brilliantly clear where I had been going wrong. The Break-Up Babe wrote that the natural response of most women right after a break-up is to freak out and start yelling, which only forces the man into a reactive position so that he feels he has no choice but to continue to withdraw. He withdraws further and the girl chases him harder and so a vicious cycle is born until at last he's withdrawn so far the relationship is all but over. It didn't have to be that way.

'Men don't think like us,' the Break-Up Babe continued.

'Too right,' I muttered aloud, thinking of the break-up sex that Michael had initiated the previous night. How was I supposed to take that?

'You have to practise detachment. Take a step back to give him room to move forward. Don't contact your other half for a month . . .'

Damn. Where did all these break-up gurus get this month of no contact from? I discarded the Break-Up Babe's advice and continued my Google search. I spent another $300 on e-books that promised much and delivered nothing interesting. I read more and more threads of declining literacy and increasing lunacy.

'do he still luv me'

'u gota make him pay'

'my boyfren cum back to me when I put voodoo curse on his big titty girl'

By two in the morning I was tired and frustrated, heartbroken and dehydrated, which probably explains why I fell like a starving woman upon a piece of banoffi pie when I read the following response to a reader's letter on a somewhat reputable advice site:

It turned out that my ex simply didn't believe that I loved him. Breaking up with me was a test. All it took was one grand gesture to turn everything around. I turned up at his office and told him that I loved him in front of all his workmates at the body-shop. We got back together and now we've been married for seven years.

What if that was it? What if, despite my protestations the previous night, Michael was as insecure in my love as that woman's ex had been in hers? What if he just wanted me to prove my love in public? He'd broken up with me in a public forum after all. What if I just had to declare my love for him in a public forum too? What if it was that simple?

I Googled the phrase 'grand gesture' and found a dozen similar stories.

'She said she never wanted to see me again, but I turned up at her office with some flowers and a ring and now we're having our second child.'

'We were on the point of divorcing but my brave step

pulled us back. He said what he wanted all along was real proof of my love.'

If proof was what Michael wanted, then proof was what I would give him.

12

Waking up the following morning, having managed just a couple of hours' sleep, I suppose I wasn't exactly thinking like a genius. I had that final scene from *An Officer and a Gentleman* running through my head. The one where Richard Gere goes into his lover's workplace and sweeps her off her feet. I was going to do something like that for Michael.

I took a taxi to the building where he worked, stopping en route to pick up three dozen red roses from a stand on the street. I got past the security guards at Michael's company with ease. I persuaded them against calling him up to announce my arrival by telling them that I was on my way to deliver a singing telegram for Michael's birthday and that to call him first would spoil the surprise.

One of the guards looked lasciviously down the front of my shirt. 'Like a stripping policewoman?' he asked.

'I just sing,' I told him sharply.

So, I got to the floor where Michael had his office, but I knew I wouldn't be able to get past Tina, his assistant. Unless she was on a fag break. I prayed she would be on a fag break. She wasn't on a fag break.

'W–what?' she stuttered when she saw me. 'Ashleigh. You're . . . er . . . you're in the office. And you . . . you've brought flowers. Nobody called to say you were coming up.'

'I know,' I said breezily. 'I told them not to. I wanted it to be a surprise.'

'It's certainly that,' said Tina. 'But, anyway, Michael is in a meeting . . .'

'I know you're lying,' I said. 'I know he's told you not to let me anywhere near him.'

'That's not true,' Tina swore. 'He really is in a meeting. But I promise I'll tell him you dropped by.'

Well, if he had been in a meeting, he was out of it now. My attention was attracted by movement at the end of the corridor and I turned to see the man himself, coming out of the staff kitchen with a steaming mug in his hand. Tea. Milk. One sugar. I knew the way he liked it so well. He was dipping a biscuit as he walked. He looked as though he didn't have a care in the world. He certainly didn't look as though he had just broken up with the love of his life.

'Michael,' I called out to him. 'I have to speak to you.'

Michael froze with the chocolate HobNob halfway between the mug and his mouth. In the time it took him to register who had called his name from behind all those flowers, half the biscuit had dropped back into the tea with a plop. Michael swore as the tea splashed on his tie.

'Ashleigh, what are you doing here?' he hissed. He remained at the other end of the corridor. He would not walk towards me, and Tina had come out from behind her desk and was preventing me from heading towards him like a goal defence marking goal attack on the netball court.

'You won't return my calls,' I shouted to him. 'You won't answer my emails or texts. What am I supposed to do?'

'Get the message?' said the bright spark who had the desk opposite Tina. I gave her the benefit of a glare.

'You should go,' said Michael. 'And take those flowers with you. This is not the right time for this.'

'But when will there be a right time?' I implored him. 'When will you listen to what I have to say?'

'There really isn't anything left to say, is there?'

'You're wrong,' I said. 'You're so wrong.'

Tina was still bobbing about in front of me.

'I've got so much left to say. I've got a whole novel's worth to tell you.' I tapped my hand against my heart. 'In here.'

Michael grimaced. 'Not now,' he hissed again.

'I'm not leaving until you hear me out,' I warned him. I growled at Tina, who took a step back.

By now a small crowd was beginning to gather, but Michael was standing his ground. He was determined not to bridge the gap between us, physically or metaphorically. He looked down at his tea somewhat mournfully.

'For heaven's sake, Ashleigh. You're making a fool of yourself.'

'Just let me say what I've got to say,' I persisted. 'And afterwards, if you still think you want me out of your life, then I will walk away for ever. I promise you. It's not too much to ask, is it?'

'I don't think so,' said a bespectacled chap, who had perched himself on the edge of the reception desk. He was settling in for the show. 'Let's hear what you've got to say.'

'I'm not going to talk to you here,' said Michael. He started to walk away. In that moment I dodged past Tina, chased him down the grey-carpeted hall and made a grab for his elbow. I jogged the tea mug, sending more of the milky-brown liquid over what I knew to be Michael's favourite suit. One of the single-breasted bespoke suits he had been wearing since his big image change.

'For heaven's sake.' He tried to jump backwards to avoid the splash. He turned to snarl at me. I had never seen him look quite so mad. I have to admit I was a little bit scared.

'But this is it,' said the little voice inside my head. 'It's now or never. Give him the speech.' I took a deep breath and spewed out the speech. Quickly. After all, at any moment someone might call a security guard.

'Michael, from the moment I saw you, I knew that you would play an important part in my life. When my eyes met yours, it was as if the final piece of the jigsaw had been fitted into place. If you still feel that we should be apart, then I understand that I will have to accept your decision, but if you have the slightest doubt, then I want you to know that we can work it out. And if you feel the same way as me, then let's spend the rest of our lives together. Michael . . .' It was time for my grand gesture. I got down on one knee. 'Will you marry me?'

'Oh, no,' said Tina.

'Jesus Christ,' said the man who was perching on the reception desk.

Someone actually applauded, but their exuberance was quickly cut short as Michael glared at his colleagues. He grabbed me by the arm, pulled me to my feet and hustled me into his office.

'Are you out of your fucking mind?' he asked.

That wasn't exactly the response I had been hoping for.

Michael's office was glazed on three sides. He shut the blinds abruptly.

Even in the shadow I could see that his face was as bright red as the roses that he dumped in the waste bin with a dangerous mixture of embarrassment and anger. Though I had been awake for much of the night, I was only just beginning to wake up.

'I'm sorry,' I said pre-emptively. 'I didn't mean to embarrass you.'

'Well, you did. What were you thinking? What on earth was that all about, Ashleigh? Have you had a stroke? Who do you think you are? Asking me to marry you? Have you been smoking crack?'

'I was trying to speak to you in your own language,' I said, remembering what the Break-Up Babe had said about talking in man-speak.

'You could try speaking to me in bloody English for a start.'

'Then let me start again,' I pleaded. 'I wanted to be sure you understood how much you mean to me.'

'I don't have time for this.'

'I just don't think you know what you're throwing away.' I continued to try to convince him, long after all reasonable hope was gone. 'I thought that my grand gesture might bring you to your senses. If you let me walk out of the office right now, you'll regret it. I know you will. You'll regret it for the rest of your life.'

'Ashleigh, what I always liked about you was that you seemed to be reasonably sane. For a woman. All this nonsense is just making me more certain than ever that I was right to call it a day. In fact I should have done it quite some time ago.'

'Oh, Michael,' I wailed. 'For God's sake, give me another chance. Let me come round and talk about this in your flat. I just want to see you.'

'You can't,' he told me then. 'Because I'm seeing someone else.'

Is it possible that hearts really do break? Because I thought I felt mine tear in two right in that moment. And as the song goes, when hearts break, they don't break even. I knew that I could no longer comfort myself with the idea that Michael was somehow hurting too. He had already moved on.

'Who is she?' I wailed. 'Who?'

'You don't really want to know that,' said Michael. 'What possible good could it do you to know?'

'It's Tina.'

'Of course it's not Tina.'

'Then it's one of my friends,' was the obvious conclusion.

'It is not one of your freaky, boring friends,' said Michael. 'I would never do that to you. What kind of man do you think I am?'

'The kind of man who would have sex with a woman moments after telling her he wants to break-up,' I reminded him. 'Does your new woman know about that? You should tell her. See how excited she is about dating you then.' My voice got higher and higher as I berated him for his faithlessness.

'I don't have to listen to this,' said Michael. 'And I'm not going to. Get some help, Ashleigh. Get a life. You've got to start getting over this. Because we're finished. It's over. We're D-O-N-E. Done.'

13

I left Michael's building in a state of shock. As I passed Tina's desk, my legs almost buckled beneath me. Despite having guarded Michael like a pit bull, Tina very kindly offered to walk me to the Tube station, but I waved her help away. I just wanted to be out of there and on my own. I sat on the Tube in a daze. If I closed my eyes, all I could see was Michael's face as he snarled at me in his office. All I could hear was our last conversation and that terrible bombshell. He had someone else!

I called Becky at school. She was teaching a class, of course, but I had the school secretary drag her out, this time by pretending I had just been involved in a car accident. I told myself that I had been in some sort of mental car wreck and if I didn't speak to her right then, I didn't know what I'd do.

'For heaven's sake,' Becky said when she found out that I wasn't in accident and emergency after all. 'You said you had had a car crash! Ashleigh, that is one sick joke.'

'I'm sorry,' I said. 'But I had to talk to you right away. If I'd said anything else, you might not have come out of your lesson.'

'Too right. I've left eighteen A-level students with an exam next Monday to talk to you. What do you have to say about that?'

I said, 'I think I'm going to die.'

'What have you done?' Becky sounded suddenly panicked. 'Have you tried to kill yourself? Have you taken something?'

'Not yet,' I said.

'Right. That's it. I'm coming over,' Becky told me. 'I'll be there as soon as I can. Just promise that you won't do anything stupid while I'm on my way.'

I swore that I wouldn't do anything more than sit and stare into space. And that was all I managed. That and a bit of rocking backwards and forwards with my knees pulled to my chest. Oh, and a spot of lying on my side on the carpet in the foetal position, full of primeval pain.

'Jesus, Ashleigh,' said Becky when she saw me. 'You look like you've got shell shock.'

'Michael has got a new girlfriend.'

'Ah.' Becky nodded grimly. She sat down on the sofa while I remained on the floor. She leaned over and stroked my hair. 'I see,' she said. 'I guessed as much. Well.' She adopted her teaching voice, the 'no point crying over spilt milk' demeanour that she used for her final-year students when they didn't get into the university of their choice. 'It's a horrible thing to hear but at least now you know exactly where you stand.'

'But what should I do?'

'Do? You should do nothing except do your best to get over him as quickly as you can. I had hoped that Michael was just having a bit of a wobble about commitment and would come to his senses, but it's clear now that there's more to this break-up than that. There's no point wasting another second on him now. If he's telling you that he's got someone else this quickly, then you can bet she was on the scene long before he got rid of you. It sounds as though he was trying to make sure that things were working out with this new girl before he gave up on the comfort of having you in his life. Talk about having your cake . . .'

'But . . . but there must be something I can do?'

Becky just shook her head. 'Forget him. He's got someone else. That's all you need to know. Now come here.'

She pulled me up to sit on the sofa beside her and enfolded me in her arms.

Concerned that I wouldn't be safe on my own, Becky insisted on taking me back to the house she shared with Henry. There she tucked me up in a bed in her spare room and fed me soup and Ben & Jerry's from Henry's secret supply. She sent Henry down the pub for the evening (he couldn't believe his luck) while she listened to me repeat the tale of my terrible day again and again and again.

'You think I'm an idiot,' I said when I'd told her about my proposal for the twentieth time.

'I think you were naïve,' she said. 'But I'm glad that Michael showed his true colours so quickly. It will make it easier to move on. More ice cream?'

I refused another spoonful of Phish Food.

'I shouldn't either,' said Becky. 'I'll never get into my wedding dress.'

I'd almost forgotten that Becky and Henry were going to be married in less than three months. I felt tears well up at the thought of it.

'You're getting married and I've just been dumped,' I wailed.

'Oh, hey,' said Becky, placing her hand on mine. 'My wedding's ages away. You'll be *so* over Michael Parker by then. You'll have a good time.'

I nodded bravely in agreement.

At the sound of Henry's key in the door, Becky's face lit up. 'I'd better go and see how drunk he is. Have you got everything you need? You can stay here for as long as you want, you know. I don't want you to be on your own a moment before you feel you're ready for it.'

I believed it. Becky gave me a heartfelt hug. She truly was my best friend.

*　　*　　*

I stayed at Becky and Henry's house for the whole weekend. Becky even cancelled a visit to a wedding fair near Croydon to spend Sunday afternoon with me.

'I think I know what a sugared almond looks like,' she said.

I really don't know how I could have got through that first weekend *sans* Michael without my best friend's support. She made sure that I was fed and drinking enough water. She ensured that I got out of bed and showered. She reminded me to brush my teeth. She confiscated my iPhone to make sure I didn't buckle and give Michael a call. She cut short the viewing of half a dozen romantic comedies on DVD whenever they came to a happy part I couldn't quite stomach. She even spoke to my mother to reassure her that I was going to be just fine.

'I know you'd do the same for me,' she said.

Becky listened to me endlessly, nodding with empathy and declaring that Michael was an idiot at exactly the right time every time. But she took a hard line when I insisted that I wanted to know who Michael had replaced me with.

'You can't expect ever to know what really went on in his mind. You have to tell yourself that you'll never hear from him again. You don't need to. You know all there is to know. He doesn't want to be with you because he's met someone else. You don't need her name. You don't need to know how old she is. You don't need to know what she looks like. All you need to know is that Michael Parker is a rat.'

I had to repeat that phrase a dozen times, with gusto, before Becky would agree that it was safe to let me go home.

14

So, I'd convinced Becky that I was going to be fine without round-the-clock surveillance, but back home, my resolve to forget about Michael Parker soon crumbled. As did my promise not to call him. I left another fifteen messages on his voicemail in the hour after Becky dropped me off. I also sent him three emails and started drafting a poem.

I'm sure that a more sensible woman would have agreed with Becky that she didn't need to know who had replaced her in someone's affections and obviously overlapped in them too. It was almost certain that Michael had met and started seeing someone new before we officially parted. Did his new girl know that Michael and I had been an item so very recently? I doubted it. He had probably told her that he was free and single. If she knew that he had two-timed her, then perhaps she wouldn't be quite so pleased she'd got her claws into him . . . But how could she know unless I told her? And I didn't even know who she was.

I had to know.

Away from Becky's reasonable influence, the madness soon set in. Michael wouldn't talk to me, but that didn't mean the trail was dead. The following day, having called into work and claimed illness yet again, I picked up my mobile and starting calling all those people in my contacts list who had some connection to my ex-boyfriend. Michael's sister was first. I'd never really liked her and it was clear that the feeling was mutual. She told me quite primly that I couldn't possibly expect her to be anything other than loyal to her brother and I should delete her number from my phone forthwith. I told her it would be my pleasure.

A couple of others (including an old schoolfriend of Michael's who had given me his number in case I ever wanted to 'upgrade' from his childhood pal) put me straight through to voicemail. I did get through to Michael's tailor (I had that number because I'd picked up some altered shirts – sleeves shortened), but though Ahmed was very sweet and claimed he was sad to hear my news, he assured me that he knew nothing about Michael except his inside-leg measurement.

'But I hope you find a nice husband soon,' he told me kindly. 'You are a very pretty girl.'

The compliment washed over me. I was on a mission.

Having exhausted all other possible leads, I called Helen, the friend who had introduced me to Michael at her birthday party all those months ago.

'Oh, I'm sorry you guys broke up,' she said. Of course, she must have heard about the incident in the office but was tactful enough to pretend otherwise.

'Who is he seeing?' I begged her.

'Ashleigh,' she said, 'I promise you I have no idea. I left the firm on maternity leave four months ago. At the time that I left, the pair of you seemed to be going strong.'

'Are you sure? Did he talk about any women in the office in a way you thought inappropriate? Was there anyone in the office he seemed especially close to?'

'How would I have known? It's a big company. Thousands of people work there. And after Michael got promoted to partner, we were working on different floors. We were four floors apart. He could have been having an affair with Kylie Minogue and I wouldn't have heard a thing. I'm sorry. Look, I've got to go.'

'Really?' I asked.

'Yes,' she said. 'I've got a new baby, remember? Poor thing's been wailing for the past fifteen minutes.'

Another day off work. A huge increase in my phone bill. And I had achieved exactly nothing.

But I was not to be discouraged. It struck me as I looked at old photographs of me and Michael on holiday, and tried to work out if he looked unhappy even then, that if Michael had announced the end of our relationship via Facebook, there was a very strong chance that he would announce the beginning of his new relationship in the same way. The problem with that was that I no longer had access to his Facebook page. The only Facebook 'friend' we had in common was my assistant, Ellie. Michael had signed her up after meeting her at my thirtieth birthday party, back in the day when we were all trying to get as many Facebook contacts as we could and were making friends with all-comers, even actively hunting down people we had once spoken to at a bus-stop.

But I couldn't ask Ellie to let me know what Michael was doing. I was supposed to be off work with a virulent stomach bug, for a start. Asking her to help would mean telling her the truth and that I did not want to do. Not yet. Ellie was like a Komodo dragon that merely nips its prey on the ankle and waits for sepsis to set in. Whenever I showed the least sign of weakness, I would feel her gaze upon me, as though she were calculating just how much longer she would have to wait before I keeled over and she could have my job, my desk and my view of the executive car park. Though I wasn't thinking straight by any means, I was *compos mentis* enough to know that I did not want to show any weakness in front of Ellie.

So how would I get access to Michael's Facebook account? At about eleven o'clock that night I had a small stroke of genius. I didn't have to ask any of my real friends to check up on Michael for me when I could create a stalking horse in the form of one of his own acquaintances.

Sitting in front of my laptop, I concentrated hard as I tried to remember the faces on Michael's friends list and fit them to the names I knew. I was looking for just one member of his crowd who didn't yet have a Facebook profile. Someone who had pooh-poohed the idea. There was bound to be one. Michael's friends were mostly accountants. They pooh-poohed a lot of things.

After much thought and much Googling, I thought that at last I had found the perfect alias to use.

I would pretend to be Helen's husband, Kevin. I remembered how, at the Christmas party at which Michael had danced with that big-haired tart who was redoing the company's lobby, Kevin had ranted about the evils of social-networking sites. He had claimed that at the very best they were for children. Twittering was for the feeble-minded. And any personal information you plugged into a site like Facebook was doubtless being used by the CIA in an infringement of your basic human rights. Well, unbeknown to him, Kevin was about to change his mind . . .

It took me just a few minutes to set up a profile page for Kevin, using a fake Gmail address. It was easy to make the profile look convincing. I knew Kevin's contact details and place of work and quickly plugged those into the 'info' section. I didn't need to add a photograph: Kevin was a new dad; he had better things to do with his time than upload photos to Facebook. If Michael asked why there was no pic, I would say that I (or rather Kevin) would be adding lots of photographs over the weekend, which would give me plenty of time to have used the fake profile for my own evil means and closed it down. I chuckled at my own cleverness. Now all I had to do was 'friend' Michael and hope that he 'friended' me back.

And he did. It took him less than an hour. I was delighted. Not least because if Michael had time to check out his new friend requests on Facebook, then he obviously wasn't making mad, passionate love to his new girlfriend that night.

'Hey, Kevin!' he said in a message sent via the site. 'Fancy seeing you here. I thought you said that Facebook was evil! What made you change your mind? How's Helen? How's the new baby? How's life as a dad?'

I wrote back, 'I decided that I was missing something. If everyone is on Facebook, then the CIA will hardly have time to check us all out, right? Helen is well, as is the baby.'

'What flavour did you have?' Michael wrote back.

'Flavour?' I responded.

'What sex is your first-born, dufus?'

At which point it occurred to me that I had no idea.

Despite having bent Helen's ear for the best part of an hour that day, I couldn't have told you with certainty whether she'd had a boy, a girl or a baby elephant. I frowned at Michael's question, which blinked at me accusingly from the screen. How come I didn't know the answer? Was my alias about to fail at the first hurdle?

I toyed with the idea of calling up Helen and asking her again. But that would be wrong for several reasons. Firstly, it was almost one in the morning. If Helen wasn't up feeding the baby, then she would be trying to get some desperately needed sleep, and if she was up and she did answer my call, then I could hardly bear to think of how the conversation would go. Did I really want Helen to know that I had so little interest in her life that I didn't know whether she'd had a boy or a girl?

I did not. So I did some more detective work. I trawled through my old emails, sure that somewhere among them there must be an email announcing the birth of Helen and Kevin's first child. And there was. I breathed a sigh of relief.

'Helen and Kevin are pleased to announce the birth of baby Alex!' the email exclaimed. 'Nine pounds two ounces. Mother and baby doing fine. Father suffering from shell shock.' Kevin was such a wag. Anyway, I prepared to take that information and regurgitate it for Michael, except that even as I opened the message window to respond to Michael's question in my cyber-disguise, I realised that I still didn't know what sex the baby was. There was a name. An unhelpfully gender-neutral name. And a weight. Nothing more.

'Bum,' I muttered to myself. I searched through all the other emails I had had from Helen before or since the baby's birth. In one she talked about the scan but added, 'They asked us if we wanted to know what sex the baby is. Of course we told them we didn't.' In the one email she had written after the baby was born, a round robin to all her friends thanking them for their kind wishes and gifts (I imagine she included me to induce some gift-buying guilt), she continued to refer to the child in a thoroughly gender-neutral way. 'Alex' or 'the baby'. She never once used 'he' or 'she'. Kevin had written a similar email but there were no clues there either. He didn't mention his glee at having someone to take to the football or his disappointment at the years of ballet lessons ahead. Unusually mature for Kevin and exceptionally unhelpful for me.

Michael's question was still waiting for an answer. And if I didn't answer his question, how would I be able to start asking questions of my own? I would have to take a chance. After all, I had a fifty-fifty chance of getting it right. Alex. Over nine pounds. It had to be a boy.

'A bouncing boy!' I wrote back. 'I've already got him in a CFC romper,' I added for authenticity. Kevin was rabidly devoted to Chelsea.

'Congratulations,' came Michael's reply. 'Can't wait to meet the little fella at his barbecue next week.'

Oh! I gasped. Helen and Kevin were having a barbecue and they hadn't invited me. Which could only mean . . .

My hands trembled as I typed, 'Will you be bringing anyone with you?' into the message box. I pressed send and leaned on my desk with my head in my hands while I waited for an answer. An answer that would surely be the answer I was looking for and yet dreading with every fibre of my being. But it didn't come. After a while I dared to look up and saw that Michael was no longer online. He had logged off Facebook without responding to my/Kevin's question and I was still in the dark. Damn.

I hadn't finished snooping for the night.

Now that Michael was offline, I clicked on to his friends list and looked at all the faces there, searching the thumbnail pictures for more clues. Michael had not yet updated his relationship status. About thirty of the seventy-four people Michael had friended were women. Any one of them could be his new girlfriend. I had to go through that list in a systematic way.

There were quite a few I could discount immediately. No matter how evil I thought Michael was, it was unlikely he was having an affair with his teenage cousin. Likewise his sister-in-law. I knew also that he thought his office manager was a cast-iron cow. He'd told me he'd only added her to his list because he was too afraid not to.

By the time the light of dawn was beginning to filter through the window, I had narrowed the suspects down to three. Two were women I didn't recognise at all. Michael had added them both to his list in the past month. The third was the woman I had seen him talking to at the Christmas party. The interior designer with the Grand Canyon cleavage and the candyfloss hair. Her name was Giselle Kleinbeck.

15

Unfortunately, by the time morning rolled around Michael had still not responded to me/Kevin as to whether he would be taking a plus-one to the baby's barbecue. That barbecue haunted me. Why hadn't I heard about it before? As soon as it was decent, I called Helen and tried to engage her in a conversation that might lead to an invitation for me too. I don't know what I thought I would do if she did ask me along, but it seemed like a good idea to have the option. I wanted to see Michael again. There was no other event on the horizon to which I could casually rock up and bump into him.

'So,' I said, 'now that you're through the first sticky month, you must want to celebrate. Are you having Alex christened?'

'Oh, no,' said Helen. 'Kevin doesn't believe in that sort of thing.'

'But you must want to do something to mark such a momentous occasion as the birth of your first child. How about some sort of secular naming ceremony? Or just a party?'

'Honestly,' Helen sighed. 'Right now a party is the last thing on my mind. We're just too exhausted with all the three a.m. feeds and the constant nappy-changing. I had no idea . . .'

'So you're not even going to do something really simple?' I pushed. 'Like a barbecue?'

Helen drew breath. I thought that she was about to cave

but instead she said, 'I've got to go. It's time for the baby's feed. I'm trying to establish some kind of routine.'

She put the phone down before I could say goodbye.

Foiled by Helen, I sent Michael another message via Facebook, as Kevin, explaining that it was important to know numbers for the barbecue because there were sausages to be ordered. Still nothing.

I couldn't just sit there and wait. I had accessed the limited profiles of the three women I suspected of stealing my man. I had Googled their names and found out a surprising and frightening amount of information about all three.

It turned out to be fairly easy to discount two more of the women. I quickly found photographs of one's very recent wedding online. I know that being married didn't entirely rule her out of the running, but the fact that she had married another woman suggested to me that Michael would not float her boat even with his nascent six-pack and new penchant for handmade shoes. The other woman resided in São Paulo. If Michael had been having a relationship with her, I had no idea how and when. Michael had been morbidly afraid of flying anywhere near South America since the outbreak of swine flu. In fact he was rather girly about flying at all. No, I decided, if Miss São Paulo was his new girlfriend, she was not likely to last.

That left me with one more candidate. The interior designer.

I went half blind looking at that tiny photograph I could see, trying to work out if she was more attractive than I was. It was hard to tell, since she was wearing a pair of comedy eyeglasses with those plastic eyes that boing out on springs. All I could see was her mouth. She had a very big smile.

Using what IT skills I had, I lifted Giselle Kleinbeck's picture from her profile and enlarged it to the maximum possible size. Then I printed out the picture and took it with me to the bathroom, where I pinned it on the wall next to the magnifying mirror and prepared to make a proper comparison. As I said, unfortunately her eyes were disguised, but I gave myself at least an equal score for eyebrows. Her hair looked good, but mine could look just as nice straight out of the hairdresser's. I had a better jaw-line, I decided, and while my rival's smile was cheerful, it was overly gummy. My teeth were a better shape, and when I smiled, you could see hardly any gum at all. I was a little comforted by the thought that my smile would age better, since her big gums would eventually recede and leave her looking like a horse.

Big gums or not, this was almost certainly the woman that Michael had chosen over me.

I got more information later that evening when Michael posted some photographs downloaded from his phone on his Facebook page. Among them was a group shot that included Giselle Kleinbeck without her comedy glasses.

I pored over those grainy shots for hours. I guessed from the background that the photograph was taken in the Gaucho Grill. I recognised the cow-hide fabric on the bench upon which she was sitting. It was a restaurant that Michael had taken me to often. I suppose you could say it was one of 'our places'. I tortured myself with the thought of that woman taking my place at 'our table'. Over the time that I had been with Michael, I had come to know what he would order in various places off by heart. In the Gaucho, he always went for an eight-ounce steak and asked me to share a salad. Had he shared a salad with her?

Finally that night came the last piece of the jigsaw. Michael responded to Kevin's question about numbers for the barbecue. 'Yes,' he said. 'I will be plus one. I'm going to bring my new girlfriend, Giselle.'

16

Oh, the agony. Not only had I been replaced in Michael's affections, I had lost my place in my social life too. I couldn't believe that Helen would have chosen to have Michael and his new girlfriend at her barbecue rather than invite me. I had known Helen for a decade. What kind of friend was she to drop me from her guest list and invite my evil ex instead? I was the one who had been dumped. Weren't all my girlfriends supposed to rally to my side and refuse even to meet the new girl? It was what I would have done. Well, I thought, as I wiped away another flurry of tears, Helen had better hope that Kevin didn't dump her when the pressure of raising a newborn got too much. She'd find out who her friends were then.

Becky was unsympathetic. She reminded me that I had promised I would not try to find out who Michael was seeing. 'And in such a dodgy way, Ash. You know that's borderline stalking . . . Actually, forget borderline,' she added. 'It is stalking full stop. And has it made you happy?'

I admitted that it hadn't.

'You are nuts.'

She made me promise that would be the end of it. 'You know her name. You know what she looks like. Anything else is only going to torture you.'

But it turned out I'd developed a taste for torture.

Of course, knowing Giselle Kleinbeck's name and having access to a picture of her with spinach between her big teeth on Michael's Facebook page was not enough for me. I had to find out more. With her name, unusual as it was for London, my earlier investigations had made it very easy to find out where she worked. Well-Sprung Interiors, south-east area representatives for Well-Sprung Upholstery, had their premises in Wimbledon, a mere two miles from my flat. I investigated their website further. It was very dull. It explained that they specialised in office interiors, and there was the name of Michael's firm among the company's list of clients. The sight of it made me clench my jaw.

He really had met her while she refurbished his office. To think I had thought that between the hours of nine and five each day I had nothing much to worry about as far as my boyfriend was concerned: there was very little totty in an office full of people who got excited about tax codes. I hadn't allowed for in-comers. Now I thought back to the first time Michael mentioned that his office was being decorated. Of course I'd thought nothing of it at the time, but now I wondered if the decorating had coincided with Michael's visit to the personal shopper at Harvey Nics and his sudden renewed interest in weight training.

I visited Well-Sprung Interiors website about a hundred times that week, from home and from the office, when I should have been dealing with the Effortless Bathing project. But the website wasn't enough for me. By the end of the week I knew that I would have to go to Well-Sprung's office.

The urge had not left me when Saturday rolled around. I just wanted to get some idea of the world Miss Well-Sprung (it seemed like a good nickname given her 'assets') moved in. I told myself it would do no harm.

All the same, a disguise seemed like a good idea. It was a Saturday and, according to the website, Well-Sprung didn't open at the weekend, but I couldn't take the risk. What if she lived over the shop? There was a strong possibility that if she saw me, she would recognise me. Michael may not have officially introduced us at the Christmas party where Miss Well-Sprung first came to my attention, but, especially if they had already begun their flirtation, she must have seen me clinging to him on the dance floor. Clinging because I had noticed her circling him like a shark. Yes, I would have to wear a disguise.

I stood in front of my wardrobe and waited for inspiration. Unfortunately, it was not quite so fruitful a cupboard of disguises as Mr Benn's. I did have a nurse's uniform, but I'd bought it from Ann Summers, the sex shop, in an attempt to cheer Michael up when he had man-flu. With its pussy pelmet skirt in highly flammable nylon, that outfit was going to fool nobody. Had it been the winter, I would have been fine. I had plenty of coats with hoods and jumpers with big roll necks that I could have pulled up to my nose. But it was the beginning of May and unusually hot. Definitely not balaclava weather. Wrapping up would draw more attention than it diverted. Only nutters wear too many layers in the warm.

Soon my options had been narrowed down to a pair of big sunglasses with a loose lens in the left eye and a head-scarf, bought when I had the notion that channelling the glamour of Grace Kelly might be a suitable fashion direction for me. I'd spent the best part of two hundred pounds in Hermès, but it hadn't quite worked as I hoped. On the three occasions I'd ventured out with that scarf, I'd looked less Princess Grace than palace washerwoman. I didn't look much better when I tied it round my head now, but it would have to do. With the sunglasses clamped firmly to my nose, most of my face was covered. The scarf hid my hair colour. I was ready to go.

*   *   *

The premises of Well-Sprung Interiors were surprisingly uninspiring. They occupied the ground floor of a building in a little parade of shops that also contained a dry-cleaner, a halal butcher and a newsagent offering mobile-phone top-ups and Oyster cards. Opposite was a hairdressing salon so out of date that it still offered a shampoo and set. I was immediately cheered by the fact that my rival obviously wasn't making Kelly Hoppen lose any sleep.

As it was a Saturday and the shop appeared to be empty, I pressed my nose against the picture window for a proper look inside. There were a couple of very ordinary-looking desks. Possibly Ikea. Neither especially tidy. The bookshelves were bowing under the weight of hundreds of dull lever-arch files. Against the wall were piled carpet and wallpaper sample books. A tower of interiors magazines was topped by a dirty mug. The mug claimed it was a present from New York. There was nothing to focus on. It was just an ordinary interiors shop, really. No more clues as to what Michael found so compelling about its inhabitant. I'd had a wasted journey. Or so I thought . . .

Just as I had satisfied myself that I could glean nothing more from staring into the closed shop, I became aware of a car pulling up to the kerb behind me. Watching the driver in the reflection on the big picture window, I realised to my horror that it was her: Miss Well-Sprung herself.

I should have hopped on to my bike, but I was paralysed with anxiety. I couldn't pretend I had just been browsing, could I? Well-Sprung Interiors didn't exactly have an inviting window display.

'Can I help you?' she asked. It was the first time I'd heard her voice. It was as husky and exotic as I had dreaded from the moment I heard she came from Brazil. Damn.

I snapped my sunglasses back down over my eyes like a visor before I dare turn round. When I did, I found her just a couple of feet away from me, her head cocked to one side as if to ask, 'What have we here?' I had to make my excuses and quickly.

'I was just . . .' I glanced across the street and the salon caught my eye. 'Just waiting for my hairdressing appointment. Hence the . . .' I indicated the scarf on my head.

'Oh, OK,' said Well-Sprung, looking me up and down. My incongruous Hermès scarf and sunglasses were accessorising a very tatty pair of combat trousers. She was wearing a white shirt knotted at the waist, tailored Capri pants and open-toed sandals. Her pedicure was flawless. 'Excuse me,' she said. She wiggled past me to open the door. As I jumped out of her way, the loose lens in my sunglasses fell to the floor and was crunched beneath her foot.

'Oh, I'm sorry.' She knelt to pick it up.

'It's OK,' I said, running across the street before she had a chance to look at me without the Polaroid shield. 'They were old.'

'But . . . your sunglasses!'

Damn. And double damn. I couldn't have drawn more attention to myself if I'd tried. And now, as I pushed my way into the salon (it took a moment before I realised the notice on the door said, 'Pull'), I became aware that she was still watching me. Of course, she was wondering about my broken sunglasses, but perhaps something about me had jogged her memory and she was beginning to work out exactly where she'd last seen me. As I hovered at the salon's reception desk, she was still watching. I couldn't just turn round and leave.

'You got an appointment?' the girl at the desk asked.

'No.'

'Kylie can fit you in when she's finished Mrs Brown's blow-dry.'

What could I do except agree? Sneaking a peek back at

Well-Sprung Interiors, I saw that my rival was still outside her office. She was talking on her mobile. Was she calling Michael? Had she worked out who I was? Would she know for sure who I was if I took my headscarf off?

'Take a seat over there.' The receptionist ushered me to a chair at the back of the salon. Momentary relief. But how long was Miss Well-Sprung going to spend hanging around outside her office that afternoon? My exit could be my undoing.

Which is why when Kylie asked me what I wanted 'done', I asked her to dye my hair brown.

'Are you sure?'

Kylie wasn't. She suggested a full head of highlights instead, but I knew that wouldn't work. Miss Well-Sprung was still in and out of her shop, carrying files to and from her car, or just sitting on the bonnet to take phone calls or have a cigarette. She was making the most of the sunshine.

'It's going to look rubbish,' said Kylie.

I said I just wanted a change. As I watched Miss Well-Sprung to see if she was still watching me, a transformation from blonde to brunette didn't seem like such a bad idea anyway. Apart from the amount of cleavage she was proudly displaying with her artfully unbuttoned shirt, the main difference between me and Miss Well-Sprung was that her hair was brown. Now that I thought about it, whenever Michael and I had spoken about those actresses he admired (for 'admired' read 'fancied') they had always been brunettes. Someone Latin-looking. Penélope Cruz was one of his favourites. He liked Salma Hayek too. And Catherine Zeta-Jones (OK, she's not very Latin, but she had a fair bash at it in *Zorro*). Michael had never gone for the girls that I modelled myself on: Gwyneth or Cate Blanchett. They were insipid. Not like Miss Well-Sprung at all.

'Can't you do a wash in, wash out?' I suggested. 'Just so I can get an idea?'

'It won't suit you,' Kylie insisted. 'And as it washes out, it will start to take on reddish tones, which will look even worse. I tell all my clients the same thing. If you dramatically change your hair colour, it's not the only thing you're going to have to alter. You have to be prepared to change your make-up too, and the colours of the clothes you wear. I had one client who even had to change the colour of the walls in her house after she went from blonde to brown.'

'I'm ready for it,' I said. I couldn't help wondering what kind of walls didn't go with brown hair.

'All right. But I am doing this at your insistence,' Kylie said one more time.

In actual fact it didn't look bad. The hair, at least, looked great. It looked magnificent. It had a depth of shine that I never could have achieved with my previous mousy colour, even if I slept in leave-in conditioner for a month. My hair was beautiful. It was the sort of hair you see being tossed in an advertisement for Laboratoires Garnier. It was sumptuous and silky. It reflected the light like a mirror. It was the kind of hair I defy any man to keep his hands out of . . . Unfortunately, it just didn't go with my face.

'I knew it,' said Kylie. 'It's way too dark.'

I didn't look like Penélope Cruz or Salma Hayek. I didn't even look like Catherine Zeta-Jones. With my pale skin under that ravishing brunette mop, I looked as though I was going to a fancy-dress party as my grandmother's favourite comedian, Max Wall. But I was in denial. As far as I was concerned, I had the kind of hair that would make Michael fall in love.

'Nothing that a bit of blusher can't fix!' I said, full of sudden foolish optimism.

Kylie shook her head. 'Let me know when you want me to add some highlights.'

I paid for my new do and left the salon. Miss Well-Sprung was outside having another cigarette, but this time she didn't even glance in my direction. I grabbed my bike and started pedalling. I'd got away with it.

17

Becky was not so sure.

I spent the rest of Saturday adjusting to my new look. Kylie had been right about needing a new look to go with my new locks. So, high on having got past Miss Well-Sprung with my cunning disguise, I spent five hundred pounds in Debenhams on new make-up and a red dress. When I got home, I put on the outfit and the make-up and sat in front of my dressing-table mirror practising pouting and hair-tossing. Anything Miss Well-Sprung could do . . . I'd have her out of my side of Michael's bed before she could say, '*Ay, caramba.*'

On Sunday Becky had invited me to lunch. Over the phone she sounded impressed when I told her that I had updated my image as my first step in getting over Michael. 'Good for you,' she said. 'Out with the old. I'm very proud of you.' In person, her reaction was rather different.

'For goodness' sake,' said Becky. 'What on earth have you done to yourself? You look just like Nancy Dell'Olio.'

It wasn't the reaction I had hoped for.

'I thought I might try being a brunette for a while.'

'But why? You have the kind of natural colour that people would die for! This' – she waved her hands at my hair with a faint expression of disgust on her face – 'is just horrible.'

'I thought it was OK.'

'Look, I know you probably want to have a new start. A new image. But the whole point of changing your hair after a break-up is to look better than before, so that if the idiot who dumped you should bump into you on the street, he is instantly filled with remorse and regret.'

'Yes. But this is what Michael goes for now . . .'

Becky did a double-take. 'You what?'

'His new girlfriend is a brunette.'

'So you dyed your hair to look like her!'

I nodded mutely.

'You absolute idiot.'

'Makes sense to me. He wants a brunette.'

'You think that's the only difference?'

'It's a start at levelling the playing field.'

'Why are you even bothering?'

'Wouldn't you?' I asked. 'If Henry left you.'

Becky shuddered. Even though her wedding invitations had been sent out, I could tell that she was superstitious about even saying such a thing. She changed the subject.

'Apart from anything else, this stupid new hair colour is going to look absolutely terrible with the bridesmaid's dress. Didn't you even think about that?'

Obviously I hadn't thought about that.

'For God's sake, Ashleigh. What am I supposed to do? It's too late to get the dress changed. You'll have to have your hair dyed blonde again. If that's even possible. Or wear a wig.'

As a result of my image change, Sunday lunch looked set to be a trial. Every few minutes or so Becky would look up at my hair, frown and shake her head. Henry tried to be kind. He told me I looked like one of the sisters from that Irish band the Corrs. Becky told him he was being ridiculous.

'She looks a fright. I can't believe it. I've spent nearly four hundred pounds on that bridesmaid's dress and now she's gone and changed her hair colour.'

'I am here,' I reminded her. 'And I've said I'm sorry. I'll get it sorted out. I swear.'

That seemed to mollify her, but by the time the roast was ready, I was starting to feel quite angry and thought that perhaps I would keep my hair brown just to spite her. It wasn't as though I was ever going to look good in that bridesmaid's dress in any case. What is it about sensible, fashionable women that makes them lose their fashion sense the moment they get an engagement ring on their finger? I foolishly suggested as much in what I thought was a joking tone. Becky spat her response, which was that she would cancel my floral headdress and buy me a brown-paper bag to wear at the wedding instead. 'You can wear it next time you go stalking as well.'

I told her I didn't feel hungry after that and left. Though the lunch had been intended to cheer me up, I left her house feeling much worse. And given how bad the last couple of weeks had been, that was really saying something.

The day was to get even worse. Skipping lunch with the happy couple left me with a rumble in my stomach and a lot of free time that only mischief could fill. The walk from Becky's house took me past Helen and Kevin's. How could I forget that they were going to be hosting a barbecue to celebrate their new arrival that very afternoon?

It was half past one when I got to the top of Helen and Kevin's street. Even from a hundred metres away I could smell the scent of lighter fluid that marks the start of any successful barbecue. Since I was still NFI (as in 'not f*cking invited'), I couldn't just rock up, but I decided that there was no law against walking down their street (though an alternative route would have been easy enough to find). And there was no law against stopping to have a rest. Behind their neighbour's hedge.

About ten minutes after I took up my vigil, Helen appeared

at the doorway. In her hand she held three silver heart-shaped balloons to welcome baby Alex. She had just finished tying the balloons to the gatepost when Michael's red sports car pulled up at the kerb and out he got, holding one more silver balloon (also heart-shaped). But where Helen's balloons declared in pretty pink letters 'It's a girl', Michael's bore 'It's a boy' in baby blue.

There was little time for me to savour Michael's confusion and embarrassment, because even as he was handing over his gift, to Helen's obvious confusion, Michael's passenger was getting out of the car. With a shake of her hair, as though she were in a shampoo advert, Miss Well-Sprung stepped on to the pavement.

'You've brought a guest?' I heard Helen say. 'But . . .'

'Didn't Kevin tell you?'

'He didn't, but . . .'

Michael held out his arm. Miss Well-Sprung slipped under it and snuggled into his side.

'I like your house,' said Miss Well-Sprung to Helen. 'Very interesting colour, your front door.'

Helen gave a little shimmy, as though praise for her front door from an interior designer were as good as being praised for the figure she hadn't regained since the baby was born.

'Well, come on in,' said Helen. 'It's lovely to meet you. I've heard a lot about you.'

I hated Helen then. Almost as much as I hated Miss Well-Sprung and Michael.

Oh, my feckless friend, my faithless boyfriend and that slut. How my heart ached as I stumbled from my hiding place behind Helen's neighbour's hedge. I stumbled the rest of the way back to my flat. People with small children crossed the road to avoid me with my face bright red from tears and the great honking noise of my sobs.

Once in the flat, further humiliation was to greet me. I got under the shower, desperate to wash the brown out of my hair now that I had seen Miss Well-Sprung again and knew that being a brunette would not help at all. But the ugly colour would not wash out. So much for semi-permanent, though I stood beneath the shower for hours and hours, shampooing twenty-three times. I had been abandoned by my boyfriend, betrayed by my friends, and to cap it all, my hair, as Kylie had promised, was an ugly shade of browny-orange.

I needed comfort badly, but I couldn't call Becky, my so-called best friend. The last thing I needed was to hear 'I told you so'. It was too late to call Mum and Dad. I could have called the Samaritans. I had called them once before, many years ago, when I first moved into the flat and thought I might be losing my job just as I signed a year-long lease. But as I recalled that dark night, I also remembered that the Samaritans are trained to be wonderfully sympathetic but also utterly impartial. They don't offer advice. And that was what I really needed, wasn't it? Proper solid advice. I needed someone to tell me what to do. Better yet, I needed someone to tell me what was going to *happen*. It didn't take much searching on the Internet before I found someone who promised to do exactly that. With my credit card in hand, I called Personal Psychics Connection.

18

'We have three psychics available to talk to you right now,' said the girl on the other end of the line. 'There's Julie, Erica and Martha.'

'Which one is best?' I asked.

'Oh, I can't say that!' the girl laughed. 'A lot of it depends on whether the spirits you want to connect with are ready to communicate with you. But I can tell you the methods of seeing that they use if you like. Julie will base her reading on your horoscope . . .'

Boring, I thought. Horoscopes were too vague.

'Erica specialises in the runes . . .'

That didn't sound especially specific either.

'And Martha takes instructions directly from a spirit cat . . .'

'A spirit cat?'

'Yes,' said the telephone operator. 'But don't worry, the cat communicates in English.'

A spirit cat. It was, of course, the daftest thing I'd ever heard, but at that time of the night it seemed as though it was more likely to get me the results I wanted than crunching numbers or throwing tiles. It was good enough for me. 'I'll have Martha,' I said.

'All right, Ashleigh. I'll just need your credit-card details and then I'll ask her to give you a call.'

I read out the long number on the front of my Mastercard.

'OK. It's twenty-nine pounds ninety-five for the first

twenty minutes, then one pound fifty a minute for every minute or fraction of a minute after that. Still want me to go ahead?'

I told her that I did. The figures she had quoted didn't mean much to me right then. Having seen Michael and Miss Well-Sprung looking so very together, I thought I might actually die from the pain of it. I wanted answers. I wanted good news for the future and I would have paid just about anything to hear them. Even from a stranger and her spirit moggy.

'All right,' said the chirpy telephonist. 'That's gone through. Martha will call you back in the next ten minutes.'

I waited eagerly, with the phone receiver still in my hand. It rang at the seven-minute mark, just as I was about to call the switchboard back and make sure the girl had taken down the right number.

'Hello?' I said quickly.

'Ashleigh,' said my mother. 'It's your mother.'

'It's eleven at night,' I pointed out. 'You're always asleep by eleven.'

'I know, dear, but I just had a feeling you wanted to talk.'

'Eh?'

'Call me a silly old woman, perhaps it's a mother thing, I just thought, I'm going to call my little girl and remind her how much I love her.'

'Thanks, Mum,' I said. 'That's really great, but can I call you back? I'm waiting for someone else to call.'

'What? At this time of night?'

'Yes.'

'Who's calling you now?'

'You did,' I suggested. 'But, seriously, I'm sorry to shove you off the phone but I'm waiting for a very important call from Los Angeles.'

'About work?'

'A possible client,' I lied.

'In that case . . .' She put her hand over the receiver but I could still hear her very clearly as she yelled to my father, 'She's waiting for a call about work. From Los Angeles! That sounds exciting,' she said to me.

'It is. OK, Mum. Thanks for calling. I have to clear the line for this really important call. But I love you too.'

'All right, darling. You know that any time you want to talk, we're here for you, your dad and me. We may be silly old duffers . . .'

'I'm not!' Dad shouted.

'. . . but we're your parents and we love you, and whatever we can do to make your life better, we will.'

'Thanks,' I said. 'I'll call you tomorrow.' Then I put the phone down before Mum could start off another thread of conversation. I didn't want or need motherly love right then. I needed that spirit cat! I felt compelled to hear its views and decided that wish – to get my mother off the phone so that the psychic cat could talk to me – must be in some way SIGNIFICANT. It meant that the cat must be picking up messages for me already.

As soon as I got rid of Mum, the phone rang again almost immediately. I stabbed the green accept button and prepared for the future to unfurl.

The phone was quiet, except for the sound of someone mouth-breathing.

'Hello,' I said, hoping this was the psychic and not just a plain psycho.

'*Miaow*,' said the caller.

'Martha?' I asked.

'No. *Miaow*. I am Tiberius, the great spirit cat. *Miaow*. Rrrooowwwlll. But in my last earthly lifetime I was Princess Fifi, the Burmese cat belonging to Martha, yes. Purr. Purr.'

'Oh. I see.'

'Do not be afraid,' Martha as Tiberius intoned. 'I have inhabited Martha's mortal corporeal being in order to be able to speak with you today. What . . . *miaow* . . . is your question?'

The question should have been, what on earth was I doing spending £29.95 to have a telephone conversation with a woman from South London who thought herself inhabited by the spirit of her dead pet? Instead I said, 'I want to know what's going to happen in my love life.'

'*Miaow*,' said Martha. 'Very well.' A pause. 'Do you want to be more specific?' the psychic asked in her normal voice.

'I'd rather hear what you pick up in the other world,' I suggested. I didn't want to give her any clues in case they influenced what she said. I'd heard that telephone psychics tried to pump people for information and adapt their readings accordingly.

'OK. *Miaow* . . . I can tell at once that you have been wronged by a man.'

Spot on. I was hooked.

'Tell me his name.'

'Aren't you getting it from the spirits?' I asked.

'They're not always that forthcoming, but wait . . .' She miaowed again. 'I am getting some letters. I'm getting an A. No, I'm getting an L. The letter N.'

'Did you say M?' I asked.

'Maybe that was it.'

'His name is Michael.'

'Aaaaah.' Suddenly Martha/Tiberius hissed. She sounded exactly like a cat that had been cornered by a dog-lover with a broom. 'I feel bad energy coming from this person,' she said. 'Is he allergic to felines?'

Amazingly, he was. In fact, Michael was allergic to just about everything. He had to have some kind of antihistamine shot in his buttock once a year in order to be able to go outside once the pollen was flying. As for animals, cat dander made his eyes as red as an experimental rabbit's,' a lick from a Labrador could kill him.

'What else are you getting?' I asked Martha.

'I will try to tune in to his aura,' she told me.

Another minute passed.

'Oh, it's dark. It's very dark in here.'

'Really?' I asked.

'Oh, yes. Bad energy,' she said. 'Bad energy indeed. *Miaow, miaowwwwwwww,*' she added. 'What do you want to know about this man? Michael.' She gave a little hiss again.

'He was my boyfriend,' I told her. 'And I want to know if he's going to come back to me.'

'He did you harm,' she said again.

'I know, but . . .'

'He's not entirely out of your life, right? And you want to know whether he will come back to you? And whether he will give you the commitment that you so desire?'

'I do,' I admitted.

'Well, the Great Ceiling Cat says that we can have anything that we wish for, but we should be careful *what* we wish for.'

Ceiling Cat? Wasn't that lolcat code for God?

'What does that mean?' I asked.

'It means . . .' Martha purred for a moment. 'It means that you need to look deep into your heart and try to see where the right path lies for you. Lift up your heart to the Great Cat in the Sky and ask him to pour light over you so that you may see.'

'Right,' I said. 'But can't you be a bit more specific? Could you tell me, for instance, whether he is in love with someone else?' I clung to the hope that Miss Well-Sprung had broken up with him on the way home from the barbecue.

'I can only tell you what I am shown,' said Martha. 'But I will look once more into the silver glass.' She did some more purring for good measure. I waited, Biro-tip poised over my notepad to start taking down any revelations. The purring continued for quite some time.

'Are you still there?' I asked, in case it was a fault on the line.

'*Rrrrrrroooooaaaaawwwww*,' said Martha. I took that to mean that I should try to be more patient.

'Er . . .' I tried again, after another three minutes.

'Something is coming,' Martha assured me. 'Something you very much need to know. Be patient. Be patient.' She slipped back into cat noises again.

I kept the phone pressed against my ear as I glanced at my watch. My twenty minutes were over. I was now listening to a grown woman purring at a cost of seventy-five pence every thirty seconds. I had absolutely lost it.

But still I hung on. On the other end of the line, Martha/Tiberius squeaked and rumbled. She rawled and miaowed. She sounded at one point as though she might be having a kitty stroke. The clock ticked. Still nothing. Nothing. And then . . .

'The Great Cat in the Sky says,' she intoned at last, 'that there is a strong female energy around him. I sense the spirit of a capybara!' she added triumphantly.

A what?

'A capybara,' she repeated. 'But all is not well. Ah, no . . .'

I heard a mobile phone trilling in the background, somewhere in Martha's house.

'The spirit is leaving me!'

'But . . . Tiberius.'

The mobile in the background was insistent.

'I'm Martha again now,' she said. 'Was that all right for you, Ashleigh? Did you get everything you needed?'

'Thanks,' I said. 'I think so.'

I had been on the phone for forty minutes. Sixty quid for a capybara. What on earth did that mean?

19

Capybara. I looked at the word written on my notepad and tried to make sense of it. Wasn't a capybara some kind of rat? Or was the word an anagram? *Bar capay? Yap a crab?* I couldn't come up with anything sensible, so I opened up my laptop again and plugged the letters in, guessing the spelling. And there it was. A capybara. I had been right. It was a cross between a beaver and a rat. And it was one of the most common wild animals to be found in Brazil.

'Brazil!' I exclaimed when I read the word. My God. It was too ridiculous to be a coincidence. Tiberius must have tuned in to Miss Well-Sprung. She was a Brazilian! It was the only explanation. Of course her spirit was represented by an animal from her homeland. I hadn't told Martha that Miss Well-Sprung was Brazilian. This was proof that the telephone psychic had not been giving me some pre-set speech.

I needed to know more. I picked up the telephone and dialled the psychic hotline again. To my irritation, the switchboard operator informed me that Martha was on another call and would not be available for at least an hour.

'Do you want me to put you on to one of the other readers?' she asked.

'No,' I said. 'It has to be Martha. I think she has a message for me. From Tiberius.'

'I understand,' said the switchboard operator, sounding as though she really did understand. 'I'll make sure that you're next in the queue.'

I didn't know what to do with myself while I waited for Martha to call back. I typed 'capybara' into Google again and brought up a couple of pictures. I looked into the shiny black eyes of a female capybara and imagined it sitting in Michael's lap. It looked like a malevolent sort of thing. I decided that the malevolence of the capybara's spirit was what was making Michael's aura so dark. He'd been bewitched by a rodent in human form.

Martha finally rang me back at a quarter to three in the morning. I was disappointed when she addressed me in her normal speaking voice rather than in the miaows of Tiberius this time, but she assured me that there was no problem. She had no doubt, since the capybara image had been so accurate, that Tiberius had more to say to me and would be back before I knew it.

Unfortunately, she was wrong. Tiberius was not back for the whole of my expensive twenty minutes.

'Aren't you getting anything from Tiberius at all?' I begged as the clock ticked into overtime.

'You can't hurry the spirits, love,' Martha told me. 'Maybe you should call back tomorrow.'

I did. I called back the next evening. And the next and the next. But Tiberius was on an extended catnap. Unable to get through to the spirits without him, Martha offered me the benefit of her personal female wisdom on men instead.

'What you have to understand, my love,' she said, 'is that all of them are bastards. It just takes some of them longer than others to prove it.'

On Thursday night Martha thought that Tiberius might be coming back, but just as she started to purr, she got a text to say that her eldest son had been picked up by the rozzers and she was needed at the police station.

93

Still I kept calling, at a cost of £29.95 for the first twenty minutes in the hope that something, anything, useful or at least hopeful, would be revealed. And finally, finally, on Saturday night, Tiberius returned.

Martha cut short a long speech about her bastard ex-husband and let out a miaow that sounded distinctly like a miaow of irritation. 'He's here,' she informed me. Then she settled into a long bout of purring.

'I'm sorry,' I said as the clock hit nineteen minutes again, 'but twenty minutes have almost passed and I don't have a lot of money. I just have to know what to do next.'

'You're sure that you still want to get back together with your ex-boyfriend?'

'Yes,' I said. 'It's what I want more than anything in the world.'

I wanted to be with Michael. I had wished for that ever since our first kiss. Being dumped had not changed how I felt at all. Neither had seeing him taking Miss Well-Sprung to my friend's barbecue. Be careful what you wish for meant nothing to me right then. I felt sure that if I got what I wanted, I would live happily ever after.

'*Miaow*,' said Tiberius. Martha's South London accent had been replaced by a luxuriously deep growl. 'Then I can help you. I can cast a spell that will bring him back to you and ensure that your rival never bothers you again. It will be an easy process for me. I can see into any human heart. But you have to do your part as well.'

'What is it?' I asked. 'I'll do anything.'

'This is what you must do.'

Tiberius gave me my instructions.

'You have been chosen,' said the psychic cat. 'To receive the blessings of the Great Ceiling Cat. But in order to receive those blessings, you must first make an offering. You must come to my mortal home for a personal consultation.'

Martha slipped back into her real voice to give me an address. I wrote down the address. Then Martha became Tiberius again to tell me, 'I will see you there when you are ready.'

'Anything else?' I asked.

'Yes,' said Tiberius. 'You must bring a thousand pounds. In cash.'

The phone line went dead. Tiberius had hung up on me.

20

I know, I know. Madness is the only word for it. I'd already spent five hundred pounds on improving my image to match Miss Well-Sprung. That week alone I had spent a further three hundred pounds on calling a psychic hotline. And now said telephone psychic had asked me for a thousand pounds and I was seriously considering giving it to her. So that she would cast a *spell*.

But haven't you ever wanted something so much that money became irrelevant? It's not as though I was thinking about blowing a grand on a pair of shoes. The way I saw it, I was considering an investment in my future happiness, and that of Michael. If we were meant to be together and a thousand pounds was what it would take to bring us back together, then it seemed like a bargain to me.

Unfortunately, I didn't have a thousand pounds. In the month since Michael dumped me, I had just about melted my credit card. I had never been much of a saver and had nothing left in my current account at all after paying that month's rent. It was with that in mind that I had gratefully accepted my mother's invitation to have Sunday lunch in the family home in Croydon. I could spend three pounds on a train fare or a fiver on a ready meal to eat all by myself. The train fare was all I could manage. I could not afford to spend a grand on juju.

I tried to forget all about it.

*   *   *

The downside to not having to cook my own lunch that Sunday was that lunch with my parents always meant lunch with my brother as well. Lucas, or 'the Accident' as he was affectionately known, coming into our lives as he did shortly after my mother first told me of the dangers of men and the importance of contraception, still lived with Mum and Dad. Not so surprising, I suppose, given that he was only twenty. There were twelve years between us.

My relationship with Lucas had always been somewhat difficult. He was cute enough as a toddler, but when I was going through those tricky teen years, Lucas was just coming into his own as the master of the practical joke. I didn't appreciate finding snails in my brand-new pixie boots. Neither did I appreciate a six-year-old Lucas and his friends using my trainer bras as catapults.

Now Lucas was twenty, he was at college, studying for an art foundation course that he hoped would help him make it to film school. Lucas looked every inch the art student that day. He would not have seemed out of place on the arm of Amy Winehouse or one of the Geldof girls. He wore his dirty blond hair straggly and long beneath a greasy old hat that had belonged to our grandfather (his gardening hat). His tight jeans were pulled bizarrely low so that his underpants were clearly visible over his waistband. Not such a good look, as far as I was concerned. Especially since I had no doubt that the underpants he was showing off had been bought by our mum. But Lucas's bizarre fashion habits were apparently very hip and they didn't seem to be costing him success with the girls. Since his voice broke (and actually before. He was a very sweet child when he wasn't tormenting me), he had been surrounded by girls. When I arrived that Sunday, one of the latest batch of girls was just leaving. She sloped away from the house as though she were sneaking past the paps outside the home of Russell Brand.

'Did that girl stay the night?' I asked Lucas. She had a distinct walk-of-shame air about her.

'Uh-huh,' said Lucas.

'What? In your room?'

'Mm-hmm.'

That would never have happened when I was living at home. I wasn't even allowed to sit at the same end of the sofa as my boyfriend if Mum and Dad were around. I tried not to be bothered by the fact that it seemed so unfair. After all, aged thirty-two, it was a long time since I'd had to answer to anyone with regard to who shared my bed at night.

'Is she your girlfriend?' I asked.

Lucas look horrified. 'Why do you people have to label everything?' he asked me.

You people? I felt incredibly old.

'And what have you done to your hair? It looks horrible.'

'Thank you very much,' I said.

'I hope that's a wash in, wash out,' said my mother.

Dad was in the kitchen that day. Mum had bought him a cookery course for his sixtieth birthday, since she was determined that things would change before my father retired. She told me she wanted him to be able to cook because she had no intention of spending the rest of her life chained to the kitchen. When she retired, she was going to write a book and learn to fly. Dad would have to make his own toast.

Dad cottoned on at once to Mum's plan but he had gone ahead and taken the course with good grace and discovered, to his surprise (and mine), that he really rather enjoyed it. Ever since, it had been hard to keep him out of the kitchen. That day he was doing something complicated with beef. Though Mum joined me for an aperitif (Cinzano and lemonade) in the living room, I could tell that she was itching to be in the kitchen, overseeing what was bound (in her eyes) to be a disaster.

It wasn't a disaster. Even Lucas managed to grunt his approval as he shovelled his food away in record time.

Now that Dad was doing the cooking, Mum had to do the washing-up. This was a part of the deal she hadn't bargained for and she pulled the rubber gloves on with a hint of disdain. She'd forgotten that the best part of cooking Sunday lunch was getting to slob out in the conservatory afterwards, while Dad and Lucas cleared away. I sensed she was wondering if delegating lunch was worth the sacrifice.

I joined Mum at the sink. They didn't have a dishwasher. It was something to do with the lecture they'd received from the vicar who married them. He'd told them that the glue that held marriages together was making sure that you washed up together. As far as the vicar was concerned, there was nothing that couldn't be resolved when you had to stand side by side for at least fifteen minutes a day. One washing, one wiping. It was for that reason that Mum and Dad didn't have a dishwasher fitted when they bought a new kitchen. Mum refused to budge on the matter, though I argued that when the vicar delivered his lecture, dishwashers had yet to be invented. Surely they could substitute washing-up for going for a walk with the dog. The elderly family dog, called Ben, was a very fat spaniel and would have benefited enormously from that.

The washing-up did, however, provide the opportunity for me to have a conversation with my mother. It was the first time I had managed to get her on her own. Dad was snoozing under the newspaper. Lucas was upstairs doing coursework, or rather playing some zombie game on the Net.

'I don't know what possessed you to dye your hair brown,' she said. She had been tutting about my new look all lunchtime. 'You always had such nice hair.'

'I wanted a change, you know. After Michael.'

'For God's sake, don't go letting him ruin your life now that he's left you. Have it dyed back how it was. Have you heard from him?'

'No.'

Mum had been remarkably kind and sensitive since the break-up, never once suggesting to me that time was running out if I ever hoped to have a husband and children. In fact, she once said to me that had she her time again, she would like to try out a life like mine. No responsibilities. No one to tell you you can't have a satin frill around the dressing table. I suggested to her that very fanciest frill around the dressing table couldn't, in my view, compare with having someone to come home to.

'Ha! The dog acts more pleased to see me than your father does. Unless your brother has already fed him.'

Ben the dog was in love with Lucas, which was only right, I supposed, since the dog had been bought to make up for the fact that after I left for university, when Lucas was just six and a half, he was effectively an only child. Their bond was unbreakable. When Lucas was upstairs, Ben would position himself at the bottom of the stairs, as if to keep guard over his master. I knew that everyone dreaded the day when the smelly old mutt finally passed on.

'You know we'll always do our best to help you,' said Mum then.

And that's when I had a very bad idea.

'Mum,' I began, 'do you really mean that?'

'Yes,' Mum answered cautiously.

'Because you know how I've always said that I wanted to get ahead on my own and would never consider asking you for anything more than your love?'

'Yes.'

'Well, it turns out I need a little more than love right now.'

Mum whirled round to face me. Her hands were still in the washing-up bowl.

'I need to borrow some money.'

'How much?'

'A thousand pounds.' I said it quickly, as if that might make the amount seem smaller.

'Are you in trouble?' Mum asked. Her eyes widened hopefully as she asked me and I noticed that her gaze had drifted down to my stomach. After all those years spent lecturing me on how not to get into trouble, I knew that she wanted nothing more than for me to announce that Michael had left me 'with child'. 'Because you don't have to do anything rash, sweetheart. You know that your father and I would be delighted—'

'I'm not pregnant,' I said quickly.

'Oh.' Mum's eyes lost their grandma glow. 'Then what do you need a thousand pounds for?'

'I want to do a course,' I lied.

'A course on what?'

'On . . . er . . .' I had to think on my feet. Rather stupidly, I hadn't planned for this very obvious question. As I hesitated, Ben nudged the back of my knee in the hope of a titbit and it came to me. The perfect answer. 'Dog grooming,' I said.

'Dog grooming?'

'Yes.'

I hoped that would be the end of it, but of course it wasn't.

'What do you want to do a course in dog grooming for?'

'For my career.'

'But you work in advertising. You've got a good job. A proper career.'

'Yes,' I said. 'But it's tough out there. People are talking redundancies all the time.'

'Is your firm talking about redundancies?' my mother asked. She still had her hands in the washing-up bowl. 'Phil! Ashleigh's firm is talking about redundancies!' she yelled to my father, who was snoozing beneath the business pages. My father spluttered awake.

'They're not talking about redundancies,' I said, 'but I don't think that anyone can really afford to be complacent right now. That's all. I'm just trying to make sure that if anything were to go wrong, I would be in the best possible position to look for work elsewhere.'

'Then why don't you take a course in cake decorating?' said my mother. 'You'd find that more interesting. And you already know you have a talent! People will always want wedding cakes. You get a qualification in cake-making and you could charge the earth for three tiers. That cake you did for your grandma's eightieth birthday was a triumph.'

'Thanks, Mum.'

'That's what you ought to be doing if you're worried about your job. Cake-making. There are courses all over the place, and I'm sure they don't cost anything like a thousand pounds. A thousand pounds for a course in dog grooming!' She raised her eyebrows.

I could see the money I needed slipping away from me. I wish I hadn't started it.

'I understand what you're saying, Mum, but I don't think I'll be able to make anywhere near as much money in cakes.'

'But I should think that dog grooming is the first thing to go when people trim their household budgets.'

'Not necessarily. You know how much people love their pets,' I said, indicating Ben with a nod of my head. Mum always bought Ben birthday and Christmas presents. 'There are lots of lonely people who treat their dogs like children. They're not going to cut back on them. So I think my idea, to do the dog-grooming course, is the best one for now. Can you help me?'

'I'll have to ask your father.'

Thankfully, though he was officially the breadwinner, Dad deferred to Mum on all matters financial. When she gave her consent, he merely shrugged and said, 'Dog grooming,' with a shake of the head, as though it were some obscure branch of psychology he had never previously heard of.

Mum wrote the cheque.

'I'll pay you back as soon as I can,' I promised her. 'Thank you so much. I can't tell you what this means to me.'

That much was true.

That night I put the cheque in the middle of the kitchen table and looked at it guiltily. Was I going mad? I was planning to hand over a thousand pounds to a voodoo priestess in an attempt to win back Michael's heart. Would I have been better advised to take a grand out of the bank in fifty-pound notes and toss them off Battersea Bridge and into the Thames?

I should have handed the cheque back and told Mum that she was right. It would be more sensible for me to do a cake course. But I thought of the promises that Martha/Tiberius had made to me over the phone. To get Michael back, a thousand pounds seemed a very small price to pay. Practically peanuts. And I was sure that if Martha did manage to work her magic and Michael and I eventually married, Mum would be only too pleased and amused to hear how she had made her contribution to my happiness.

The following morning I took the cheque to the bank and made an appointment to see Martha four days later, by which time the cheque should have cleared.

With that appointment in my diary, I actually managed to make it into the office for the next four days and did some useful work between looking at the Well-Sprung Interiors website and checking Michael's updates on Facebook. (He seemed to think that 'Kevin' had told him Alex was a boy for a joke.) Oh, Facebook. Source of such agony and comfort. Each time I logged on I held my breath and hardly dare open my eyes beyond a squint until I could be sure that Michael hadn't changed his relationship status again, to engaged.

21

Back before Michael broke up with me, back when my brain was still working (just), I would have turned and fled home the minute I emerged from the Tube station nearest to the address that Martha the cat psychic had given me. I was carrying a thousand pounds in cash through a part of London that even the hardest character Ray Winstone ever played would not have chanced to walk through alone. And I was carrying my one and only real designer handbag: a Prada number I'd found on eBay. Though I doubted that any of the local footpads would have believed that anyone who ventured into their hood would be so daft as to carry real Prada, I didn't want to lose it.

I walked quickly, praying that I could get to Martha's door without incident. I was on such high alert that when a twenty-something lad opened his mouth to say something (like 'Gimme your handbag', I assumed), I barrelled on past him at high speed, so that he had to shout after me to tell me that my shoelace was undone, right as I tripped over it. Then I managed to get lost. The battery on my iPhone had died and I had to call Martha from a phone box while another fierce-eyed boy-man waited outside. A drug dealer arranging a drop-off, I was sure. When he opened the door, I handed my bag straight over.

'What are you doing?' he asked, giving the bag back to me. 'I only want to know how long you're going to be. I need to call my mum to remind her to record *Britain's Got Talent*.'

When he'd finished calling his mum, he directed me to the block where Martha lived. I had been standing right in front of it.

Martha opened the door.

'I knew the Great Ceiling Cat would help you find your way here,' she said as she ushered me inside.

She was, in so many ways, exactly as I had expected her to be. She was shorter than me. About five feet one. She was wearing a floor-length purple robe that was edged with black lace. Her hair, which was dyed red with a thick grey stripe of roots, was decorated with a black ribbon. Inside, her flat was also exactly as I had imagined. Though it was sunny outside, the place was dark as a cellar. Purple velvet was draped at every window. There was an overwhelming smell of incense and cat pee. It reminded me of the shops that Becky and I had frequented as teens, before emo had its own name.

'Did you bring the money?' Martha got straight to the point.

I nodded.

Martha counted out the thousand pounds in cash on to a table covered in a velvet curtain as though she had been a croupier in a previous existence. She pursed her lips when the first count came to nine hundred and ninety and I waited anxiously as she counted the wad again.

'Good,' she said.

'So, you can get Michael to come back to me now.'

'If it is what the spirits will,' Martha said.

'But . . .' I gestured to the money.

'Your money only buys my intervention with the spirits,' she explained. 'I can guarantee nothing unless it is part of your life's destined path.'

I was tempted to ask why I had just handed over a grand

in that case. Was she telling me that if Michael was going to come back on to my life's path, he would return regardless of whether or not I coughed up? And if the spirits didn't will it, then vice versa? What exactly was her part in the whole thing?

'But I can hurry things along,' said Martha, as though she had sensed that I might be cottoning on to the futility of the transaction.

'Can you?' I asked.

'Yes. But I will need some things from you. I can perform a "go away" spell on this new woman in your lover's life, but in order to be able to do that, I will need you to bring me a lock of her hair.'

'How can I do that?'

'You'll find a way. Just one hair from her head will make the difference. You will add it to this' – she held up what looked like a grey sock – 'which contains all the other ingredients you need to make her leave. Once you have all the ingredients, you must bury this talisman beneath the threshold to your lover's house. She will be unable to step over it and eventually she must give him up for you once more.'

Martha handed me the grey sock. For it was a sock after all. I dared to peer inside it. As I opened the sock, there was a strong whiff of something unpleasant. Possibly feet. It occurred to me then that perhaps this was an actual dead man's sock, taken straight from a corpse!

'You want to know what's inside?' said Martha.

I half shook my head, but she went ahead and told me anyway. 'The pouch' – pouch! That was a sophisticated word for it – 'contains a small glass bottle, inside which there are nine pins, nine needles and nine nails to bring discomfort, anger and pain. There is also the hair of a black dog and the hair of a black cat to make them fight like cat and dog.

There is a small bundle of hyssop and hotfoot powder to make your rival run away.'

It sounded pretty serious.

'Are you sure you are ready to unleash the spell's power?'

I looked at my hand. It was shaking as I held the stinking pouch.

Martha threw her head back and laughed. It was a proper Bond-baddy laugh, which shook her entire body and mine. Her current living cat jumped up from the table and fled for the safety of the curtains. I dropped the pouch on the floor.

'Careful!' Martha shouted. 'You don't want to release the djinni.'

Now I really didn't want to pick it up. I just stood and stared until Martha had to pick the sock up from the floor and press it into my hand herself. Having done that, she suddenly rubbed at her ear as though she were a cat beginning to clean itself.

'*Miaow*,' she said. The spirit cat was back.

'Tiberius?'

'Tiberius says that no harm can come to anyone who follows his advice. When your lover and his new woman part, they will believe that they are doing the right thing. They will be happy they are no longer together. Everything will be as it should be.'

'In that case—'

'But you have to follow the instructions. Get the hair and bury the spell. It must be outside his house. They have to step over it.' Then she hissed. 'Tiberius is tired now. You must go.'

I didn't need to be asked twice. I couldn't wait to be out of that place. I felt as though the atmosphere in Martha's house, with all those sickly, smoky smells, had been embalming me from the inside out. I could still smell the scent in my hair as I took the Tube back home.

Back in my flat, I tipped the contents of the pouch out on to a white plate and examined them. There was nothing that looked obviously harmful, but I still felt a shudder as I put it all back together again.

Part of me wanted it to be hokum, but another part of me wanted it to work very badly indeed. And it wouldn't work until I got the hair.

22

How on earth was I going to get the hair?

I knew where to find Miss Well-Sprung, but I couldn't just walk into her shop and pull it straight from head. I would have to get her to come to me.

I called Becky and told her my plan.

'No,' she said. 'Ashleigh, this is nut-job behaviour. It *is* stalking. It is illegal. And it probably carries a prison term.'

'So, you're saying you won't help me?'

I had asked Becky if she would invite Michael's new girl-friend over to her house to measure up her sofas for some new soft covers. She would be bound to lose a hair in the process. All I had to do was turn up at Becky's house right after she left and find that hair. Unfortunately, Becky was not about to 'enable me', as she put it.

'No,' she said right away.

'Come on,' I pleaded. 'It's just half an hour of your time.'

'I don't understand why you want to see her. I mean, Ashleigh, how is it going to help you? Really?'

I hadn't even told her about the needing-hair-for-a-voodoo-spell part of the equation. Neither did she know that I had already seen my rival in the flesh twice before.

'I just need to know that there's nothing I can do to get Michael back. If his new woman and I are completely different from one another, then I will know that it's a lost cause, won't I?'

'Stop!' Becky commanded. 'You are going insane. It doesn't

matter what she's like. It matters what Michael is like. And we've established, over the past month and a half, that Michael Parker is a Class-A Twat. End of story.'

'You don't really think it's that simple. You remember what you were like when you broke up with Rob.'

I heard a sharp intake of breath on the other end of the phone. Prior to meeting her fiancé, Henry, Becky would have told anyone who asked that Rob Young was the love of her life and always would be. Becky had spilled a lot of tears over Rob Young. She nearly spilled actual blood, as well, when she heard that he'd replaced her with a former friend from teacher-training college.

'I do remember what I was like,' she said softly. 'And with the benefit of hindsight, I can see that all that crying was a total waste of time. Rob was right to end our relationship. It was going nowhere. As soon as one of you wants out, it is over. When I think how much happier I am now that I'm with Henry, and how I might never even have met him if Rob hadn't dumped me and I hadn't forced myself to go on that singles boating weekend. I shudder to think I might have missed out on meeting the real man of my dreams . . .' Her voice quavered a little, as though she were actually shuddering. 'Benefit from my hard lessons, Ashleigh. Do not attempt to see Michael's new girlfriend or inveigle your way into her life in any way. If I hear that you have attempted to become her new best friend in order to find out what's going on, I will call the hospital and have you sectioned.'

'So, you're really not going to help me . . .'

'But I am helping you,' said Becky. 'I am refusing to enable you in making an utter fool of yourself.'

I didn't see it. What I saw was Becky being unreasonably squeamish about helping me do whatever it took to get

Michael back, or, as far as she was concerned, start moving on. And hadn't she spent the past few weeks telling me that move on was exactly what I needed to do?

Had she asked the same of me, I would have done it. In fact, I had done something similar on her behalf! I remembered now that I had hidden in a bush outside Rob Young's house to get a positive ID on the woman who had replaced Becky in his affections. At Becky's request! She had conveniently forgotten about that. I called her back and reminded her.

'Ashleigh,' she sighed, 'what can I do but apologise for having involved you in my madness? There are still days when I wake up in a cold sweat as I remember the depths that I sank to over that stupid man. I would not wish that feeling on anybody. Especially not you, my best friend. And that is why I am going to save you the misery. You may not thank me now, but you will. Good night.'

I was not very pleased. But she was not my last resort. I could still ask for help from the one person who was contractually unable to refuse. My personal assistant, Ellie. I would give her my instructions first thing the following day.

'You want me to call this upholsterer woman and ask her to come in and look at the company's sofas?' she repeated as though I were some kind of idiot.

'Yes,' I said. 'What's so funny about that?'

'But they were new last year,' Ellie pointed out. 'There's nothing wrong with them.'

'I know,' I said. 'But I can't help thinking that the black leather and tubular steel combo is a bit flash. A bit eighties. Too Loadsamoney. It's not very new austerity, is it? Not very "credit crunchy".'

'Neither is spending even more money to recover a sofa

that's only twelve months old, with no obvious wear to it,' said the clever little cow.

'Ellie,' I said, 'don't worry yourself about it. You're not expected to know anything about the budgets. Just call the number and make an appointment. It won't cost anything to get a quote.'

Ellie gave me that weird look again. 'If you insist,' she said.

'I do insist,' I told her.

Bloody Ellie. Every day I wondered why I had given Ellie the job rather than any one of the other eight candidates I interviewed for the position. At the time she had seemed the most simpatico. I daresay she reminded me a little of myself. She was quietly spoken. She seemed a little shy. I wanted to give her a leg-up. I wanted to help her get ahead, just as my first boss had been kind enough to see potential in me. And for the first month of Ellie's tenure (her probation month) I thought I had been proved right. She was sweet and deferential and eager to please, but after that, when her probation period was over and she knew I wouldn't be able to get rid of her without a fight, it was as though she had had a personality transplant. She became chippy and sarcastic. She did her best to undermine me at every turn. I swear I even overheard her telling another assistant in the company that she thought of me less as her mentor than 'plain mental'. 'I really don't know how she got to such a senior position,' Ellie had continued. But the fact was, I was in a senior position to her and I had to remember that. If I asked her to jump, Ellie was only supposed to ask, 'How high?' There was to be no questioning of my authority. Right?

About ten minutes later Ellie poked her head round the office door and told me, 'They're sending someone round on Friday at four thirty.'

'Someone?' My ears pricked up. 'Didn't they specify who?'

'No,' Ellie shrugged. 'Why would they?'

'I want the woman I asked you to call. Her specifically.'

'So, let me get this straight, you want this woman in particular to come in and quote for recovering our sofas, which don't need recovering. You don't want to have to deal with her yourself but she has to come in when you're in the office.'

'What's so difficult about that?' I asked in exasperation.

'There's nothing difficult about it,' said Ellie. 'I can fix just about anything. But it's weird.'

'It's not weird. I'm too busy to deal with the upholstery myself, but I want to be sure that they don't send some monkey apprentice who's going to get the measurements wrong. Someone gave me her name and told me she's the one to use.'

'Have you passed this with Barry?' Ellie asked. Barry was the MD. 'Only surely there's no point going through this rigmarole at all if he's just going to turn round and say that we're not allowed to spend any money on office furnishings. You remember that meeting we had at the beginning of the year. "Careless spending costs jobs" and all that.'

How could I forget? Barry's Second World War style of dealing with the credit crunch had caused a great deal of hilarity for us all. He'd tried to set an example by bringing in homemade sandwiches for a week before reverting to using the local Pizza Express as his canteen. Neither did he seem to see the irony in exhorting us all to save money, then wasting a sheaf of A4 by insisting that we all have printed copies of the three-page email memo he sent on the subject, so that we could pin them above our desks and see his 'Careless spending costs jobs' slogan every time we looked up.

I addressed Ellie's concern. 'If and only if this upholsterer woman is up to my exacting standards, I will let Barry know what I think, which is that a little money spent now on making the office look more *à la vent* could be a valuable long-term investment, as visiting clients will see that we've moved on from the age of bachelor-pad-style bling.'

'*À la vent?*' said Ellie.

'It's French,' I told her. 'Look it up.'

Exit Ellie with much eye-rolling. But she did report back later that afternoon to confirm that the proprietor of Well-Sprung herself would be taking the appointment on Friday.

'Good,' I said. 'Now, wasn't that easy? And think how much easier it would have been if you'd just done what I asked in the first place.'

'Weirdo,' said Ellie under her breath. She thought I didn't hear.

Really, she was shaping up for a very bad half-yearly review indeed. Assuming I dared give her a bad review when we found ourselves eyeball to eyeball over the board table.

Having arranged a meeting, or at least a chance to see Miss Well-Sprung up close again, I had a new sense of focus.

When Friday rolled around, I spent most of the day feeling slightly sick as I waited for the moment for my rival to arrive. I'd had my hair done that lunchtime. It was an extravagance, but if Miss Well-Sprung worked out who I was, then I wanted her to be able to report back to Michael that I was looking great. Fabulous even. Obviously doing very well without him, thank you very much. What's more, I wanted her to feel intimidated. I also changed into a DVF wrap dress.

Ellie frowned when she saw me. 'Have you got a meeting that I don't know about?' she asked. I could tell that this was a source of anxiety for Ellie, who did not like to be left out of anything that might aid her rise to the top of the company tree. 'Or' – and this she said with an air of disbelief – 'a date to go to after work?'

'I just wanted to wear a dress, OK?' I snapped back at her. 'What's wrong with that?'

'Nothing.' Ellie shrugged. But later on I heard her utter the word 'menopause' while she was on the phone to one of her mates.

Menopause? For heaven's sake. I was thirty-two.

Anyway, I got absolutely nothing done that day. How on earth could I concentrate on anything but the arrival of Miss Well-Sprung? I practised a hundred thousand casual lines in my head.

'Do I know you?' she might ask me.

'I don't think so,' I'd say.

'Hold on,' she'd reply. 'I definitely do know you. Or, rather, I know your face. Michael still has your picture by his bedside.'

There was fat chance that she would actually say that, but at least if she did I knew I would be able to laugh a lightly disdainful laugh at the thought and tell her, 'Michael? Oh, you must mean Michael Parker. That's ancient history! But please do give him my regards.'

At half past three the buzzer rang. She was right on time. I positioned myself near the open door to my office and pretended to be tidying my bookshelf so that I would be able to get a good look at her.

Miss Well-Sprung was in the office for just twenty minutes. She took a few measurements of the black leather sofas and left Ellie with a folder of fabric samples and a company brochure. I watched as Ellie shook hands with her and pointed her in the direction of the office. Miss Well-Sprung did not even glance in my direction. What a waste of well-practised, witty one-liners.

I rushed out of my office. 'What was she like?' I asked Ellie.

Ellie shrugged. 'What do you mean? She seemed to know what she was doing.'

'Yes, but what was she *like*?'

'She seemed like a nice enough person. She left this' – Ellie handed me a book of swatches – 'for you to choose the material you want. Assuming Barry approves.'

'Of course Barry won't approve,' I said. 'You may as well have this couriered back to her.'

I was certain that I would have what I needed soon enough.

I had to wait until everyone had left the office to look for my precious hair. There was bound to be one. I'd seen plenty of forensic-science documentaries. I knew that we're all shedding hundreds of hairs each and every day. Unfortunately, bloody Miss Well-Sprung didn't seem to be. There were no hairs whatsoever on the black leather sofa. I pounced on a long hair that lay across Ellie's desk, but close examination of said hair against a sheet of white paper seemed to suggest that it was more likely to be mine than my rival's.

I scoured the floor around Ellie's desk and did an inch-by-inch search of the lobby, where I happened upon a hair that looked decidedly pubic. I discarded that with a shudder. After a further hour on my knees I found another hair, slightly darker than any I had on my head and longer than any that might have belonged to Ellie. It wasn't very long, but I decided it had to be one of Miss Well-Sprung's. I pressed it between two sheets of notepaper and put it in my diary for safekeeping as I headed home.

Back in my kitchen, I opened the sock and quickly slipped that single hair inside alongside the curious ingredients that Martha had promised would make my wish come true. To do the rest, I had to wait until darkness fell, which was late as we were almost at the summer solstice. When darkness did arrive, I donned my scarf and my sunglasses (with the single lens), then cycled to Michael's apartment complex and tried to work out where I could plant the sock to best effect.

How had I not noticed before that River Heights was part of a concrete jungle? There were two tiny flower beds on either side of the main gate, but neither was any good. If I understood Martha correctly, then the spell sock had to be placed somewhere Michael and Miss Well-Sprung would actually step over it each time they went into River Heights. They were unlikely to clamber over the flower beds when a perfectly good path ran between them.

As I pondered my dilemma, the night guard stepped out of his gatehouse for a cigarette break and I realised that he had spotted me. Hanging around the gate with my face covered by the scarf and my one-lensed sunglasses, I must have looked a little odd to say the least. The guard extinguished his cigarette and walked towards the gate.

'Wrong building,' I said, and with a cheerful little wave, I hopped on my bike and continued down to the end of the cul de sac in the hope that the guard would be satisfied that I was just an innocent cyclist who'd got lost.

I was too spooked to do anything that night. The following evening I returned only to be foiled by the guard again. This time he was standing right outside the gates on his cigarette break. On the third night he was there once more and definitely spotted me on my approach, still wearing the sunglasses and scarf. I was desperate to get the curse underway by now, so I brazened it out and decided to hang around until he went back inside. I cycled on by as though going to the other building again.

At the bottom of the cul de sac, I waited for five minutes in the shadow of the large bushes that surround Riverside Point, the slightly nicer building that Michael hadn't been able to afford to buy into. I watched and waited for my moment. As soon as the guard at Michael's complex went back into his hut, I was on my bike and pedalling like Lance Armstrong, pausing only to drop the voodoo sock through the grate outside the main gates. If the guard noticed, there was nothing he could do about it. I had deployed my curse.

'Hey! Watch out!' I was so busy making my getaway that I almost cycled into Michael as he walked down the pavement towards home.

'You could have bloody killed me!' he shouted after me.

I laughed out loud. I actually cackled! Perhaps the curse had already started working.

23

So, I had delivered the spell to Michael's door. All I could do now was wait. And worry. The more I thought about it, the more it occurred to me that I had made a mistake by dropping the sock into the grate. Grates mean drains and that drain doubtless led down to the sewer. In all probability the sock had been washed out into the Thames within hours of being dropped through the grate. Michael and Miss Well-Sprung would not have to step over it at all.

After a week had passed without Michael calling to tell me that Miss Well-Sprung had left and he wanted me back, I began to think that the thousand pounds from Mum's loan had been well and truly wasted. I'd been an idiot. Not only was Michael still happily apart from me, every time I spoke to Mum on the phone I had to tell her what I'd learned at my dog-grooming course.

Worse was to come when Mum and Dad threw a buffet lunch to celebrate their thirty-fifth wedding anniversary. As soon as I walked in, I was cornered by one of my parents' neighbours, Mrs Charlton, proud owner of two standard poodles called Roxy and Satin (or Rocky and Satan to anyone who had the misfortune to cross them).

'Your mother tells me you've been doing a dog-grooming course.'

'Er, that's right.' What else could I say?

'She said that you're going to need lots of dogs to practise on, so I told her you could borrow Roxy and Satin. I can't afford to take them to the proper grooming salon anyway. Not now I'm a pensioner.' She paused.

I knew I was expected to sympathise.

'If you want to do them this afternoon, I can give you my keys and you can go round there while your mum's getting the buffet ready.'

'But I've got my party clothes on,' I said by way of an excuse.

'You can borrow my apron.'

'Perhaps another day.'

'They really need to be done now. It's going to get hot next week.'

'Oh, go on,' said my mother who had appeared at my side with a dish full of cocktail sausages. 'It'll only take half an hour, won't it? You could even bring the dogs over here. So we could all watch.'

I felt the walls closing in. Never have I been so grateful for the intervention of my brother, who said first, 'You can't bring Rocky and Satan over. Ben hates them.'

'If Ben was properly trained . . .' Mrs Charlton began.

Then Lucas scored another point. 'Auntie Joyce is here,' he said to me. 'Come and help me get her out of the taxi.'

I may have pulled a muscle helping her out of the back of the cab, but Auntie Joyce was and always had been one of my favourite relatives. She was actually my great-auntie Joyce. Her sister, my maternal grandmother, had been a judgemental old bag, given to such outrageous pronouncements on my love life as 'Why don't you just give up and become a lesbian?' But Joyce was sweet and disinclined to cause a fight. My grandmother said it was because she had overdone the sherry.

Anyway, Auntie Joyce had never married. As far as I knew, she had never had a man in her life at all, which perhaps

explained her unlined forehead and the generally untrou-
bled demeanour that she had carried with her well into her
eighties.

Which isn't to say that Auntie Joyce was altogether cut
off from the world. Oh, no, she engaged herself fully with
the community and was an active member of her church.
When she arrived at Mum and Dad's that lunchtime, she
was carrying a knitting bag, and from the second she sat
down until the moment she left, excluding the fifteen minutes
it took for her to eat lunch, her fingers never stopped moving.
Click, click, clickety click.

She explained that she was making small knitted figures
for the church's Christmas fair. Christmas was still a good
six months off, but she had promised to make three hundred
of the things. She was working on number seventeen that
afternoon, having started her epic task only the previous
evening.

While Dad and Mum prepared their sumptuous buffet, I
was charged with keeping Joyce well supplied with gin and
tonic. She asked me how I was getting on with that 'lovely
boyfriend' of mine. I told her that 'lovely boyfriend' had
dumped me without warning and was now shagging a
Brazilian upholsterer. OK, I didn't use the word 'shagging'.

'Oh dear,' she said. 'That is a pity. Shagging a Brazilian . . .'

My mouth dropped open. Auntie Joyce's vocabulary
had expanded. Perhaps it's true what they say about the
onset of senility being marked by a loss of social grace
and inhibition.

'I just can't keep my mind off it,' I said. 'I've been trying
to block him out of my head but he just keeps creeping back
in. With the pneumatic Miss Well-Sprung close behind.'

'Is that her name?' asked Auntie Joyce.

'It's the name of her company.'

'Funny,' said Auntie Joyce.

'Not really. It's driving me totally nuts.'

'What you need to do is keep occupied. Why do you think I've taken on all this knitting?'

'For the children?' I said.

'No,' she said. 'It's to keep my mind off *him*.'

Auntie Joyce's angelic face was suddenly twisted with annoyance.

'Him?'

There was a 'him'. It was the first I'd heard of it.

'Frank Farmer.'

'The church caretaker?' She'd talked about him before.

'The very same. The smooth-talking, self-centred shyster. Getting me and Emily Barclay to cook for him, both of us thinking that we had something serious going on . . . and all the time he's thinking that just because we're both in our eighties, we're going to be grateful to share the attentions of some jumped-up seventy-two-year-old. Absolute bastard.'

My mouth dropped open in shock again.

'I had no idea!'

'That I was seeing someone?'

I nodded.

'Well, a lady likes to keep some things close to her chest. But it's all over now.' She clicked through three more stitches. 'When I found out what was going on, I called Emily and I told her we had to do something. She agreed and we came up with a plan. We had a showdown. Me, Emily and Frank. I thought we were going to tell him that we were both done with him, but then she said, "You have to choose between us, Frank," and he bloody well chose her!'

'Unbelievable,' I said.

'That was not what we'd agreed. I can't tell you how hurt I was.'

'I can imagine.'

'I'm not sure which is worse, losing Frank or being

betrayed by my fellow woman. Where is the sisterhood in that! And so this is how I keep my mind off it. With all this bloody knitting. Because God knows I would not be doing it otherwise. I'll never be able to go down the senior citizens' club again.'

Her pain was clear. I wasn't sure what to say. 'You can't give up the club,' I said.

'I've got to. I've got my pride.'

'You know what, Auntie Joyce,' I said then, 'I think that you're the lucky one, not Emily. I don't know what she was thinking. Why on earth would you want a man who you knew had cheated on you?' Though even as I said it I knew that, had Miss Well-Sprung and I stood in front of Michael, and he'd chosen me, I wouldn't have given a second thought to the fact that he thought it was perfectly acceptable to sleep with both of us at the same time. I would have done a lap of victory round Clapham Common and got straight back to the business of prostrating myself before his worthless arse.

Still, for a matter of seconds I was able to step out of myself and give some sensible advice. I laid my hands on Auntie Joyce's, quieting that click-clicking for a while, and said, 'He wasn't worth it. You deserve so much better.'

'And so do you, my dear,' she said. 'So do you.'

It was sweet and, at the same time, profoundly depressing. Here we were, sharing a universal girly moment and yet how awful to think that at eighty-three years old, Auntie Joyce was still falling for the same old schtick, still breaking her heart and losing a friend over a man who wasn't worthy of carrying her knitting bag. I uttered a little prayer: Please, God, let me have it figured out before I reach retirement age.

Still, I did come away from that afternoon with some new wisdom. Auntie Joyce was right about one thing: I needed to keep my brain occupied with a task that so fully absorbed me there was no room for ruminations about Michael. I needed to experience what psychologists refer to as 'flow'. At work, there were moments when I had to concentrate hard enough to shut anything else out, but when I was left to my own devices, it was hopeless. I certainly wasn't getting any sense of flow from my lonely evenings spent reading endless threads of woe on break-up websites or from obsessively clicking through the pictures on Michael's Facebook page. Perhaps knitting was the ideal task. I hadn't picked up a set of knitting needles for years. Before I left the house, I asked Auntie Joyce to show me the basic stitches again.

'But what will I knit?' I asked her.

Auntie Joyce gestured towards her enormous knitting bag. 'I've got two hundred and eighty-three to go. Why don't you take the pink wool and these needles and make some little people dressed as angels or the Virgin Mary? They're very easy. You just have to knit one big tube for the body and the head, and four smaller tubes to make the arms and legs.'

She gave me the pattern, which she had made up herself. It looked pretty simple. Knit and purl, stocking stitch . . . nothing fancy. I could easily stitch on little facial features in black wool.

'OK,' I said. 'I'll do ten.'

24

Easier said than done. I got started on the knitting as soon as I got home. Three hours later my fingers were red and sore and I had completed just one little woolly body in the time it would have taken Auntie Joyce to make three. The lurid pink tube, which I'd stuffed with a pair of old laddered tights, looked far from human. At least, it didn't look like a whole human. It looked altogether more obscene – a fat little penis in hundred per cent washable acrylic.

But while I wasn't exactly thrilled with what I had managed to create so far, it had kept my mind occupied. The concentration that knitting had required of me was even greater than I imagined, and I was determined not to be defeated.

Though I had work the next day, I sat up for the rest of the night to make the arms and the legs. I attached them as Auntie Joyce's pattern instructed. Then it was time to create the eyes, the nose and the mouth with neat stitching.

It wasn't until I finished that I realised there was something strangely familiar about my little woolly creation.

Oh God! I thought. He looks like Michael!

There was something about the black wool eyes that reminded me of Michael's lashes (overly luxuriant for a man), and the grim red line of the mouth reminded me of Michael's mouth as he told me so proudly me that he had 'never made any promises' to me. My treacherous subconscious had forced me to knit my ex-boyfriend!

Ugh. I stabbed the fat woollen body with a knitting needle. 'Never made any promises! Take that, you cow-lashed git.'

Stab, stab, stab. Stab. Stab. Stab. Stab. Stab.

I stopped and slumped back on to the sofa. I was surprised at my sudden outburst of violence and slightly shocked. And yet . . .

Perhaps there was something in this crafts thing. It really was therapeutic.

And that was how I accidentally made my first voodoo doll. The children of the church would have to be one woolly angel short.

I christened him Mini-Michael and spent the next few evenings and lunch hours customising him so that he resembled my ex even more closely. I made him a black jumper – like the cashmere sweater Michael was hardly ever seen without since his Harvey Nics makeover – by cutting off the end of a cashmere sock that had long since lost its mate and snipping two little slits for Mini-Michael's arms. I found a scrap of brown wool in the bag that Auntie Joyce had given me and used that to make the doll's hair, complete with a thinning patch on the crown. I made him a pair of trousers out of a piece of material from the sample book that Miss Well-Sprung had left behind, which Ellie had yet to return. That gave me a little grim satisfaction. I even made him a silver necklace to match the one that some previous hapless girlfriend had given him when she got back from a holiday in India, using a section of chain from an old broken bracelet of mine.

Mini-Michael was perfect in every way. And that was when the fun started. One evening I popped out to the corner shop to buy a pint of milk and saw, on one of those revolving displays by the till, a packet of a hundred pins, each with the different coloured head. They had almost certainly been there since the seventies. I bought them, feeling a faint flutter of excitement and embarrassment as the girl behind the counter rang them up. Though she could never have guessed the carnage I intended to inflict, could she?

I decided that this was something that had to be conducted with a degree of ceremony. I needed candles, which meant opening the fig scented candle from Diptyque that I had been saving for some romantic interlude. It meant significant music. It meant a big glass of red wine.

This was much more fun than the voodoo sock. What a jolly evening I had, decorating Mini-Michael all over with those pins. I stuck them in his eyes. I stuck them where his ears should have been, in his arms, his legs, all over his chest and his torso. I stuck them in his feet. I stuck twelve of them in his crotch, as I shouted something along the lines of 'Die! Die! Die!!!' And then I put the doll into a biscuit tin and buried him at the bottom of my wardrobe.

Afterwards I danced around the living room to a mix of triumphant girl hits, including, of course, 'I Will Survive' and my personal favourite, Beyoncé's 'Irreplaceable'. I loved that girl. As I danced, I swigged from my glass of red wine, getting plenty of it on the cream rug, but I felt good. I felt as though I was actually taking some action to claim back my happiness.

Regardless of whether my latest spot of voodoo would really work or not, I felt a great deal better.

The following day I was to get a surprise.

The first thing I did every morning was check Michael's status on Facebook. Unbelievably, he had yet to root out and eliminate my fake Kevin profile. That day 'Feeling under the weather and working from home' was Michael's status, updated at eight o'clock that morning. Under the weather? That meant he felt ill! Was it possible that the damage I'd inflicted on my little woolly Mini-Michael had something to do with it?

A ridiculous notion. If Martha's voodoo sock hadn't worked, then it was unlikely that I had managed to achieve anything with my knitting. All the same, I felt guiltily gleeful.

Later, when I logged on to Facebook again, Michael had changed his status to 'Still feeling really bad. Must be man-flu!'

'Oh, ha, ha, ha,' I said. I bet he thought that man-flu comment was really funny.

I noticed that Miss Well-Sprung had added a comment beneath his status update: 'Hope you feel better by tonight, my love.'

I felt my right eye twitch as I read that. So they had a date planned. I had to make sure that Michael didn't feel better in time.

What would it take? I wondered. How embarrassing an ailment would Michael have to have before he would cancel their evening together?

When I got back from the office that night, I went straight to the wardrobe, pulled out Mini-Michael in his biscuit tin coffin and, using a red felt-tip pen, gave him a nasty set of spots all around the crotch. I dotted another spot on the end of his nose, just for luck. I sat up until the early hours of the morning hoping he would post an update about his condition, but I suppose even Michael would draw the line at reporting a genital rash in his status update.

Common wisdom states that time heals all wounds and that eventually everyone who ever had their heart broken starts to get over it, but at two months and a day I was nowhere near that stage.

Rather, I was entering a truly dark phase. Two weeks after I created the Mini-Michael, which I subjected to nightly torments, my usual round-up of Internet snooping on Michael's life culminated in my typing 'when will Michael die' into the Google box at the top of my browser. Even more disturbing was the number of websites that were willing to tell me exactly when it would happen. Alas, the general consensus was that he had at least another twenty-five years, even if I factored in his allergies.

I was a woman obsessed. I thought about Michael every moment of every day. Especially at night, when Michael was almost certainly in bed with Miss Well-Sprung. She was the one getting the benefit of the crisp white linen on his bed and the freshly ground coffee in his kitchen. I didn't even have a cat to snuggle up to. I was turning into a cat woman without a kitten.

One Monday morning as I took the Tube into the office, I realised that I had not spoken to a single living person since the previous Friday night.

'You could have come over to our place!' Becky protested when I told her.

'You didn't call me.'

'You know how busy I've been with the wedding. The time just flies. But you should have called me. We would have been very happy to see you.'

'I can't just keep coming over and playing gooseberry,' I moaned.

'Don't be silly,' said Becky. 'Henry and I would have been glad of the distraction.'

I gave a sceptical grunt.

'Never mind. This week is going to be much better. Think of how much fun we're going to have on Thursday night!'

Ah, yes. Thursday night.

As I walked home from work that afternoon, the sun was still shining and it seemed that the world and his missus were out enjoying it. The birds, the bees, even the wasps were out there two by two. I was reminded of my single status at every turn. I had forgotten how bloody awful it was to be on your own in a world that had been made for pairs ever since Noah. Especially during the summer.

What is the best time of year to have your heart broken? The annals of female experience are packed with tales of chronologically thoughtless dumpings. Christmas and New Year seem to be favourites. I suppose it makes great sense if you've decided that you no longer want to be with someone to call it a day before you have to buy them a Christmas present, or before they get you something ridiculously thoughtful and expensive that ties you in for another six months.

New Year must be a rough time to be dumped as well. There you are, looking forward to seeing in the New Year with the man of your dreams, then suddenly it's over and you find yourself in a corner at midnight. At best, you're fighting back the tears while you watch all the couples who did make it to 1 January together. At worst, you're avoiding the one single bloke at the party, a geek with a cold sore, who thinks you're there expressly for the purpose of breaking his three-year sex drought with a shag in the host's airing cupboard.

Valentine's Day is another baddy. There's nothing worse than being single on Valentine's Day. Except perhaps a card from your mother. I can see how being dumped on your birthday would scar you for life as well. Especially if it's a big birthday, like forty. You might as well have opened a birthday card to discover it says, 'Get a cat.'

Nevertheless I decided that the misery of finding yourself single on Christmas, New Year or Valentine's Day had nothing on what I was going through. It seemed that I alone in the whole of England knew the pain of being dumped in the wedding season.

It wasn't as though I hadn't been single during the wedding season before. I had known the horror of the invitation to which your neatly calligraphed name is appended with the words every girl dreads: 'plus one'. Without that elusive 'plus one' by my side, I had known the horror of being seated at the 'singles' table, only to find that the other guests at said table were only single because they were widowed. In the Second World War.

What Michael had plunged me into was a whole new level of horror. Prior to our break-up, just that summer alone I had accepted invitations to four weddings on behalf of us both. Admittedly, I hadn't told him about three of them, but I had felt sure that he would be there by my side and so I had confidently added his name to my RSVPs.

Becky had threatened castration when she realised that Michael really was going to leave a gap in one of her carefully put-together tables of eight. I knew that at some point I would have to let the other brides know that Michael was intent on monkeying with their numbers.

'Don't leave it too long,' Becky had warned me. 'There is nothing, nothing on earth more distressing for a bride-to-be than last-minute changes to the guest list.'

'What? Nothing?' I'd responded. 'Even the groom getting killed in a freak stag-night accident.'

'That's not even slightly funny,' said Becky. 'I can't believe you would joke about my fiancé being dead!' She crossed her fingers and knocked on wood as though that would make things better.

I felt suitably chastised, but I would be lying if I said that I didn't secretly wish that one of the prospective brides would call me and tell me that her wedding had been cancelled. Not because of a death, of course, but perhaps an outbreak of chickenpox, or a surprise pregnancy that meant she wouldn't be able to get into her dress and had thus decided to postpone the wedding until the following year. Anything, anything at all that would save me having to explain that Michael and I had split up. I just didn't want to have to go to all those bloody weddings on my own.

The four weddings would begin with Becky's wedding, which was to take place in less than three weeks. Thursday was to be her hen night.

25

As Becky's best friend and chief bridesmaid, I had been charged with arranging her send-off. Back when she first announced her engagement, I had happily taken on the project, though, despite the fact that we'd been friends since childhood, there were very few other girls whom I knew properly on the guest list. Since she met Henry, Becky had, inevitably I suppose, spent more time cultivating his pals than vice versa.

Still I realised that I was in trouble when I sent out the first round-robin email, asking everyone on Becky's list to let me know what might be a suitable date. I had no idea how difficult it was going to be to dovetail the school/holiday/fertility arrangements of a dozen assorted London ladies. Just when I thought I had the perfect day, one of Becky's invitees (someone who was married to one of Henry's former workmates) wrote to tell me that she would be unable to attend on that particular evening as it coincided with her ovulation. I resisted the urge to write back and tell her that coming out and getting rat-arsed with the girls might actually increase her chances of getting laid at the right time.

'Amanda can't make the eighteenth,' I told Becky.

'Oh, no,' said Becky. 'We have to have Amanda. Her husband is really high up in a company that Henry's applying for a job with.'

I got out my diary again.

And that's how Becky's hen night came to be on a Thursday, rather than the more traditional weekend evening as I had envisioned. Likewise, my plan to spend an afternoon doing the wine-tasting tour at Vinopolis was swiftly voted out in favour of a meal at a smart restaurant in Mayfair. Once Amanda the ovulator got her way over the date of the hen night, she started moving in on the other arrangements too. She sent an email to everyone on the list raving about the restaurant where she'd had her own 'extremely grown-up' hen party and everyone agreed it would be perfect for Becky's send-off too. I had no choice but to agree, though the sight of the menu made me blanch. I had organised group outings before and was well used to the fact that someone would skip off without paying their share. If that happened on this hen night, I would be unable to pay my rent. For months. But Becky was really excited about the idea and so that was that.

Thursday rolled around.

I felt like the slowest girl in school when I met Becky's friends. I knew immediately that I had worn the wrong outfit. My skinny jeans and sparkly top combo, which got a grudging nod of approval from Ellie, was way too casual for the venue and the crowd. I swear that one of them was wearing a black velvet Alice band (and not in an ironic nod to the eighties, which was what I had been aiming for with my pixie boots).

When the woman who turned out to be Amanda arrived, she actually handed me her coat as she walked into the room. 'Oh, I'm sorry,' she said. 'You look as though you work here.'

I gritted my teeth behind a smile and made a mental note to make sure I was sitting a very, very long way away from that cow. But Amanda wasn't the only one I didn't fancy sitting next to. Perhaps it was because I had arranged the evening that Becky's new friends acted as though I was the hired help. I tried and failed to break into several conversations as we milled in the bar, sipping cocktails (largely virgin ones). I was met with looks of pure horror when I attempted to get the party started by suggesting that we all don novelty headgear from Claire's Accessories.

'I suppose I'd better have one,' said Becky, picking out the least horrifying pair of deely-boppers. 'Since I am the bride-to-be.'

But I could tell even she was embarrassed.

'Your table's ready,' said the woman who really was in charge of the restaurant. Not a moment too soon.

I let the other women seat themselves and squeezed in at the very end of the table, opposite an empty seat. There'd been a cancellation. One of Becky's hens was ovulating a day earlier than expected.

Though all of the women were in theory my contemporaries, they seemed from a different generation. To my left was Isabelle. Her husband had been at university with Henry. As I understood it, she'd just celebrated her thirty-third birthday, but she looked much older. For most of the first course she was engaged in a conversation about prep schools with the woman opposite her. When that woman got up (six months pregnant, bladder fit to burst), Isabelle turned her politest smile on me.

'Do you have children?' she asked.

'No,' I replied.

'Would your husband like to have some?'

'I don't have a husband,' I admitted. 'In fact, I don't even have a boyfriend right now. I just got dumped!' I said gaily. I tried to chink my glass against hers, as if to toast my hopelessness. She smiled tightly, as though I'd said something slightly distasteful.

'Oh, poor you,' she said, but there was little sympathy in her voice.

'Turned out he'd been seeing someone else for the last few months,' I continued. 'She's an interior designer. She was doing up his office. You think you're safe when they're at work, right? How wrong could I have been . . .'

Isabelle nodded along, but she was noticeably relieved when the pregnant woman came back from the ladies' and complained about her stretchmarks. That seemed to be infinitely preferable to talking about my faithless ex-boyfriend.

What is it about single women that makes married women so nervous? I wondered as the conversation carried on without me. Did Isabelle think that being dumped was catching? Did she think I was on the prowl for a new man? It wasn't as though her husband was there to steal, if I suddenly decided that I had to have a man right at that very moment. I wondered if Becky would stop inviting me to her house as soon as she had a wedding ring on her finger. Probably not. At least, not while Henry's best mate, Julian, was still single. In fact, since I split up with Michael, I think on balance Becky had actually invited me over more often. I was a welcome addition to her table plans while Julian continued to muck up the nice even numbers.

But the other women at Becky's hen night seemed to have no interest in wasting talk on me. Isabelle was quickly engrossed in conversation with the woman who had stretchmarks and I felt, not for the first time, that marriage and children was an exclusive club for which I never seemed to be wearing the right outfit.

A little later I tried to infiltrate the conversation by offering to refill Isabelle's glass. She glared at me and looked pointedly at the pregnant girl's stomach.

'I'm sorry,' I joked, 'I had no idea that you're not supposed to drink while sitting next to a pregnant woman.'

'Actually, I'm trying for another baby,' Isabelle explained before she turned back to her companion with a roll of her eyes that I couldn't miss.

A brief but horrible image of Isabelle trying for a baby flitted through my mind. I imagined her face straining as she mounted her husband. 'Come on! Come on! I'm ovulating right now!'

I filled my own glass and tried to drink my mind blank again. There was plenty of booze to get through. I'd ordered three bottles of white and three bottles of red, but as far as I could see no one was drinking except me and the bride-to-be.

I don't think that anyone addressed another comment to me all evening. It was just me and the sauvignon blanc from then on. When I got to my feet to raise a toast to our mutual friend, the bride-to-be, I felt such a lurch that I had to sit straight back down again and Becky went un-toasted until Amanda, who had chosen the restaurant, noticed the omission and made a little speech of her own.

'Dear Becky,' she said, 'I remember the first day we met, when Henry brought you to our little garden party and I said to Tristan, "This is her. This is Henry's little Miss Right." Well, I'm so glad that I was right and that I can be here today to celebrate your forthcoming marriage. I've known you for just a couple of years, but I truly feel, Becky, with my hand on my *little* heart, that you and I are good friends. I'm sure that everyone around this table tonight would like to join me in wishing you all happiness for your future. To Becky!' She raised a glass of cranberry juice.

'Thank you,' Becky replied. 'And thank you, Amanda, for choosing this lovely restaurant. I've had a truly special night.'

The women around the table congratulated Amanda on her organisational ability. It was clear that my diarising spreadsheet was long forgotten. As were my novelty hen-night gifts. Even Becky had disguarded her deely-boppers and L-plate.

I couldn't wait to get out of there.

'Did you have a good time?' Becky hiccupped as we put the last of the yummies into a cab and started looking for one of our own.

'They all hated me,' I complained.

'Don't be silly.'

'I'm serious. Nobody had anything to say to me,' I said.

Subconsciously, I was offering Becky the chance to jump in and say that Henry's friends' wives had nothing to say to *anyone*, that they were dull and she hated them too. Instead, she said, 'You weren't going on about Michael, were you?'

'No, I was not!' I exclaimed.

'Are you sure?'

'Becky, you're supposed to be my friend. I was not going on about Michael. In fact, I only mentioned him once. To Isabelle.'

'Oh, Isabelle!' Becky's face practically lit up as she breathed the other woman's name. 'She's really lovely. You know, she is setting up her own business selling nearly new children's clothes. It's called the Angel Exchange.'

'Great,' I said.

'She used to be a fund manager.'

'Fabulous.'

'Until she married Tim, who is one of the few remaining bankers who can afford to take a house in the South of France for the *whole* summer.'

'Of course . . . Well, I still thought she was a cow.'

Becky looked as though I had personally insulted her. 'Perhaps you didn't give her a proper chance.'

'Perhaps she didn't give me one.'

Becky just shook her head. 'I thought when we turned up at the restaurant tonight that you seemed really chirpy,' she said somewhat accusingly.

'I was, until they all refused to get into the swing of things.'

'They're not the kind of women who get a kick out of wearing silly headgear. I'm sorry, but I enjoyed myself and I'm really grateful that you put the evening together. You have to admit that until you came up against the tee-total Mummy Mafia, you were doing fine. I was really glad to see it. I'm happy that you're starting to get back to your old self again.'

I knew what she was doing. She was trying to talk me out of my funk, trying to convince me that I felt better than I did. It probably worked on her year elevens.

'Actually,' I told her, 'I've been feeling worse than ever. If it hadn't been for your hen night, I could have spent the entire week in bed, just staring at the ceiling and wondering whether I had enough aspirin in the cupboard to kill myself, assuming I could bring myself to get out of bed to swallow them.'

Becky frowned. 'You don't really mean that,' she said.

'I do. I don't think you believe quite how badly my heart was broken.'

'It was quite a while ago now,' Becky tried.

I didn't take the hint. 'Just a couple of months! And the way people talk, you would think that I'm just supposed to get up and carry on like I never even met the man. Nobody wants to listen to me any more. Not even you.'

'I've listened to you quite a bit,' Becky pointed out.

'You're supposed to. You're supposed to be my best friend. I can't get hold of you half the time. Truth is, I don't think you really care.'

It was a red rag to a bull. Becky's expression changed from sympathetic to a bit pissed off.

'Come on, Ashleigh,' said Becky. 'You have to see why it's difficult for me to keep sympathising with you so long after Michael actually dumped you. It's not as though we're talking about the end of a marriage. You weren't married. You weren't engaged. You weren't even living together. The way I see it, you and Michael weren't even having a proper relationship. You were just dating.'

'For two and a half years?'

'Yes. Did you ever spend Christmas together? No. Did he ever introduce you to his parents? No. Did he ever talk about the future? Not beyond the next weekend. You were dating. Just dating.'

I didn't know how to respond. Was that really what Becky thought? Was that what everybody really thought?

'It wasn't that important,' she continued.

'It was two and a half years of my life! Two and a half years! We both know plenty of people who got together, got married and got divorced in the space of two and a half years. Are you saying they have more reason to be upset?'

'It's not the length of time you were with someone that counts,' said Becky. 'It's the depth of the commitment. Getting married is commitment. Living together is commitment. Anything else . . . For goodness' sake. Look at it realistically. It's ridiculous, grieving like this over a couple years of going to the cinema on Saturdays and having the odd mini-break. When Michael's schedule allowed it, I hasten to add. You got foolishly attached to a man who thought of nothing but his own happiness and squeezed you in when it suited him. He never took your needs into consideration. It's time for you to put it behind you. I need you to put it behind you because it is bloody well driving me mad!'

I could only open and close my mouth in soundless agony.

'Since the day you met Michael he has dominated your life. When you were with him, it was bad enough. I don't think you have any idea how much time you spent analysing every date, every night you spent together, every phone call. It was obvious to me from very early on that you were on to a loser, but I did my best to support you and I have to admit that when you called to tell me that he'd dumped you, I was glad. No more bloody Michael, I thought. How wrong could I have been? How on earth can you still have so much to say about a man who walked out of your life over two months ago? There is no new information here. He's gone. It's over. It's done. Now, I'm sure you'd rather talk about something more cheerful. I know I would. When are we going to get together and get in some practice for opening the dancing at the reception? Henry isn't too bad, but Julian is awful and since he's the best man . . .'

'I don't feel much like dancing,' I said.

Becky frowned. 'Ashleigh, I don't mean to hurt you. I'm just telling you the truth as I see it. And sometimes the truth sets us free. I want you to be happy and I think the first step to being happy is for you to let go of this ridiculous fiction that you've lost the love of your life. Michael certainly didn't see it that way.'

'But . . .'

She laid a hand on my arm. 'Michael was a shit for dumping you like he did,' she said, 'but the fact that you're still so miserable so long after he's gone is entirely your fault. Your recovery is up to you. You have got to move on. Do it for me. As my wedding present.'

Her face took on the approximate expression of one who was concerned for my welfare, but all I could focus on was a peculiar little upward twist at the corner of her mouth that suggested what she really wanted to do was laugh in my face. Was this my best friend? If she thought so little of my heartache, then why would anyone else think any more of it?

I moved my arm so that her hand slipped away.

'Ashleigh, don't be like that.'

'Like what? Hurt? Get someone else to be your bloody chief bridesmaid,' I spat. 'That's all you care about, isn't it? Your sodding wedding. As if I didn't know that before your nasty little speech. Well, thank you very much for showing me what a true friend is like. You can forget about me being at your wedding at all.'

I didn't wait for a taxi. I stomped off in the opposite direction, leaving Becky to go home alone.

When I got home, my answer machine was flashing angrily. Becky had left six messages to go with the three she had left on my mobile. I knew that I had scared her with my threat that I wouldn't be at the wedding. It wasn't just that I was her chief bridesmaid, I was also making the cake. I imagined her panicking that there would be nothing for the guests to watch her cut with her new husband. Her perfect day would be ruined. But I wasn't about to call her and put her out of her misery. Not when I was so miserable myself.

I knew that I should just go to bed. On the other hand, I was pretty sure that I wouldn't be able to sleep. I knew I would just lie there staring at the ceiling, ruminating on all the things that were wrong with my life. Especially in comparison with Mrs Isabelle Extremely Loaded and Mrs Amanda Perfect and the rest of Becky's new snotty yummy friends. I was in the kind of mood where it seems like a good idea to open another bottle of wine and drink the lot. All on your own.

As I drank, I replayed Becky's accusations. One thing in particular had struck me as cruel. 'Michael was a shit for dumping you like he did,' she said, 'but the fact that you're still so miserable so long after he's gone is entirely your fault. Your recovery is up to you.'

But I was trying, I told myself. I was doing everything humanly possible to get myself back on track. I had tried everything, from knitting to voodoo. That day at work I had even created a PowerPoint presentation on Michael's bad points, as per the advice of another break-up website. The idea was that I should watch the presentation every day until those points sank in and started to feel real, until I started to believe that I was well shot of him.

I needed to see that presentation now. I poured myself another glass of wine and opened my laptop. Then I spent a jolly three hours adding to the page entitled 'Michael's Physical Shortcomings' in Getting Over Michael.doc. It almost made me smile. Especially when, following the advice that the more clearly you can visualise something, the more effective your visualisations will be, I decided to search the Internet for amusing illustrations for 'odd-shaped toes', 'cold sores' and, my favourite of them all, 'short dick'.

Oh, yes, I got quite creative in the wee small hours. Really, it is astonishing what you can find on the Internet. I quickly learned that Michael fell well inside the parameters deemed 'average' for penis size, but where's the fun in that? To illustrate my opinion that his penis was not all that it should have been, I chose a picture of a willy so small that I think it would hardly have qualified as a clitoris.

That night, I very much enjoyed running my Getting Over Michael presentation. I decided that it was beginning to work. I even managed to laugh when the slide entitled 'He Has an Unusually Small Cock' popped up. I watched it eleven times before I fell asleep at my kitchen table.

26

The following morning I woke with 'QWERTY' imprinted on my forehead and a mouth that tasted like a camel's backside, a whole hour after I should have been at work and just half an hour before I was due to give a presentation to the people from Effortless Bathing. You cannot imagine the speed with which I left the house. Fortunately, having fallen asleep in my clothes, I didn't have to bother dressing.

'Fuck's sake, Ashleigh,' said Ellie when I arrived in the office, 'they've been here for half an hour. What happened to you?'

'Tube,' I said. 'Northern Line.'

'I came in on the Northern Line,' said Ellie. 'It was fine for me.'

'Then it must have gone wrong right after you got off,' I told her.

'And what are you wearing?' She screwed up her nose at my jeans.

'We're an advertising agency. Can't I look creative?'

'It would help if you looked clean,' she said. 'Weren't you wearing that exact outfit last night?'

'Of course not,' I told her.

Really, it was too much, the way my assistant kept questioning me. We would have to have a conversation about her impertinence after the meeting. Right then I didn't have time to argue. I asked Ellie to get me a coffee.

'You'll probably need something stronger,' she said.

'Why's that?' I asked.

'The big boss is sitting in on this one.'

'What?'

Ellie nodded.

'Why didn't anybody tell me?'

'None of us knew. But Clare thinks it's because he has a crush on the Effortless Bathing marketing guy.'

'Who? Jeffrey?'

He wasn't what I would have called a hunk.

Ellie nodded again.

'Christ,' I said. 'That's all I need.'

'You'll have to hope that the lovely Jeff takes Barry's mind off your terrible presentation.'

'My presentation is not going to be terrible. Honestly, Ellie, anyone would think I hadn't given you your first job. I'm your mentor. You're supposed to look up to me.'

'Remind me why,' said Ellie. 'Exactly.'

If I hadn't had a meeting room full of people waiting for me, I would have torn a strip off her. But I didn't have the luxury of time to fight. Also, part of me was certain that I was going to ace the presentation I had worked so hard to finish. In fact, by the time Ellie stepped out to get cappuccinos for everyone (except Jeffrey, who had lived in France for six months and thought it was the most disgusting thing imaginable to have milk in your coffee after ten), she would have to admit that I rocked.

'Sorry I'm a little late,' I said to everyone as I stepped into the boardroom. 'Northern Line.'

'Terrible,' everyone agreed without question.

I ignored Ellie's eye-roll.

'I hope you haven't been too bored while you've been waiting, and I hope I'm going to make it up to you now with my presentation.' I gave them my winning smile and was gratified to receive winning smiles all round in return.

Even from Barry. I guessed that he was merely trying to make himself seem like a cheerful sort of chap while in the presence of Jeffrey, but who cared? If bio-feedback meant that fake smile made Barry feel even half a per cent warmer towards me too, then I was happy to see it.

I plugged my laptop into the room's built-in presentation equipment, opened PowerPoint, selected the last file I had been working on and got started.

I had gone through this presentation so many times that I didn't even need to look at the screen. Instead, I boldly looked out on my audience and rattled off the spiel like a true performer.

My audience was transfixed.

'Next slide,' I said to Ellie. 'Now, as you can see,' I continued, 'Effortless Bathing's share of the easy-access bathing market currently stands at thirteen per cent, but I'm confident that we can change that.'

I looked at Clare the account director. She had her eyes fixed on my slide. Her brow was wrinkled in concentration.

'I know what you're thinking,' I said. 'It can't really be true.'

I looked at Jeffrey. He was leaning forward. Squinting.

'But trust me, twenty per cent is not an unrealistic target. In fact, I have looked at the competition and come to the conclusion that even this figure is way too small.'

Barry was also transfixed. And slack-jawed.

I was flying. I had them all. Even Ellie's expression had changed from its default smug setting to stunned. The campaign I was proposing was daring, but it could work. I knew that. I could already imagine the end of the meeting. Jeffrey and his team would leave happy. Barry would slap me on the back. He might even give me Clare's job. She wanted to spend more time with her horses.

'Next slide,' I said.

Ellie diligently flicked through the slides until I came to the end.

'And that,' I said to the assembled, 'is all I have to say on the matter. Does anyone have any questions?'

Barry, I could tell, was bursting to ask something.

'Barry?' I opened the floor to him.

'What on earth is that?'

Have you ever found yourself behind the wheel of a car as it spins out of control? The moment you realise that you're losing it, something quite peculiar happens. Time slows down, as if to afford you a valuable extra heartbeat in which to make the right decision. An illusory nano-second in which to wrench the wheel in the opposite direction and keep out of the path of the oncoming juggernaut.

That's exactly what it felt like to me when Barry pointed at the image on the projector behind me and, in the same moment, I glanced down at the smaller, identical image on my laptop.

'What . . . on . . . earth . . . is . . . that . . . ?' Barry repeated.

It was like that moment when you realise, as you're halfway through walking across the restaurant from the ladies' to your seat that people aren't looking at you because you're working that little black dress so dramatically. They're staring at the trail of loo paper, or at the way your skirt is tucked into your knickers, giving everyone a great view of your arse and the big grey Spanx you had been meaning to throw away for months.

'Oh. Bum,' I said.

'I think you owe us an explanation,' said Barry.

'I don't think she needs to explain anything,' said Jeffrey, almost gallantly. 'It's all perfectly clear to me.'

'Yeah. But, *seriously*, what is that?' asked Ellie. She was genuinely curious.

The PowerPoint presentation had paused on my picture of the world's smallest cock. In such a hurry had I been to get the meeting started, I hadn't noticed that the last PowerPoint presentation I'd viewed before getting to the office was not my presentation on how to make Effortless Bathing's new Easy Bath a household name in an ageing nation, but Getting Over Michael.doc. I felt distinctly nauseous as I recalled the other slides to which I'd treated my co-workers and clients.

'Don't worry,' said Jeffrey. 'I thought it was all very funny.'

'Well, yes,' said Barry. 'It had its moments. But I would hate for you to think that it's always like this in our office.'

'Our meetings with Ashleigh are the highlight of my life,' said Jeffrey.

Was Jeffrey flirting with me? I hoped he wasn't. That could only make things worse.

'I don't know how this happened,' I said hopelessly. 'I worked on my presentation all night. Maybe I've got a computer virus . . .'

'I'll email you the proper presentation,' said Ellie quickly. 'So you can watch it at your own convenience. We're really very sorry.'

'There's no need for *you* to be sorry,' Barry told Ellie. 'You were just following instructions.' She wriggled like a tickled kitten.

'Send me a copy of this presentation too,' said Jeffrey. 'So I can remind myself how to be a better man.'

'I don't think you need any lessons on that,' said Barry.

Jeffrey blushed. Barry blushed too. I just wanted to die.

I remained in the meeting room long after everyone else had filed out, with the picture of the micro-penis still projected on the wall behind me. I leaned heavily against the desk, too horrified to do anything but stare at the untouched pile of croissants in the centre of the board table. It crossed my mind briefly that, since no one ever touched the croissants, we might as well have a couple of plastic ones on permanent display. Then I went back to being horrified. How had I made such a stupid mistake? Instead of my killer presentation, I had given a display of such outstanding incompetence it would probably go down in the annals of advertising as the ultimate example of what not to do. I was for the high jump, wasn't I?

But I heard laughter in the hallway. Barry's laughter. That was a good sign. Jeffrey had been very sweet. He had made light of my cock-up – my mini-cock-up – and Barry was so keen to please Jeffrey. Perhaps that would save my neck. Another gale of laughter reached me. For a moment I thought that everything would be all right.

But then Barry was back in the boardroom. Before I had time to turn off my laptop.

'That,' he said, pointing at the micro-cock in its full, technicolour glory, 'is the saddest thing I have ever seen.'

Seeing the chance to inject some more levity, I agreed with him. 'I know. And I dated it.'

Barry smiled, but it was not the smile of someone who was enjoying a joke. It was the sad smile of someone who knows something you don't know and what they do know is not good. At all.

'When you have finished in here,' he said, 'I think that you and I should have a long-overdue chat. In my office.'

He left.

As a nervous reaction, I stuffed one of the perennial croissants into my mouth and chewed it desperately as the tears came to my eyes. I suddenly knew exactly what was coming.

27

Barry didn't put on the black cap of a hanging judge, but he might as well have done. Clare was already there with him when I walked into the office. She had the look of a concerned social worker about her as she tapped her fingers nervously on the manila folder in her lap. My name was written upon it in thick, black pen. I was horrified by the sight of it. I had no idea they already had an actual *file* on me.

'I'm sorry,' I said at once.

'Sit down,' said Barry. 'Have a glass of water.'

Water. That didn't bode well. Not even an offer of tea?

Clare and Barry swapped glances and Clare gave a tiny nod to cue Barry that she was ready to start.

'We all know how much Michael meant to you,' said Barry. 'And hard as you may think I am, Ashleigh, I do know what it's like to have loved and lost. We all do.'

Clare nodded.

'And we all know that it takes time to get over these things. Especially as one gets older and the hopes and dreams we once had of a happy ever after seem ever more elusive.'

Oh, no, I was going to cry.

'It's harder and harder to bounce back each time,' Barry continued. 'But, Ashleigh, you're starting to be a liability. Sure, the Effortless Bathing people made light of your mistake in the presentation today, but we all know that won't be the end of it. Their account manager is about as discreet as Katie Price on truth serum. By close of play tonight there won't be a single person in the British advertising industry who doesn't know what happened here today. In fact, I wouldn't be surprised if it goes global.'

Clare stood up abruptly. 'I'm going to talk to Ellie before she puts that presentation on YouTube.'

'She wouldn't. She can't,' I said. 'It was on my laptop. Nowhere else.'

Clare sat down, but she stood up again equally quickly. 'I believe you, but I would also put money on Ellie knowing how to get into your files.' She left the office for a moment. While she was gone, Barry took a call from his mother (she was safely home from the dentist) and I sat on my hands. When Clare came back, she announced, 'Ellie has promised not to tell anyone, on pain of death. And the promise of a pay-grade review.'

Good old Ellie. I'd been right to think that she was one clever girl when I offered her the job. She sure knew how to make lemonade out of the lemons I had been handed that day.

'So.' Barry was ready to begin again. He leaned forward on the desk, fingers interlocked, eyebrows interlocked. He regarded me seriously. 'What are we going to do?'

'I'll make a written apology to the people from Effortless Bathing. I really am sorry,' I said.

'I don't doubt it. But the fact is that we would be within our rights to ask you to leave right away. Being made to look at a picture of a stranger's penis could be seen as harassment by some more delicate souls.'

'No one in this office is that delicate!' I protested.

'I can't take the risk of being seen to be irresponsible by not taking firm enough action.'

Clare reached across and took my hand. It was then that I realised.

'You're asking me to fall on my sword, aren't you?'

Clare and Barry nodded in unison.

'But . . .'

'You need some time off,' said Clare.

'I could just take some leave,' I suggested hopefully.

'You need a *lot* of time off,' said Barry. 'We'll look after you,' he promised. 'We'll make sure that you don't walk away from here empty-handed. We'll even throw in a few sessions with a shrink. How about that? I'm sure Clare knows a good one.'

Clare gave him her 'look'. She was not the type of woman who wanted it to be known that she knew the number of a therapist.

'What do you think, Ashleigh?' Barry asked me.

I couldn't answer him. My brain simply shut down in horror. I had never been given the sack before in my life. Unless you count the time I was let go from my Saturday job for turning up late three weeks in a row.

'According to your contract, you have a four-week notice period,' said Clare. 'But there's really no need for you to work through it. Ellie is on top of all your projects, I think. And I'm sure you'll agree that she can phone you if there's anything she doesn't understand.'

'Of course,' I said in a very small voice.

'Is that everything?' Barry looked at Clare.

'That's everything.' Clare gave me another sympathetic smile. 'You've been a valuable member of the team, Ashleigh.'

'But not any more.'

She stopped short of agreeing with me.

Barry stood up. 'I've . . . er . . . I've got to visit the gents'.'

'I should be getting back to work too,' said Clare. 'You can go home now,' she told me. 'If you like. Get Ellie to call you a taxi on account.'

I just about managed to walk out of Barry's office and back to my desk without falling down. Still, I looked distressed enough to bring Ellie scuttling back from the photocopier at once. She brought sweet tea.

'For shock. You look like you've had one.' She even offered me a HobNob from her secret stash of carbs.

'They've given me the sack.'

'Noooo!' said Ellie. 'Why on earth? Anyone could make a mistake with the files on their laptop. Anyone. I can't believe they didn't cut you some slack.' She wrapped her arm round my shoulder. 'This is really bad, Ashleigh. I'm with you every step of the way. Do you need a cardboard box for your stuff? I'll go and see if I can find one in the stationery cupboard.'

Ellie even helped me to pack my things away. She made herself incredibly useful, but as I left the office that afternoon, I knew she was already trying out my swivel chair for size.

28

As if life couldn't get worse, when I got home, Becky was waiting on the doorstep.

'Why won't you return my calls?' she snapped. 'You're so selfish! I have been going out of my mind!'

'And I have been getting the sack.'

'What? What the hell did you do to get the sack?'

Becky had clearly forgotten that the correct reaction in such circumstances was to be sympathetic.

'I cocked up a presentation, all right? Quite literally, if you must know.'

'I must know,' said Becky. 'Let me buy you a drink.'

I dumped my laptop just inside the front door and let her take me to the pub, where I had a big glass of sauvignon blanc and told her the tale.

'Ashleigh,' she said, 'that's not actually funny. What are you going to do for work?'

'Make wedding cakes?' I suggested.

Becky cast her eyes down to the table. 'Talking of which . . . It's really late in the day for me to order another cake. Even if you don't want to be my bridesmaid . . . if you're willing to finish it, I'll pay you. It would get you started in your new career.' She smiled a little nervously.

'Oh, for heaven's sake,' I said, 'that cake is my wedding present to you.'

'But you're not coming to—'

'Of course I'm coming to your wedding.'

'Oh, thank God.' Becky heaved a sigh of relief.

'I've got nothing else to do.'

At last Becky's big day arrived. Feeling all traditional, she had decided to go back to her parents' house for the night before the wedding and insisted that I should go with her. When asking me to be her chief bridesmaid, she had given me a little book outlining my duties in the run-up to the wedding and on the day itself. From the moment she woke up at six in the morning (the wedding wasn't until three in the afternoon), she made the most of her exalted position as bride. She started by ordering me downstairs for a cup of tea before I'd even opened my eyes.

'Make you tea?' I moaned.

'It's my perfect day,' she reminded me.

When I returned with Becky's Earl Grey and a bottle of champagne, I found her with her mother. They were going through Becky's wedding folder like a pair of generals preparing to take a small country. Or a large country, for that matter.

'The little bridesmaids will be here at nine. The hairdresser arrives at nine thirty,' said Becky's mum. 'And the cake is in place?' she said to me, looking over the top of her glasses.

'Of course it is,' I said. 'I delivered it to the hotel kitchen last night.'

'Good. Ashleigh, I'm so glad you came to your senses and agreed to be here today. You know that if you hadn't come, you would have regretted it for the rest of your life, don't you?'

I nodded and helped myself to another glass of champagne. Becky's mother pulled a mildly disapproving face but quickly reset to 'smile' when she realised that I had noticed.

'Just so long as you don't step on my train on the way down the aisle!' Becky said.

The morning passed in a flurry of hairdressing and make-up appointments. It was largely without event, except that one of the younger bridesmaids ate too many of the fairy cakes Becky's mother had provided for elevenses and was sick down the front of her dress. Fortunately, the worst of the damage sponged off easily. Then it was time to get Becky into her dress: a proper fairytale number with lacing all the way up the back. I was surprised she could breathe by the time all the lacing was done, but she could still breathe *and* give instructions.

'Before I forget,' she said to me, 'I need you to give this CD to the DJ for our first dance.'

The first dance had been such a big secret, but when I saw the CD, I wasn't in the least bit surprised. If I'd gone into Ladbrokes and asked for odds on this particular song *not* being the first dance, I would have got an incredible deal.

James Blunt.

'It's track—'

'Number five,' I said. '"You're Beautiful".'

'How did you guess?' Becky asked.

Full marks for bloody originality. I wondered, yet again, why no one ever seemed to notice that 'You're Beautiful' isn't an uplifting love song. It's tragic. The last line says, 'I'll never be with you.' In fact, the only person I knew who ever got that was Michael, who sang the song to me as we walked back to his place from the Tube one night. I was charmed at the time, but looking back, I understood at last what he had been getting at. The emphasis was definitely on 'I'll never be with you' as far as he was concerned. The memory made the champagne in my mouth seem suddenly flat.

'Ashleigh. Ashleigh!' Becky clicked her fingers in front of my face. 'You were zoning out. Remember what you promised? Today is a happy day, so I don't want to see you without a smile on your face for one second. We can go back to *moaning about Michael* when I get back from my honeymoon.'

The way she said it, 'Moaning about Michael', with her comedy sad face, made me feel very stupid and small.

'You're right,' I told her. 'It's your day and you're my best friend. Here's my happy face just for you.' I poked my fingers into my cheeks to lift up the sides of my mouth into a smile.

'Be careful of your make-up,' she said, inspecting me for damage.

'The cars are here!' one of the younger bridesmaids called up the stairs.

We bridesmaids would be travelling to the church in a limo. Becky and her dad would follow in a Bentley a little later.

'I'll see you at the church,' I told her. 'Keep smiling. Remember it's a happy day!'

'It's *my* happy day,' Becky agreed.

29

So, I walked down the aisle behind my best friend, to the tune of 'Sheep May Safely Graze' (so much classier than 'The Wedding March', Becky told me), feeling like a loser in my bright-pink dress and trying desperately hard to convince myself that the congregation were too busy admiring Becky in her 'cost-of-a-small-car' wedding dress to be looking at me. Nevertheless I was sure that I saw a couple of the hen-night harridans nudge each other as I passed by. *Always the sodding bridesmaid.* And they weren't in the least bit surprised . . .

Up at the altar, Henry was waiting, looking slightly constipated in his morning dress. Though he wore a suit and tie five days a week and I don't think I had ever seen him wear a shirt without a collar, even he looked uncomfortable in a waistcoat and cravat. Perhaps it was the colour of his cravat and cummerbund that made him look so ill. Though Becky had been shrugging off the vestiges of our distinctly lower-middle-class upbringing since meeting her distinctly upper-class man, she hadn't been able to resist insisting that Henry match his accessories to her flowers. Which were pink. I could only imagine what Henry's mother had to say about that.

Standing next to Henry was his best man, Julian. As Becky and her father did the handing-over palaver, Julian looked at me in a way that was positively ravenous. I looked straight ahead. I may have been at my lowest point ever, but I was not so low that Julian, with his hamster cheeks covered in ruddy gin blossoms, should think he had a chance.

I took Becky's bouquet and stepped back into my place in the front pew.

'Dearly beloved . . .' the vicar began.

It was an emotional wedding. Becky was crying from the off. Henry cried. Julian caught my eye and seemed to be crying too, though that may have been down to his hangover. I felt the tears spring to my eyes for a variety of reasons. The romance in Becky's life and the corresponding lack of it in mine. The thought that I might never find myself standing at an altar with a man whom I loved. And the fact that my Jimmy Choos were too tight.

Becky and Henry exited the church to the triumphant pealing of bells. The rain held off for the photographs: an endless series of group tableaux in the graveyard to be followed by yet more shots at the reception venue. A double-decker bus had been hired to take the guests between the church and the reception, which was being held at a country house hotel, but first I had to get Becky safely into the Bentley and make sure that her skirt didn't get stuck in the door. It sounds easier than it was.

On arrival at the reception, I knocked back two glasses of champagne in quick succession before I continued my chief bridesmaid's duties, marshalling the smaller bridesmaids for photos and making a pretty arrangement of our bouquets on a table in the dining room once the photographs were done.

For the wedding breakfast, I sat at the head table, between Henry's father and his fourth wife. I soon gave up trying to make conversation with Henry's father because his hearing aid was on the blink. The fourth wife was friendly enough, but she had only recently arrived in the UK from the Ukraine and her English was limited to the names of all the designer concessions in Harvey Nichols. When I showed her the Jimmy Choos that had been killing me, she frowned. 'Last season's collection.'

After the meal came the speeches. Becky's father embarrassed both his daughter and me with tales from our Croydon childhood. Henry gave a speech that was moving in its incompetence. It was so obvious that he loved his wife. Julian gave a surprisingly PG-rated best man's speech. Actually, perhaps I shouldn't have been so surprised, since Becky had vetoed any strip-club shenanigans for Henry's stag party. Instead, he and his closest male friends had spent a day on a golf course and were home by 7 p.m.

'Thank God that's over,' said Julian, when his speech was done and he could at last risk having a glass or six of champers.

'You did very well,' I assured him. My moment in the spotlight was still to come.

30

'It's time for the cake,' said Becky's mother, grabbing my arm with her heavily be-ringed fingers. 'We're all very excited to see it.'

I felt a little sick. I had worked so hard to make Becky's wedding cake perfect. I had made the fruitcake a month before. The flowers, all made of icing, were also entirely fashioned by me. The previous evening I had watched nervously as two members of staff from the hotel kitchen helped me stack the three layers on top of each other. Objectively, I knew that the cake was a triumph. Becky couldn't have got better if she'd paid a professional the best part of a grand. But part of me still worried that it wasn't good enough for my friend or that something terrible might happen between the moment I added the last pink sugar flower and the moment it was wheeled into the ballroom. I had been into the kitchen to check on that cake at least five times during dinner. Now the moment of truth had come.

'You know,' Becky's mother continued, 'I was so worried that you were going to ruin Becky's special day. Naturally, she's kept me up to date with all the developments in your love life and the way that you've been dealing with them. We all felt very sorry for you, but at one point I actually asked Becky whether it was really such a good idea, having you in the wedding party at all. You would probably be much better off sitting at the back of the church, I told her. So you didn't feel as though you were on display when you were finding things so difficult. Though of course nobody looks at anyone except the bride really. But Becky insisted. She said that your friendship was more important to her than that, and even if you did stomp up the aisle with a face like thunder, she would find it in her heart to forgive you.'

'That's nice,' I said.

Becky's mother swayed towards me as though to impart something confidential. 'But let me tell you that I told her that I would definitely *not* forgive you if you didn't pull yourself together and act like a grown-up and it didn't matter if it was her wedding day, if you weren't smiling when you walked up the aisle behind my daughter, I would give you what for at the reception.'

'Well, thank goodness you don't have to.'

'That's what I said to Henry's mother. And she agreed. Because trust me she was worried too after hearing from Henry how ridiculous you were being about that man.'

'*Ridiculous*,' I echoed.

'We were both quite convinced you'd make a scene.'

'You were?'

'Oh, yes. You always were the kind to make a scene. Even when you were a little girl. The times that Becky came home crying because you'd had one of your tantrums. You were lucky that I never slapped you. I really don't know why she bothered with you. But at least we can laugh about it now, eh? Now, let's go and get that cake.' She practically pulled me to my feet. I shook off her hand.

'There's no need for you to come,' I told her. 'I'd rather do a last-minute check by myself. I want to make sure that everything is perfect before I let *anyone* see it. And I want Becky to be the first. Since it is her special day.'

'If you're sure?'

'Really, don't worry yourself about it at all. You should

be entertaining the other guests. Mother-of-the-bride is a very important role.'

'You're right.' Becky's mother beamed. 'Well, I can't wait to see this cake of yours!'

She planted a powdery kiss on my cheek and headed back to her seat, lurching dramatically from side to side. She'd had way too much Roederer.

Meanwhile I headed for the kitchen, where Becky's wedding cake waited for me. All three magnificent tiers of it.

31

In the kitchen, two waiters who were having a sneaky fag by the back door snapped to attention when I walked in.

'It's time for the cake,' I said. 'I'm going to need some help wheeling the trolley.'

'At your service,' said the younger guy, dusting cigarette ash from the cuff of his jacket.

'Not quite yet,' I said. 'I need to add some finishing touches.'

The waiter nodded and went back for another fag.

I looked at the cake, like an artist appraising a sculpture. What was missing? What would make this cake utterly unique and an extra-special gift for Becky? What would it take to make sure that this cake made Becky's wedding reception one that no one who had attended it would ever forget?

The previous evening I had asked the chef if it would be OK to leave a Tupperware box in one of his larders. I fetched it now. It contained a few things I might need in a cake-related emergency. There were some spare sugar flowers in case I decided that less wasn't more after all. There was the little tube of icing I had used to glue the miniature bride and groom (also made of sugar) to the top tier. That icing was what I needed.

My hand began to shake as I contemplated piping a special message round the side of each and every tier. I held my right wrist with my left hand to help steady it and began to pipe letters in neat capitals. The icing I piped was white, but the message could be seen clearly if you looked closely. The fact that the bride and groom would have to look closely was part of the fun.

It took quite a while and I have to admit that the last few letters were a little wonky, but the overall effect was amazing. I stood back to admire my handiwork. The two waiters joined me, silent with awe. I knew that the cake looked incredible. I could already imagine the delight on Becky's face as we pushed the trolley out into the ballroom.

'Let's go,' I said.

The two waiters positioned themselves one on either end of the trolley and slowly, carefully, began to move the cake towards the door. I walked out ahead of them with my head held high. Julian, the best man, saw us appear and tapped the side of his glass for silence.

'Ladies and gentlemen, it's time to cut the cake!'

The bride and groom met up again in the middle of the room – they had been circulating among their guests – and walked hand in hand to where I waited next to my master-piece.

'Thank you so much,' Becky said to me. 'I knew you'd come through in the end.'

Henry just grinned. He was sozzled.

'Have you got a knife?' Becky asked.

'Here you go.' I handed her the enormous knife with a porcelain handle big enough for two newly wedded hands that the hotel kept for just such an occasion. Becky and Henry stepped forward and rested the tip of the knife lightly on the icing so that everyone could take a snap. My stomach gurgled as I waited for her to stop posing and take a proper look at what she was actually cutting into.

It was a moment or two before Becky realised that there were actually words in the delicate tracery of icing that surrounded the carefully rendered sugar figures of her and her new husband. She squinted to read them.

'Oh, you've written something,' she said.

What was she expecting? Their names? The date of the wedding? Just 'Congratulations', perhaps? That would have been the obvious choice. She definitely wasn't expecting what I had really iced on to her wedding cake.

'I give it six months.'

That's what I had written. In elegant iced script, again and again and again and again. Round and round the sugar lovers like a labyrinth, and all over the sides of each tier. I had thought, as I was doing it, that I should write my message in red, but I decided that white on white was more subtle and artistic. In any case, I could tell that it was having just as dramatic an effect.

Becky looked first at me and then at her husband. In his half-cut state, Henry had yet to register what was wrong with the otherwise perfect picture. Becky's face crumpled. The cake knife dropped to the floor with a clatter. Henry narrowly missed losing a toe. Becky gathered up her enormous skirt and ran from the room.

'What's wrong?' Henry called after her.

'What's happened?' asked Becky's mother.

The wedding party reacted in shock.

I left moments later, but I didn't run after Becky, who had gone out into the garden to sob among the roses. I turned left, to the car park, where a taxi was already waiting. (I had asked one of the kitchen staff to order it in advance.) I went straight home.

32

Did it make me feel better? Not exactly. But in my drunken state I did manage to convince myself that my actions had been justified. I was fed up of being ridiculed or, at best, ignored. Becky's mother had talked to me as though I were still a child. Well, the worm had turned.

I pushed open the front door to my building. It was jammed, as usual, by junk mail. Pizza leaflets. Letters from our local MP. It made me even more angry than usual to see the pile of paper that no one in the building would ever read. But that day, just when I felt more alone in the world than I had ever done, I noticed that there was something for me! A pale-blue envelope with my name and address written on it in a very familiar hand.

It was a letter. From Michael!

Snatching it up from the pile of junk on the floor, I tore the envelope open and greedily devoured its contents. What did he want? Was it a love letter? Had the voodoo worked? Had he come to his senses? Did he want me back at last?

Dear Ashleigh,

I'm very sorry to have to write this letter. I can't believe it has come to this. I have reason to believe that you have been hanging around outside my apartment building at all hours, wearing a ridiculous disguise including an ugly brown wig. The security guard says he has seen you on a number of occasions. My new girlfriend also suspects that you have been lingering outside her shop and arranging phoney appointments to waste her time. This has to stop. If you persist in stalking me and my girlfriend like this, I will have no choice but to inform the police and take steps to have a restraining order taken out against you. For both our sakes, Ashleigh, but especially for yours, please try to put our relationship behind you and move on with your life.

Yours sincerely,
Michael

He had cc-ed the letter to G. Kleinbeck. And to M. Fox, whom I knew as Martin Fox, one of the lawyers at Michael's company. Martin and I had met on several occasions and he had always seemed a nice bloke. I thought he'd liked me too. The thought that he had seen the letter I now held in my shaking hands, a letter that accused me directly of being a stalker, made me feel rather sick. How could Michael do this to me! I was outraged for a moment before I started to panic. Was it possible that Michael had found out about my fake Facebook profile? Could he trace it back to me? There was bound to be CCTV coverage of me lurking around outside his building. Did Miss Well-Sprung have CCTV outside her shop? Was Michael gathering evidence to take me to court? Did he have enough already?

I decided I had to get rid of the letter at once, as though disposing of the letter would mean it had never existed. In the safety of my flat at last, I lit the scented candle in whose gentle light I had wished so many times for a reconciliation with the man I loved. I tore the hateful letter into pieces and fed them into the flames, crying bitterly all the while. I drank a bottle of wine while I was at it.

Then I went to bed, leaving the candle burning. I slept fitfully until I was woken good and proper by the smoke alarm . . .

33

'You're lucky to be alive,' was what the fireman said to me as I stood outside the block where I lived, wrapped in a grey blanket, while everything I owned in the world sizzled away to nothing. 'You don't know how fortunate you are that your landlord had fitted a smoke alarm in the first place! And that the woman from across the road saw your curtains were on fire and called us. It could have been much, much worse. You are a very lucky girl indeed.'

I nodded mutely. I didn't feel lucky. And I didn't feel very much like a girl. I felt old and stupid. My upstairs neighbour, Miranda, who had also been evacuated, glared at me, as if I needed any reminder that I was an idiot.

How could one little scented candle have done such an enormous amount of damage? The fire brigade's initial investigation suggested that leaving the candle burning was compounded by the fact that I had also left the sitting-room window open. It was a warm night but also breezy and the wind had blown the curtains inwards so that they brushed across the flame and that was all it took. Towering inferno. It took the firemen a good couple of hours to make sure the fire was out.

My neighbours and I were taken from the scene to the hospital, where we were checked over for smoke inhalation.

It was no surprise when the fire brigade confirmed that there was no way I would be able to move back into my flat anytime soon. Everybody who lived in the building had to find somewhere else to go. The flat above mine was damaged by smoke. The flat below by water. My landlord was facing a mammoth insurance claim. The combination of fire and water had left the building as shaky as a fun house at the fair. It might be months before the place would be declared safe again.

I muttered my apologies to my neighbours, who were thankfully quite restrained given the terrible situation I had brought upon us all. At last Miranda even admitted that it might have happened to her. She told me that she often used candles as part of her spells. Spells? Who knew that so many people in London practised witchcraft? She promised to cast one for the swift resolution of our sudden housing problem.

For now, however, I had nowhere to go but back to my parents. Home. The place where they have to take you in.

In the middle of the night, when the taxi the hospital had ordered dropped me off in Croydon, Mum was full of maternal concern and praised God for my safe return. The following morning, when the reality of the situation was beginning to hit me like a runaway bullet train, she was slightly less full of love and forgiveness.

'You left a candle burning! For heaven's sake.'

The ear-bashings came thick and fast. My landlord warned me that his buildings insurance might not cover my stupidity. My contents insurer told me that my claim would likely be dismissed. My mother reminded me all day long that I might have killed myself and half the street. I began to wish I had. I had lost my boyfriend, my job and now my home.

'Don't even get me started about what you did to poor Becky at the wedding,' she added when I thought things couldn't get worse. Of course Becky's mother had called to tell my mum the moment I left the reception. I was a marked woman as far as she was concerned.

My depression deepened when I saw what the firemen had managed to salvage from the flat. All my clothes had been ruined by smoke, fire or water. My books had gone the same way. My DVDs had cracked or melted. None of my favourite photographs had survived. All I had left was four mugs, including the chipped one I had been meaning to throw away for months. And one more thing.

'We found this in the bottom of the wardrobe,' said the fire officer as he handed over a charred biscuit tin. I didn't need to look inside to know that Mini-Michael would be perfectly unscathed. 'We thought it might mean something to you.'

'Thanks,' I said. 'That's just great.'

I didn't even have a bedroom in my parents' house any more. It had long since been converted into Mum and Dad's 'office' and 'gym'. The single bed I had grown up with had been replaced by a Nordic Track treadmill and a swanky desk from Ikea, complete with computer work station and printer bay. Mum had even bought some of that weird plastic stuff to put over the carpet so that she could scoot about on a wheelie office chair. There was really no room for me, even with my worldly goods reduced to nothing but a few mugs and a voodoo doll of my ex-boyfriend.

My mother tutted loudly as she watched my dad and brother move a filing cabinet out of the office and on to the landing so that I could have some space on the floor to sleep on. The Nordic Track would have to be moved as well.

'I suppose I'll have to do my exercises in the conservatory now, where anybody looking out of their back windows can see me!'

'Forget it. Leave the Nordic Track where it is and I'll get a hotel room,' I said.

'Nonsense,' said Dad, who hadn't been anywhere near the Nordic Track since the day he put his back out while assembling it. 'You're our daughter. You're more important than whether the neighbours see your mother in her tracksuit. What kind of parents would we be if we sent you to a hotel?'

Mum nodded grudgingly. 'Your father's right. You can stay with us for as long as you like,' she told me.

'And we'll be happy to have you,' said Dad.

'But you have to promise to get professional help,' was Mum's last word on the subject.

34

Professional help! I couldn't believe it. I never thought I'd hear those words from my mother. I'd always thought that as far as she was concerned, a mother's advice was about as professional as it gets. What could anyone else possibly have to tell me? But it seemed that Mum was deadly serious. Over supper that night she told me she had been hearing a lot about the wonders of counselling from one of the girls in her office who was training to volunteer for Relate.

'But I can't afford to have therapy,' I said.

'You can get it on the NHS if it's urgent enough. And I think that it is urgent now, don't you, dear?' As a result, Mum wasted no time in getting me an appointment with her local GP, who was going to be my GP for the duration of the time I had to stay in Croydon.

'Tell her everything that's happened,' Mum said. 'You want to make sure she understands how bad things have got.'

I felt ridiculous. Surely Dr Tucker did not want to be bothered with my break-up tale, but when I told her I thought I was wasting her time, she pressed me gently for more details and she seemed so kind and understanding that I poured out every detail of the story (all right, with the exception of the voodoo sock and Mini-Michael and exactly what I had done to upset my best friend) and she responded with a very sensible plan.

'Almost everybody reacts badly to a break-up,' she said.

'You'd hardly be human if you didn't. And you do seem to have been having a particularly difficult time of it. But I'm not going to give you drugs,' she continued. 'I think what you would really benefit from is talking to other people in the same boat.'

'Therapy?'

'Yes. Group therapy, to be precise. You can get going with it straight away.' She wrote down a name and number on a piece of paper. 'This is a support group for people in exactly your situation. Call this lady and ask when the next meeting is.'

The group that Dr Tucker said I should join met in a church hall on a Saturday morning. Actually, church hall is probably too grand a name for it. It was a prefabricated hut in the corner of a wide expanse of tarmac that formed a very optimistic car park around St Mary's C of E. I had walked past this particular church several times a week until I left home and moved to London and the only time I had seen the car park anywhere near full was when the local Rotary club held their twice-yearly car-boot sale.

That morning the car park was half full. As I chained my bicycle to the railings opposite the hut (which said that I shouldn't chain my bicycle there at all), I heard the sound of enthusiastically bad piano playing. Glancing in through the windows, I saw a dozen or so little girls in powder-blue leotards attempting to dance the polka, while their mummies and daddies looked on, glowing with pride.

A very different bunch of people had gathered in the lobby of the prefab. They were half in because it was drizzling that day and half out because they all needed to smoke.

'Are you here for the group?' I asked. As if I needed to. There wasn't one person among the six in the lobby who looked able to dress him- or herself properly, let alone hold down a relationship, have a child and raise a pristine junior ballerina.

At five to ten the pianist in the hall played a triumphant final note. The ballerinas curtseyed to their teacher and to each other and the class was done. When the doors to the room swang open, it was as though the gates of heaven were being opened for just a second. Lights, drama, laughter. Then the nice mummies and daddies saw the strange people in the corridor and hugged their precious children close. I chanced a smile at one little girl. Her mother picked her up and ran. I hadn't bothered to put any make-up on that morning, in anticipation of my mascara running, but did I really look that bad?

The other people seemed to know what to do. While the ballet mistress and her accompanist tidied away their equipment, the members of Broken Hearts United, or BHU, as they liked to be known for short, set up the room for a meeting. The chairs were brought into a tight little circle round a small, low table, upon which was placed a pile of photocopied leaflets and a candle. I was a little anxious to see the chairs being arranged in a neat, tight circle, having hoped to spend my first ever group therapy meeting lurking at the back of the room, in easy reach of the exit. But there was to be no chance of that, unless I bolted before the whole thing started, of course. I turned towards the door.

It was too late.

'Your first time?' asked the red-eyed girl who had arranged the leaflets on the table.

I nodded.

'We'll take care of you,' she said, taking me by the elbow and leading me towards a seat. 'My name is Enya.'

'Is this going to be like an AA meeting?' I wondered out loud.

'There are probably some similarities,' said Enya, 'in that we take it in turns to share and only offer advice if we're asked for it. No one judges.'

That was good. I was fed up of being judged.

'There's nothing to worry about. We'll look after you here.'

I thanked her and hoped she was right. As I settled into my seat, another confused-looking girl wandered in. She was a little younger than me, but I recognised the drawn look of serious heartbreak at once.

At five past ten the group leader, who was called Charles, arrived. He was in such a hurry that he didn't bother to take off his bicycle clips. No guesses as to why he was still single, I thought.

'Sorry I'm late. Do we have any newcomers?' he asked.

Tentatively, the other newbie and I put up our hands.

'Good. Perhaps you'd like to tell us a bit about yourself and why you're here?'

'I'm Katy. I'm here because I saw a flyer on the notice board at this café I go to,' said the other newbie.

'I'm Ashleigh. I'm here on the advice of my doctor,' I said. The group murmured approvingly. 'I can't seem to get over my break-up.'

'Well,' said Charles, 'you've come to the right place.'

The meeting progressed in a very orderly fashion. After Katy and I had told our stories (both of them greatly abridged), Charles asked for any other contributions. Everyone put up their hands. The group congratulated one chap who had managed to go for a whole week without calling his ex-girlfriend. Another man confessed that he had broken down and called his ex, 'but only when I knew he wouldn't be home. I hung up after listening to the message on his answer machine.'

'A good strategy,' said Charles. 'Did you disguise your number first?'

'Damn,' said the guy. 'I didn't think of that.'

Then it was the turn of Enya, the red-eyed woman who had welcomed me to the meeting that day.

'I've been coming to these meetings for quite some time,' said Enya. 'And I just want to thank you all for being my lifeline in the difficult days since my break-up.'

The group clapped at the compliment.

'Should I tell my story for the new people?' Enya asked Charles, the group leader. Charles nodded. Enya held her coffee mug tightly and looked to the ceiling, as though she were trying to prevent herself from crying. My mind was already boggling as I imagined what on earth her story could be. She looked to be in her early forties. Had she married young? Was she mourning the end of a relationship that had lasted twenty years?

Enya continued, 'Robert and I were together for eleven months.'

Oh.

'Our relationship was everything I had ever dreamed of. I gave my whole self to him. My body and my soul. I thought that we were building a union that would last for ever. I was wrong. Shortly before our first Christmas together, he called me from the hotel in Rhyl where he was staying on business' – she made little inverted commas with her fingers when she said the word 'business' – 'and told me that he didn't want to be with me any more.'

The other members of BHU sighed as they shared Enya's pain.

'I thought that I would die,' Enya continued. 'I begged and pleaded for him to tell me what I could do to turn things around, but he'd made up his mind and refused to listen to me. He told me that he didn't think he'd ever really been in love.'

A woman who had not taken her nose out of her hand-
kerchief for the entire session let out an anguished sob on
Enya's behalf.

'I couldn't believe what I was hearing. Not only had he
broken my heart, he was trying to destroy my memories. I
knew that he loved me. I knew that he was making a mistake.
But it was as though he'd been overtaken by an evil spirit.
The things that he said. So cruel and untrue. He told me I
was needy. He told me I wanted too much from him and
that was why he left.'

Charles tutted and slowly shook his head.

'And the pain just keeps on growing,' Enya said with a
shuddering intake of breath. 'Every night before I go to bed
I pray that the following morning will release me. Every
night I pray that my first thought upon waking will be of
something other than him. Him! Him! But still my torment
goes on.' She took a moment to wave her fist at the gods.
'Seven years!' she cried. 'Seven years! Am I doomed to eternal
torment?'

I had been taking a mouthful of tea as Enya made that
last revelation. The mouthful came out through my nose.

Had I understood her properly? Enya had managed to
spin out her grief over the end of an eleven-month relationship for a whole seven years! If I extrapolated from her
experience and multiplied it by the length of time that
Michael and I had been together, then I was looking at
almost twenty-one years of this misery. Longer than the
average criminal sentenced to 'life' actually spent in jail.

'I don't know what I did to deserve this,' Enya sighed. 'I
don't know why I was chosen to bear this pain.'

'Me neither,' I said in what I hoped was a supportive way.

Enya thanked me for my 'contribution'.

'But what happened to Robert?' the other newbie dared
to ask.

The entire room turned towards her with disapproval in their eyes. But Enya said it was OK. She would tell the new people the end of the story.

'He got married,' said Enya. 'He has three children. He took out a restraining order against me late last year.'

When the session had ended, Enya came across the room and grabbed both my hands. Though she had been nursing her coffee cup for the entire session, her fingers were horribly cold. I felt like Ebenezer Scrooge being grabbed by one of his ghosts. Was Enya the ghost of my future?

'You were so brave today, telling your story so stoically. We're all really proud of you,' she told me in a blast of halitosis. 'Some of us go on to Starbucks after the session, to go over what we've learned. Perhaps you'd like to come along?'

I fought the urge to tell her that I wasn't sure she had learned anything. Seven years grieving such a short relationship, while the guy who had left her had met someone else, married and had a family? Enya was ridiculous. But was she really so much more ridiculous than me?

I imagined what Michael might think if he could have heard me describing the end of our affair to this room full of odd-bods, who all had very good reason to believe that they might *never* get laid again. I wasn't like them, was I? I wasn't wearing bicycle clips. I wasn't wearing anything that looked as though it might have been made by a blind womens' collective in Ecuador. I didn't smell of mothballs or llamas. I didn't have breath that could kill a dog.

I had to get out of there. I felt as though another moment in the company of those people would only do me harm. That meeting had been what the Americans so charmingly call a 'circle jerk'. I told Enya that I had to get home. My mother was expecting me for lunch.

'OK,' she said, kissing me on both cheeks. 'Here's my card. Anytime you want to talk, just call me. Anytime. I'm always happy to talk.'

I took the card, which said that she ran a shelter for homeless cats. I wasn't in the least bit surprised.

The other newbie drew level with me as we exited the hall.

'What did you think?' I asked her.

Her eyes bugged out in horror. 'I don't know what to think,' she said. 'But I know I am *never* going back in there. Never. I am going straight home to log on to Match.com and I am going to get laid by next weekend.'

She was out of that place like a bat out of hell.

35

As I headed back to Mum and Dad's, it occurred to me that maybe the other newbie had the right idea. Voodoo hadn't worked, and group therapy was not looking promising. Perhaps simply getting laid was the answer. I could continue to allow Michael the same space in my brain that he had always occupied, or I could get someone else in to edge him out.

I needed to get back out there.

But who could I get back out there with? My social circle had been withering year on year as my friends succumbed to marriage and motherhood, even before I delivered the death blow by ruining Becky's wedding. The last time I had been on a night out had been Becky's hen night and that was hardly a raucous affair, with three of the girls not drinking because they were breastfeeding, three not drinking because they were pregnant and one not drinking because she wanted to get pregnant before December to avoid the crushing pity of her mother-in-law over Christmas lunch.

Nevertheless I did know of another hen night coming up that might be a little more fun.

My young cousin Karen was getting married in a couple of weeks' time. I wasn't going to go to the actual wedding. She was marrying a Kiwi guy she'd met in some backpackers' club in Covent Garden and the marriage was going to take place on Fiji, with just the bride, the groom and their best friends in attendance. (My aunt was absolutely livid.)

Anyway, Karen may not have invited any of her family members to her wedding, but she had invited me to her hen night, which was to take place on the August bank-holiday weekend. I had already turned the kind invitation down, thinking of nothing that would send me into a terminal depression faster than a night out with a bunch of twenty-somethings mainlining Red Bull and vodka. But needs must. I had to go out or end up like Enya. I was not yet ready to sit in a bar all by myself, though. That would be way too sad. I had to go out with a gang, and Karen's was the only gang available to me right now.

Karen was delighted to hear from me. 'I thought you had another engagement.'

'My friend's baby shower was cancelled,' I lied.

'Aw,' said Karen. 'That's a shame. But I'm really happy you're going to come on my hen night instead. We're going to have an amazing time, Ash. We're starting at Bolsheviks on the High Street. We're going to walk north, having a drink in every single bar we come across, until we get to the nightclub. Assuming that any of us are still standing by then!'

'Sounds fantastic,' I said, wondering what on earth I was letting myself in for.

'Wonderful! I'll see you next week!'

'Perhaps I should just stay in,' I said, as I had breakfast with my parents on the morning before Karen's hen do. 'I don't know any of her friends. And they probably don't want an old-timer like me tagging along with them anyway. I'm sure she only invited me to be polite.'

'Oh, go on,' said Mum. 'Karen will be really excited to have you there. She's always looked up to you. You'll have a great evening. Besides, I don't like to think of you sitting here all on your own while we're away.'

That weekend, the last bank holiday of the summer, my father was taking Mum to the hotel where they'd spent their honeymoon. They were supposed to go away for a whole week but the modest little bed and breakfast in Newquay had since become a ritzy boutique hotel and so they had cut back to two nights.

Mum had only agreed to go away that weekend because she knew that Lucas was planning to go away as well, to the Reading Festival, and that way she didn't have to worry about him inviting his feckless mates round and getting fag burns on her new sofa. Five years previously she and Dad had left Lucas on his own for just one night and come back to find that particular year's new sofa covered in new-age travellers drinking Special Brew from the best wedding-gift crystal and flicking ash from their spliffs into my deceased paternal grandmother's prized Hermès teacups.

'At least they weren't flicking the ash on the carpet,' Lucas had protested.

The pot-smoking faded into insignificance when Mum went up to her bedroom and found one of Lucas's school-friends – a very sweet girl (or so we thought) – having a threesome with her boyfriend and one of my parents' neighbours.

When Mum reminded my brother of that unfortunate party and the damage it had done to her trust in him, he pointed out to her that in actual fact I was the pyromaniac in the family.

'Thanks, Lucas.'

'It was an accident,' my mother chipped in on my behalf.

Despite my brother's attempt at stirring things up, Mum was finally persuaded to get into the Saab and hit the road down to Cornwall. She waved tearfully until the car had rounded the corner and was out of sight. Anyone would think she had never left her children at home before, despite the fact that I had lived independently for a good decade prior to setting fire to my own flat.

'The cat's away . . .' said Lucas, as we went back into the house. He cranked up the stereo.

Thank goodness it wasn't long before his friends came to collect him in an old VW camper van. Five of them were going to Reading that year. The van was piled high with rucksacks full of neatly ironed T-shirts (they all lived with their mums) and Tupperware containers of food, carefully packed into ice-boxes to keep it fresh (the mums again). Lucas added his own contribution to the stash: a hamper full of sandwiches lovingly prepared by Dad. They were less like the wild young rebels they thought they were than *Five Go Camping* without the dog. Talking of which. Ben tried hard to sneak into the back of the van but was thwarted. He was staying with me.

'Don't forget to walk him,' Lucas warned me. As if he ever remembered.

'Don't die of a drug overdose, will you?' I said as I saw him and Richard, his best friend, off the premises.

'Watch out for chlamydia,' was Richard's charming reply.

'Fat chance,' said Lucas. 'Ashleigh hasn't had a shag in a year.'

'Five months,' I pointed out, pointlessly. 'It's been less than five months.' As far as Lucas and Richard were concerned, at thirty-two I was a shrivelled old bag.

Once I had the house to myself, I turned the music *down* and settled at the kitchen table with a mug of tea and the latest copy of *Hello!* (which Mum had bought for the coverage of some hapless soap star's funeral). It didn't cheer me up.

The following afternoon I took Ben for a walk in the park. The weather wasn't too bad, considering it was a bank holiday, and every spare patch of grass played host to a picnic. It was hard to walk from one side to the other without being hit by balls, Frisbees and Jack Russell terriers in pursuit of said neon plastic discs. Ben enjoyed himself, but that walk didn't do much to improve my mood. Those people who weren't playing Frisbee or trying to keep young children out of the pond were inevitably walking in twos. I remembered how Michael and I used to walk along like that, our arms around each other, synchronising our steps so that we wouldn't bump hips.

I had a stabbing vision of Michael wrapped around Miss Well-Sprung. I wondered what they were doing that bank holiday. Perhaps they were at the carnival in Notting Hill and she was making him do some exotic Brazilian dance. I drew small comfort from the fact that he would probably look like a twit. Michael couldn't dance at all. But maybe, as I had been, Miss Well-Sprung was too much in love with him to care.

Turning for home, I retraced my steps back to Mum and Dad's. I was on the point of deciding that I was too miserable to go out that evening when my phone rang. It was Karen.

'Hiya,' she said. 'Just checking you know where we're meeting up tonight.'

'Er . . .' I began. 'I thought perhaps . . .'

'You're not going to bail out, are you? You can't pull out now. I've told all my mates that you're coming. You're the only member of my family I could ever talk to.'

How could I refuse after that?

At eight o'clock I found myself standing on the pavement outside the first venue. I hadn't seen my cousin Karen for a couple of years. In fact, I hadn't seen her in the flesh since she was doing her GCSEs. But like so many families, we kept in touch via Facebook, so I had seen pictures of a variety of hairdos, boyfriends and shots of her wearing traffic cones at the end of a long night on the town. That said, I still wondered if I would recognise her. Would she recognise me? My hair, after all, was now the reddish-brown of a scruffy city fox.

In the end, it was easy. I saw them as soon as I walked into the bar, Bolsheviks, a Russian-themed bar specialising in shots that had been an Argentinian bar just a couple of weeks earlier. (The toilet doors were still adorned with silhouettes of tango dancers.) Unlike Becky's snotty girlfriends, Karen's friends were not planning to hold back on the traditional hen-night frippery. They were already in full regalia, wearing tutus instead of skirts and pink fur-covered horns on their heads. They each had a T-shirt with the name of a Bond girl emblazoned upon it. They looked crazy. They looked ridiculous. They looked like they were ready to have a good time.

Having embraced me enthusiastically, Karen held me at arm's length and looked at my ensemble (a black dress and a pair of sensible heels I had borrowed from my mother) in dismay.

'Everything I had was ruined in the fire,' I said to excuse myself.

'Doesn't matter. You need to change into this,' said Karen's best friend and chief bridesmaid, Lola, handing me a plastic bag. I knew without looking what would be inside.

'We saved Miss Moneypenny for you,' Karen explained. 'Since you are the oldest.'

Like I needed reminding.

I followed Karen into the tango toilets to change. Reluctantly, I folded Mum's little black dress into my enormous handbag (also borrowed) and put on the outfit that Karen had provided for me instead. The stiff net ballet skirt barely covered my knickers.

'Are those cycling shorts?' Karen asked, pointing at the little black shorts that poked out from beneath the pink tulle.

'They're Spanx,' I said grimly.

'What do you need those for?' Karen asked. 'You're not fat.'

'That's what you think. Because I'm always holding my wobbly bits in.'

'Oh.'

'You'll understand when you're older,' I said.

'I'm never going to wear support underwear,' said Karen.

'I think I said that once too.'

She handed me the T-shirt. I didn't need to put it on to know that it was going to be a disaster. I held it up to my chest.

'Karen, this is a *child's* T-shirt,' I said. 'I won't even be able to get this over my head.'

'You totally will,' she said, taking it from my hands and starting to tug it over my head for me. 'It's full of Lycra. See? It's, like, really stretchy.'

True. It did stretch. And I did get it on. Though when I looked in the mirror, I was not in any way comforted by what I saw. Imagine stuffing a pair of slightly misshapen melons into an elasticated bandage.

'This T-shirt is way too small,' I said to Karen. 'In fact, I'd have to say it's borderline obscene.'

Lola had joined us. 'Oh my God,' she said. 'You have got a magnificent rack! Have you had your tits done?'

'I have not had my tits done,' I said.

'Well, it looks like you have. In a good way. You are going to stop traffic.' She jiggled my breasts *à la* the dreaded Trinny in the early days of *What Not to Wear*.

'I'm putting my dress back on.'

Karen pouted. 'Come on, Ash. It's my hen night. I'm only

going to do this once. You've got to enter into the spirit of things. We're all dressed up so people can see we're together. We're a team.'

'Yeah,' said Lola. 'Team Karen. Come on, Ash. Have a laugh while you still can.'

'While I still can?' I winced.

She took a pair of nail scissors out of her handbag.

'It's all right,' I said. 'I'll wear the T-shirt. There's no need to threaten me.'

'Hold still,' she said, getting dangerously close to my neck with the pointed blades. 'This T-shirt needs customisation.' Lola was training to be a fashion stylist.

She snipped a channel from the round neckline of the T-shirt down to the top of my cleavage. Instantly, the little cut spread into a rough-and-ready V-neck, of the kind that Jodie Marsh or some other glamour model might wear to flaunt her expensive and not entirely successful surgery.

'Oh. My. God.' I could only stare at my reflection in horror. I looked as though I was going to spend the evening working as a superannuated promotional 'model' handing out shots of vodka with a free serving of innuendo.

'Fantastic,' said Karen. Her friend agreed. 'Now you're ready. Hello, boys!'

I wrapped my arms across my chest. 'I cannot leave the ladies' looking like such a . . . such a slut!'

'Oh, come on!'

Karen and her friends were not taking no for an answer. We had been joined by two more of the girls. Daisy, whose Bond name was Solitaire, and Jools, who for that night only was Vesper Lynd.

'We're missing happy hour!' said Vesper.

I was bodily dragged back out into the bar, where one of our crew – codename Plenty O'Toole – had lined up twelve shot glasses. Behind the bar, a lad who didn't look legally old enough to be working as a barman was performing some pretty impressive juggling with two bottles. In a seamless move, he stopped juggling and began to pour liquor into our empty glasses. A layer of peach schnapps was followed by a layer of Baileys and a few drops of grenadine as a garnish. The Baileys started to curdle.

'That looks vile,' I said.

'It's a brain haemorrhage,' said the barman proudly. 'If you can drink five of these without throwing up, you get the sixth for free.'

'I can do that,' said Daisy/Solitaire. She quickly despatched four of the twelve glasses lined up along the bar. Then she covered her mouth with both her hands. She couldn't do it after all. But she did manage to keep the four she had already drunk down, which was a good thing in the circumstances.

'Ready, ladies?' Lola handed out the remaining glasses. 'Let's toast the blushing bride! Up your bum, Karen!'

I did my best to look game as I sipped at my own brain haemorrhage. Really, who comes up with these things? The combination of peach schnapps and Baileys Irish Cream was quite the most vile thing imaginable. The Baileys and schnapps wouldn't mix in the glass, resulting in a blobby emulsion that looked unspeakable and tasted worse. It was so sweet I felt sure I heard my teeth squeak. Having forced the evil stuff down, I slammed the glass back on the bar with a shudder and hoped that was the end of it. I needed a proper drink to wash the taste away.

'Another round,' someone shouted.

'Can't we have a bottle of wine?' I asked.

'Nah,' said Karen. 'It'll take us ages to get pissed drinking wine. Plus, if you do shots, you have to spend less time running backwards and forwards to the toilet.' The logic of youth . . .

A fresh round of haemorrhages had already been prepared.

'Come on, Ashleigh! Down in one this time,' yelled Lola.

I suppose I could have refused. I could have wished Karen the very best with married life, given her the 'Congratulations, you're getting married' card that I had in my handbag and high-tailed it out of there. But there was something infectious about the enthusiasm these girls had for life. They were out for a good time and, heaven knows, I needed a good time. So I stayed. Maybe if I just let go and got bladdered . . . I downed my second haemorrhage. By the time I'd had three brain haemorrhages, I was definitely starting to 'chillax', as my young cousin would have said.

The bar in which we found ourselves at around ten o'clock that long night seemed to be full of hen and stag parties. A DJ took requests for all those who were about to give up their freedom. Karen asked him to play 'Hit Me, Baby, One More Time', which is the first song she ever got into. She was just ten when the song was released and asked for the DVD for Christmas. I remembered the family party when she and her little sister dressed like hookers and performed the Britney dance for our horrified grandparents. I dread to think what Granny Polly would have thought if she'd seen Karen dancing to Britney on her hen night, lifting her overly tight Pussy Galore T-shirt emblazoned with L-plates to reveal a day-glo-pink bra.

Karen's performance was so energetic that she was soon invited to dance on a pedestal in front of the DJ's decks. Her bachelorettes whooped with delight as Karen did a bit more bump and grind and was rewarded with a bottle of cava. 'Better than champagne,' the DJ assured her.

Karen had despatched half the bottle by the time she made it back to our table. She offered me a swig and I took it. The cava was as warm and sweet as if it had been left on a sunny windowsill for a week and a half. Ordinarily I would have turned up my nose, but four brain haemorrhages into the evening, I was no Jancis Robinson. I had quickly reached the stage where I agreed with Daisy and Lola that I was happy to drink anything as long as it was alcoholic.

'My round,' I said. 'Barman, line 'em up.'

36

Four shots later, we found ourselves in a nightclub called Histeria. I wondered if the misspelling was deliberate and gave the word a double meaning that I simply couldn't see. A double meaning wasn't the only thing I was having trouble seeing by this point. Gazing up at the blackboard behind the bar in search of a new and more interesting cocktail, I found myself unable to focus on the equally creatively spelled cocktail list. Either I was going short-sighted or I had been poisoned by Baileys. Never mind.

Unable to find anything more appealing than a brain haemorrhage on the list, I had another two. Then we hens took to the dance floor, mob-handed, creating a little circle round our bags and Karen's shoes (a pair of high-heeled 'tranny' platforms, which were killing her) like early settlers on the drive to conquer the American West. Though much, much, much more drunk.

'Like this,' said Karen, showing me how to grind. 'You're not doing the Locomotion now, Auntie Ashleigh.'

'I am not old enough to have done the Locomotion!' I exclaimed. 'And stop calling me auntie. I'm your cousin.'

'I know, but I always thought of you as an auntie,' said Karen. 'With you being so much older and really boring and that.'

'You think I'm boring?'

'Not any more. You're being a really good laugh tonight.'

I thanked her for the compliment, but I was irked and the

thought of being considered dull made me go back to the bar for another round of shooters. A neck full of undiluted spirits improved my grinding technique no end. So much so that a red-faced rugby player on a stag do was inspired to press his genitals to my buttocks. I should have been outraged but I wasn't. I was that far gone. Karen whooped as I actually turned round and jiggled my breasts in the rugby player's face.

'They're real,' I added. In case he hadn't noticed. He nodded his appreciation and asked if he could have a feel. I said he couldn't. He danced off elsewhere.

Then at midnight the DJ interrupted the non-stop bump and grind to make a brief announcement.

'It's that time of the evening, boys and girls. Time for our weekly competition. Last week the boys had the chance to win a bottle of champagne by having their eyebrows shaved off. This week it's the turn of the ladies, with an old classic . . . the most popular competition *EVAH* here at Histeria nightspot. Ladies and gentlemen, your attention, please. It is time' – he played the sound effect of Big Ben bonging twelve as he intoned very seriously over the top of it – 'for the wet-T-shirt competition!'

The crowd went wild. I whooped too. It seemed appropriate.

'Come on, ladies! Step on up!' He quickly had three contestants. 'I need at least five more!'

'Hey, Ashleigh,' said Lola, 'it's your turn to win us some drinks.'

It was true. The other hens had been working very hard to keep alcohol consumption up and costs down. Lola and Daisy had already climbed on to a podium and French-kissed each other for a bottle of Lambrini. Anna – aka Plenty O'Toole – had shown a rugby player her 'chicken fillets' in return for a round of drinks for the lot of us. She let him keep one of the chicken fillets for another round after that. I had been paying my way. I'd bought three ruinous rounds at Bolsheviks, but I sensed that Lola was more concerned about my getting into the spirit of things than merely flashing the cash.

'You really think I should do the wet-T-shirt competition?'

She nodded. The other girls agreed.

'On behalf of the team,' said Lola. 'I'd do it myself but you have by far the best gazungas.'

What on earth were those?

'I can't get up there,' I said. 'I'm thirty-two years old.'

'So? That's nowhere near retirement age.'

'All the more reason to do it,' piped up Daisy. 'Have you ever done it before?'

'Of course not.'

'Do you want to grow old without ever having got your boobs out in front of an appreciative crowd?'

'That was my general plan,' I admitted.

It was Karen who piled on the pressure. She grasped my arm and told me passionately, 'Go for it, Ashleigh. We only regret the things we haven't done.'

She said it with such conviction. How could I possibly disagree? The stage was already filling with girls far less squeamish than me. I couldn't help but cast an eye over the competition and wonder what my chances really were. Certainly, the only rack up there that looked any bigger than mine was definitely not a natural one. I'd get extra points for being a hundred per cent natural, Lola suggested.

'Go on,' said Karen. 'You've got better tits than any of them.'

And so the combination of a skinful of spirits and the encouragement of my younger companions got the better of me at last. A switch flipped in my head and the sexist stupidity I would have run a mile from on any ordinary day suddenly seemed like an opportunity to strike a blow for real boobs and older women everywhere.

'I'll do it.'

'Go, Ashleigh!'

With the cheers of my fellow partygoers ringing in my ears, I took my place in the line-up of hopefuls, while the compere of the evening's festivities handed out buckets to an equal number of men. It goes without saying that there were no shortage of volunteers. He assigned one man to each of the girls before he donned a waterproof poncho and instructed, 'Now, I'm going to count to three, and when I have finished counting to three, you boys are going to—'

My bucket-holder – who looked overly keen to do his job, I thought – didn't wait for three. I didn't have time to close my eyes and brace myself for the gallon of cold water that he tipped over my head.

'Not over her head, you doughnut!' the DJ shouted. 'You're only meant to get her T-shirt wet.'

'Sorry,' my bucket boy said shamefacedly. He dug into his pocket and brought out a packet of tissues. 'Will this help?'

I dabbed at my eyes, in a pointless and futile attempt to keep my mascara from running down my face, while the other men did their duty, leaving ten girls shivering on the stage. The water was unnecessarily cold. Lola would later explain that was all about the nipples. The DJ, still wearing his poncho, stepped out from his booth again to deliver his judgement. He walked the length of the line, pretending to scribble on his clipboard as he examined the boobs on display.

'Nice rack,' he told girl number one.

'Great uplift,' he said to the next.

'Not bad for an old girl,' he said when he got to me. 'Are they real?'

'One hundred per cent,' I assured him.

'That gets extra points.' He put a tick next to my name.

He continued on down the line, putting on a pair of comedy spectacles to examine one especially unfortunate flat-chested girl. To help him make his decision, he asked the audience to give their own opinion via a 'clapometer'. I was astonished at the volume my friends managed to raise for me. They were unbelievably enthusiastic.

Still, the top prize – an envelope containing a hundred pounds – went to an Australian girl called Hazel, who was working as a nanny in London while she saved to tour the rest of Europe. Second prize went to Emma, who also worked as a nanny, for a family in South Kensington. Emma offered to take her T-shirt right off in return for a free cocktail. I imagined the yummy mummies who employed those girls would not have been impressed.

I looked down at my gang, who had been whooping my name to no avail. I shrugged my shoulders.

'And a special prize,' said the DJ, 'for tonight's *oldest* contestant.'

Another bottle of cava. I waved it above my head and stepped down to join the girls, who gathered me into their midst as though I was coming back to them with a bottle of Cristal. It was soon polished off.

'You were amazing,' said Lola, as she wrapped me in her cardigan.

'I can't believe I was the *oldest* contestant.'

'That girl in the red top was totally the same age as you,' said Daisy. 'Either that or she's spent a lot of time on a sunbed.'

'You were robbed,' said Karen.

'Perhaps if you'd taken your bra off. You know, so your nipples really showed,' Daisy suggested.

'I'll remember that for next time.'

We were interrupted by the boy who had thrown the bucket of water over my head.

'Sorry,' he said again. 'I got a bit over-excited. Threw a bit prematurely.'

'Well, if you're like that in the sack, you can piss off straight away,' said Daisy.

The boy looked hurt. He turned to me. 'Can I buy you a drink?'

'Has someone dared you?' asked Karen. Rather thoughtlessly, since it seemed to me that the slur was less about his bravery than the improbability that he might just feel like treating me.

'No,' he said. 'I just want to. Really. I do.'

'That'd be great,' I told him. 'Make it a brain haemorrhage.' I had been developing quite a taste for them.

The boy went off to the bar. I saw him counting out coins into the palm of his hand as he waited to be served.

'That's probably the last of his pocket money,' said Karen.

'Don't be so cruel,' I said.

I was strangely touched by his insistence on buying me a drink. In the decade and a half since I'd been legally able to drink, I'd found that it was often easier to get a British man to spill a drink on you than to buy you one.

The bucket boy came back with my shot.

'Thanks,' I said. 'My name's Ashleigh.'

'Jack,' he said.

We shook hands in a somewhat formal fashion given that we'd met over my wet boobs.

Karen and her friends had drawn themselves into a huddle, leaving me and my new friend alone. I could tell that they were talking about us – finding it all very funny – but I wasn't about to send the poor lad away. He was very good-looking.

'Do you come here often?' he said.

'Er . . . no. Not really. In fact,' I admitted, 'I haven't been clubbing since 2005.'

'What?' He looked at me in surprise.

I realised that he probably couldn't have got into a club in 2005, on account of having to stay home and revise for his GCSEs, or whatever it is they take these days.

'I come here every week,' he said. 'It's a great laugh.'

'Yes,' I agreed. 'I've had a good time.'

'You were a good sport, getting up there like that.'

'You mean at my age?' I filled in the gaps.

'I wasn't thinking anything about your age,' said Jack. Then he added, 'What is it?'

'I'm not telling you that.'

Karen and her friends were getting restless. Lola was sent over to fill me in on their plans. Apparently there was a club on the industrial estate that started at three and ran through until nine and that was where they were going to head next. I had to bail out. I kissed my cousin goodbye and wished her well for her upcoming marriage. Her friends had certainly given her one hell of a send-off into married life.

'How will you get home?' asked Karen.

'I'll get a cab,' I said.

'I'll wait with you if you like,' said Jack.

Karen and her friends exited with much suggestive eyebrow-raising.

37

Outside the club, the pavement was busier than on the Saturday before Christmas. All the clubs were kicking their clients out at once and the street was just as buzzing as the dance floor had been. But it was raining now. The clouds that had been gathering as I arrived at Bolsheviks were really letting loose. The competition for a taxi was going to be intense.

Jack was still beside me. He and I waited side by side on the pavement for fifteen minutes. No sign of a yellow cab light. I started to shiver. I had changed out of my hen-night outfit and back into my mum's dress, but now the rain was soaking me through again. Jack offered me his bomber jacket.

'You'll freeze,' I said. He was wearing just a T-shirt beneath.

'Not likely,' he said. 'I'm covered in hair. And fat.'

'You're not fat,' I said.

'I am. Look.' He lifted up his T-shirt to show me his tummy. Washboard abs, of course. I said, 'Nice,' and quickly turned back to scan the street for a yellow light before I was overcome with the urge to touch his muscles.

'Well, this is hopeless,' I said. 'We'll never get a cab.'

'Can I walk you home?' Jack asked.

Of course, it struck me that even compared to entering the wet-T-shirt competition, this was the most stupid thing

I had done in years. Allowing a complete stranger to walk me home? I would have advised any other woman against it, but that night I rationalised it to myself. I told myself that the entire hen party had met Jack. The club probably had CCTV footage of him throwing his bucket over my boobs. He would have to be a pretty stupid serial killer to try anything dodgy with so much evidence that he and I had left the club together. I told myself that I wouldn't let him in the house in any case. Not into my parents' place. Mum would throw a fit. But as we walked, I began to feel a little more comfortable with my gallant companion. It turned out that he knew my cousin's fiancé. They'd worked together in the compliance department of the bank that had recently made Karen's husband-to-be redundant. Jack had lost his job too and was temping to tide himself over.

'It's OK,' he said. 'I don't have many overheads. I live in a shared flat.'

'How horrible,' I said involuntarily. I could imagine nothing worse. There wasn't enough money in the world to persuade me to go back to sharing fridge space with anyone else after my five years in the flat-share universe. It was bad enough having to go back to Mum and Dad's temporarily. But Jack was much younger than me. How much younger I dared not ask, though I was guessing that he was twenty-six max. He looked as though he could grow a moustache, at least.

It took us the best part of an hour to walk back to my parents' house. As we turned into the street, Jack said, 'I think I came to a party in this street once. About five years ago. It all got a little bit wild.'

'Well,' I said, stopping outside the house, 'nothing wild happening tonight. This is me. Thank you very much for walking me home.' I gave him back his jacket. We stood there awkwardly. 'Er, goodbye,' I tried, just as Jack plucked up the courage to say, 'I was wondering if perhaps I could see you again. I could take you out for a coffee or something. I mean, only if you want to. If you'd like . . .' His voice trailed away in expectation of rejection.

My resolve finally melted like snow on a hot car bonnet. He looked so sweet and brave.

'Come in and have a coffee now,' I suggested. It didn't mean we had to do anything.

'Really? Yes, please,' said Jack.

But Jack didn't ever get that coffee. Deciding that it was now or never and ignoring Ben the dog's disapproving look, I took Jack straight into the sitting room and pulled him down on to the sofa beside me. He didn't protest. Instead he started kissing me as though he hadn't eaten in three and a half years.

It had actually been well over three years since I last took my clothes off in front of someone other than Michael. When Michael and I went to the bed for the first time, I had been fairly sober by comparison, which seemed appropriate for the gravity of the moment. It was as though I had known very early on that Michael was going to be important in my life.

When it came to taking my clothes off in front of Jack, however, there was altogether less ceremony. Any worries I had about revealing my Spanx were banished when I saw what he was wearing beneath his trousers. It was a pair of awful underpants – white running to grey – that only a mother could have bought. I could tell that he was so busy being ashamed about being caught in those scraggy old Y-fronts that he wouldn't notice if I was wearing La Perla or a Tubigrip. He helped me roll the Spanx off, which was good, as it's surprisingly hard work getting in and out of those things and, had he not helped me, I might have worn them all night.

We rolled off the sofa and on to Mum's prized rug (a gift from a trip to Istanbul), and as Ben looked on in doggy bewilderment, we got busy.

The sex was energetic and over quickly. I think it lasted the length of one track of the latest Killers album. I thought that Jack would want to leave as soon as it was over, but he didn't. Instead he snuggled into my side and said, 'Do you mind if I stay the night?'

I nodded mutely.

He propped himself up on an elbow and looked down into my face.

'You can stay,' I said, when it became clear that he'd missed the mute nod and was eager for reassurance. 'Just promise you won't puke in the bed.'

'Oh, I never puke,' he said.

'Great.' That was good enough for me. I was finding it hard to keep my eyes open in any case.

So I took him upstairs to my room. If he was surprised that I slept in a single bed – I hadn't told him this was my parents' house after all – he didn't show it. He just jumped in and rolled on to his back, looking as happy as Ben after a tummy rub.

'It's so nice to be in clean sheets,' he said. 'I haven't had clean sheets since the washing machine packed up.'

I decided that it was probably for the best I didn't ask him exactly when that was.

Jack was soon asleep. He looked even younger as he drifted into a dream. I revised my estimate of his age down from twenty-six to twenty-four. Oh dear. I had shagged a man almost a decade younger than me. It crossed my mind that made me a cougar, one of those women who prey on younger men for sex.

I blamed it on the Baileys.

38

The following day I woke with a headache and a dead arm. My single bed really wasn't big enough for two and I had spent most of the night squashed up against the wall. Realising that I wasn't alone, I gave a little start. It took a while for my brain to catch up with the situation. The night-club. The wet-T-shirt competition. The handsome young lad in the baggy grey underpants.

It hadn't been a dream.

As I inched my arm out from beneath his neck, the handsome young lad gave a little snort and another piece of the jigsaw fitted into place.

'Jack,' I whispered to myself. At least I remembered his name. But the question was, would he remember mine? I couldn't remember how many shots I'd had, but I did recall having sunk the lioness's share of at least two bottles of cava. Had Jack been similarly inebriated? My ego couldn't take the risk that he would wake up, see what he had fallen asleep next to and take fright. I edged my way out of the bed.

As I had feared, the bathroom mirror greeted me with a reflection of the face I deserved after such a big night on the town. Evidently, I had not followed the beauty editor's cardinal rule and taken my make-up off before bedding down for the night. I panicked when I saw a thick black hair sprouting from my top lip, before I realised that it was one of my false eyelashes gone very badly awry.

I forced myself into the shower and washed my hair three times, but even as I dried myself, I knew that the smell of pure alcohol was still seeping from my body and would do for the rest of the day. I examined my tongue. It was white and furry. My entire body was suffering while my liver struggled to process three Christmases' worth of wine and spirits. I had aged a decade and a half in my sleep.

And I had a young man in my bed.

Time to panic.

What was I going to do about Jack?

At least I had managed to wake up before him so I could make the best of my hung-over face before he saw me. But I didn't want him to hang around. What on earth were we going to talk about? I had to get rid of him. Mum and Dad were returning from Cornwall today.

Jack would prove harder to get rid of than I had hoped. When I came back into the bedroom after my shower, he was just where I had left him, spread out across the bed like a starfish. Dead to the world. Well, not actually dead. I did check to see if he was breathing and was relieved when he let out an almighty snore. The almighty snore didn't, however, wake him up. He carried on sleeping.

I looked at my watch – it was ten o'clock – and made some calculations. Mum and Dad would not be back until three in the afternoon at the earliest. I knew that Dad would not want to check out of the hotel until they absolutely had to. He was a great believer in getting his money's worth. Even if he drove like the devil's own horseman, Dad would not make it from Cornwall to Croydon in under five hours.

So I had until three. With that in mind, I let Jack doze on while I fed the dog and drank some extremely strong coffee. After that I raided Mum's store of Beroccas. Little by little my hangover started to recede. I decided I could handle this. When Jack woke up, I would offer him some breakfast, thank him for making sure I got home OK and send him on his way with dignity and style.

Unfortunately, Mum and Dad were not the only returning travellers I had to worry about.

The weather overnight had not been fantastic. The rain that had prevented me from getting a taxi had carried on for hours. It was still grey that morning. A grey day didn't bother me so much. As soon as I got rid of Jack, I was going to spend the rest of the day indoors doing nothing. Not even walking the dog. Ben was getting too old to want to go for a walk every day. But what I had reckoned without was the weather's effects on a series of outdoor events up and down the country. Including the Reading Festival.

It was around eleven o'clock when I heard the sound of a key in the door. I was sitting at Mum's dressing table at the time, examining my spots. I always got spots the morning after a heavy night. I jumped up and looked out of the window. Had Mum and Dad come home early? It was worse than that. Dad's Saab wasn't parked on the drive, but Lucas's friend's VW camper was.

The boys were already inside.

'I hope your sister has left us some bacon,' said someone.

'Don't worry about it,' said Lucas. 'She's a vegetarian.'

'Lucas,' I hissed down the stairs at him. He was in the hallway, kissing his dog in a very unhygienic way.

'Did she look after you properly?' Lucas addressed the hound.

'What are you doing back here?' I asked.

'It rained,' said Lucas simply. 'It got all muddy.'

'So you came back? But you paid hundreds of pounds for those tickets. What kind of wimp are you?'

'There's nothing good on today, so I thought we'd come

back here and hang out, seeing as Mum and Dad won't be back till later.'

'You can't just bring all your mates back with you.'

Two more lads, who had been good enough to stay outside to finish their skinny roll-up cigarettes, appeared on the doorstep.

'All right, Ashleigh?' Freddie called up the stairs. Freddie was a lovely boy. Very well brought up. And ordinarily it was a pleasure to see him, but not right then.

'Can't you go back to one of their houses?' I suggested.

'No. You're being weird,' my brother noted. 'What's going on? You haven't . . .' He stepped backwards with a look of mock horror on his face. 'You've got a man up there!'

'I have not,' I said, wondering how the hell I was going to get Jack out without my brother seeing. Would Jack be prepared to stay in my bedroom until Lucas and his mates were too busy with the PSP to notice him sneaking out through the front door? Or perhaps he could climb out of my bedroom window on to the flat roof of the garage below before shimmying down a drainpipe. I had done that a couple of times back when I was still at school and not allowed out because I was supposed to be concentrating on my A-levels. Oh God. What was I thinking? I couldn't ask Jack to do that. What if he fell and broke his neck?

'She's got a bloke up there!' my brother crowed. 'My sister's getting laid.'

Freddie looked a little disappointed. Later I would find out that he had a crush on me. 'Come on, Lucas,' he said. 'It's hardly very gentlemanly of you to suggest something like that . . .'

'What do you want to do, Freddie? Go up there and challenge the cad to a duel? C'mon.' Lucas jumped into the *en garde* stance.

'I just think you should be a bit more respectful to your sister, that's all.'

'Challenge me to a duel, then,' said Lucas, playfully bumping chests with his friend. Then he turned his attention back to me.

'Come on, sis. Tell us who you're hiding up there. I want to know who's been having his wicked way with you in our parents' house. *Our parents' house!*' He parodied shock and horror.

'Lucas,' I said, 'piss off. For God's sake. Will you just grow up? There's nobody up here but me.'

'Then why are you whispering?'

'I'm not whispering,' I said in a hushed tone.

'There's definitely someone in there. I'm coming up.' Lucas began to bound up the stairs two at a time. I prepared to repel him from the landing. But I needn't have bothered because before Lucas was even halfway up the stairs, Jack chose exactly the wrong moment to come out of the bedroom.

'What's going on?' he asked, rubbing the sleep from his eyes. He looked like a little boy. Much younger than he had done the previous evening. Now I could see quite clearly that he was nowhere near twenty-four. He was as young as my brother. Exactly the same age as my brother, to be entirely accurate.

'Jack Green?'

'Lucas-Pukas?' said Jack, responding with the nickname Lucas had carried all the way through school and just about managed to shake off now he was in college. 'What are you doing here, man?'

'I could ask the same of you!'

'Is he your housemate?' Jack asked me.

'She's my sister!' Lucas helpfully filled in the gaps. 'What the fuck are you doing in my house?'

Jack looked to me, as if to ask my permission to elaborate on our night's activities. I shook my head subtly. As if Lucas hadn't already guessed. Jack carried on down the stairs. He and my brother indulged in a matey, back-slapping hug. It turned out they had been in the same class at secondary school.

'Lucas is the guy who had that party I was telling you about,' Jack told me. 'Awesome, man.' He bumped fists with the other guys.

'This is so fucking unbelievable,' said Lucas. 'Come on, man. I haven't seen you in ages. Come and have some breakfast with us.'

Jack had the decency to look back up the stairs and give me an apologetic shrug before he followed Lucas into the kitchen, where they would doubtless finish all the bacon, forgetting that I had given up vegetarianism long ago because Michael thought it was silly.

39

I stayed upstairs in my room. Of all the people I could have chosen to jump back into the dating pool with, why on earth did he have to be one of Lucas's schoolfriends? Never mind that he was of a legal age. Anyone of Lucas's age was still a child, as far as I was concerned. Which meant I really was a cougar! I had lost my virginity before that boy went to secondary school. Oh, it got worse and worse, though downstairs, Lucas and Jack seemed to be having a fine time, catching up on the news and gossip since they left school after finishing their A-levels. From time to time a gust of laughter would reach my burning ears. And what else could they be laughing about but me? Lucas was almost certainly filling Jack in on my small nervous breakdown. Losing my job. Ruining my best friend's wedding. The little house fire . . .

I was in agony. I lay in bed, fully clothed, with the sheets pulled up to my ears in an attempt to block out the noise of my brother's hilarity. Tears ran down my cheeks as I thought how I would appear if Michael could see me right then. A laughing stock. Desperate. Oh, yes, if Michael heard how low I had stooped, he would be laughing too. I might just as well take myself off to a nunnery. Assuming they would even have me with my track record of immoral behaviour.

While the boys downstairs partied, I could only cry. I felt so sorry for myself I couldn't have cared if I dissolved in a saltwater puddle of my own making. Someone somewhere was having a divine joke. I saw myself in another Broken Hearts United meeting but this time Enya would be full of pity for *me*.

At about two in the afternoon there was a soft knock at my door.

'Go away,' I said. I didn't want to talk to anyone.

But the knock came again.

I got out of bed and wrenched the door open. 'What do you want?' I asked brusquely, expecting Lucas.

It was Jack.

'I'm going home now. But I thought I should come and say goodbye,' he said.

'Goodbye.' I smiled tightly.

'And thank you. I really enjoyed . . . er . . . spending the night with you.'

I nodded.

'And I'd like to do it again sometime. If you . . . er . . . Will you give me your phone number?'

'You don't really want it,' I snapped. I could imagine it all. Lucas would be at the bottom of the stairs, waiting to hear if I'd been taken in. He'd almost certainly set Jack up to ask me out again. Well, I wasn't going to fall for it.

'Oh. OK. Then I'll see you around, I guess,' said Jack.

'Bye,' I told him, closing the door in his face with a quiet but determined click.

I was never going to go out, get drunk and pick up a random bloke ever again.

I didn't go downstairs again for the rest of the afternoon. I just lay on my bed listening out for any sign that Lucas might have got rid of the rest of his stupid friends. But the

VW van stood on the driveway all afternoon while Lucas entertained his mates and made more fry-ups. The smells that drifted up the stairs made my stomach growl and grumble. By four o'clock I was beginning to hallucinate bacon sandwiches but still I could not go downstairs. My shame was greater than my need for a sarnie.

To take my mind off my humiliation and the fact that at any moment I might start to eat my pillow, I took Mini-Michael out of his hiding place in the cupboard. I was going to make him pay for my latest mistake. I twisted his limbs and punched his little woolly face. I stuck pins from his head to his toes. Just as I was stabbing Mini-Michael in the stomach, my brother walked into my bedroom without knocking on the door.

'What are you doing?' he asked.

He was holding a plate upon which were a couple of crudely made sandwiches and a handful of crisps.

'Nothing,' I said, quickly shoving Mini-Michael under my pillow.

'Were you stabbing something?'

'Don't be ridiculous.'

'It looked like you were stabbing something. Are you self-harming? You haven't gone mental, have you, sis?'

'I have not.'

'OK, then. Whatever you say. I've told the lads they've got to go now,' he said. 'And I made you this.' He held out the sandwich but I didn't take it for fear that by moving I might reveal Mini-Michael. 'I'll just leave it here. I hope you . . . er . . . start to feel better.' He put the sandwich down on my dressing table and backed out of the room, as though someone had told him that you should never turn your back on a nutter.

For that was what I had become. My brother's kindness

in bringing me that sandwich moved me to tears again. He was a great little brother. It wasn't his fault that Michael had dumped me. I resolved to be far nicer to Lucas in future.

40

My resolution to be nicer to Lucas did not last long.

A couple of days later I dragged myself to the Jobcentre for the humiliation of my fortnightly jobseeker's interview. It was a horrible thing to have to do. Personally, I found it so awful to be ticked off about my job-hunting success (or rather lack of it) by a woman who always had her cardigan buttoned up wrongly that I found it very hard to believe anyone would contrive to stay on benefits deliberately, which was what her every question seemed to imply.

Anyway, it never put me in a great mood. It was just another thing that served to remind me that my life was officially rubbish and there was no particular reason to hope that the status quo would be changing anytime soon. After the Jobcentre, I ran a few errands for Mum. I returned a couple of books to the library for Dad. While I was in the library, I browsed the self-help section to see if they had anything new. There was nothing new except a book on making the most of the menopause, which was, thankfully, just about the only problem I didn't have right then.

While I was at the library, I also took the opportunity to check my email. It was much more relaxing than checking it on Mum's laptop. Though Mum knew that there was no limit to the amount of time she could spend on the Internet for her twelve pounds a month with BT Broadband, it didn't stop her from hovering anxiously while I checked my mail. She couldn't quite shake the memory of when she and Dad still had a dial-up connection and Lucas ran up a four-figure bill playing Warcraft when he was supposed to be revising for his GCSEs.

There was little of interest in my email account that day. Some spam asking me if I wanted to improve the length/girth/hardness and/or general appearance of my penis. A couple of fundraising requests from people I knew only vaguely. I deleted those straight away, before I could read what they were fundraising for and start to feel guilty that I didn't have the money to help out.

And then there was an email from YouTube, informing me that someone I knew had just posted a new item. My little brother, Lucas.

I clicked on through. The little video window opened on a view I knew well. It was the view of my bedroom window from outside my parents' house. I felt a rising sense of dread as I wondered what on earth Lucas had been filming. Did he have some shot of me mooning out over the street like a latterday Rapunzel, waiting for a prince who would never turn up, no matter how long my hair got? No. The camera pulled in closer. I wasn't in the shot. But there was something in the window. Something that had been posed as though looking out like a prisoner. I squinted at the screen.

'Oh my God.'

It was Mini-Michael.

The computer had finished buffering and now the full horror of Lucas's latest creative endeavour began to unfold. The shot changed so that the camera was looking out from inside my room, from Mini-Michael's point of view. No wonder my brother had been so quiet for the past few days. The time and effort involved in this little stop-motion animation was obvious. It looked very slick. I had to give him that. But the content . . .

There was Mini-Michael, plucky as a Para and prickly as

a hedgehog with sewing pins as he shimmied his way down from the windowsill using a curtain as a rope. Lucas, with the skills he had learned at art college, had somehow even animated the little doll's face, so that he could convey his despair and panic as he tried to escape from my bedroom, which he managed, at last, only to run straight into the jaws of Ben the dog.

The fact that Lucas had been into my room was bad enough but it was the commentary beneath the clip that really pushed me over the edge. It was a conversation between Lucas and his art-school friends.

'Cool doll,' said one. 'Where did you get it?'

'Under my sister's bed. I think she made it. It's supposed to be her ex-boyfriend.'

'That boring accountant bloke you hated?'

'Yeah,' wrote Lucas. 'That's the one. He dumped her and went off with a Brazilian.'

'Can't say I blame him,' said Lucas's friend. 'Brazilians are hot. So, is this like some kind of weird voodoo shit or what? Your sister is *out there*.'

'I certainly wouldn't cross her,' my brother wrote.

Lucas had only one sister. It didn't take Inspector Poirot to work out that I was the voodoo knitter and Michael was my intended victim. Now I was really panicking. Just who had seen the clip? If that idiot Lucas hadn't thought to take my email address off his circulation list, then it was possible, indeed quite probable, that he had forwarded the clip to our entire extended family. And perhaps even to Michael himself if Lucas had also copied in the addresses from my contacts list, which I had allowed him to do when he was flogging his handmade Christmas cards to supplement his beer money. The ramifications were just too terrible.

'I'll kill him,' I said, jumping to my feet. 'I'll bloody kill him.'

By the time I logged out of YouTube I was foaming at the mouth. No one batted an eyelid, of course. I was, after all, in a public library. Threats of grevious bodily harm were commonplace from the weirdos who used the library as a place to keep out of the cold while the hostel was shut.

When I got back to Mum and Dad's, I was white-hot with rage.

'Where is he?' I roared as I pushed open the kitchen door so roughly that it slammed against the wall behind. The dog ran under the kitchen table for cover. 'Where's Lucas? I'm going to rip his head off.'

'Watch the paintwork,' said Mum, 'or I'll rip your head off too. Whatever's the matter with you?'

'Ask your son,' I said.

I headed on upstairs to his bedroom. Lucas had a guest. He was trying to impress some art-school girl with his indie vinyl collection (most of which had once belonged to me). As I burst into the room, they were sitting side by side on the bed. Lucas was pushing the girl's lank fringe out of her eyes. They jumped apart. I could tell that I had interrupted Lucas's killer seductive move.

'What the . . . ? Piss off,' Lucas told me.

'I will not,' I said.

'What the hell's got into you?'

'How about YouTube,' I snarled. 'A certain epic-escape adventure filmed inside my bedroom.'

'Oh, that,' said Lucas, trying to stay cool in front of his intended conquest.

'That really cool voodoo-doll thing?' asked the girl adoringly.

'It wasn't cool,' I told her. 'It was cruel. And I reckon you want to think twice about getting involved with such a dishonest, sweaty little creep as the infant who made it.'

'Oh, I . . .' The girl looked a little scared now.

'Yes, infant,' I said to Lucas. Turning back to the girl, I added, 'Did he tell you that he wet the bed until he turned fifteen?'

'Hey!' Lucas interrupted. 'That's not fair.'

'And filming my personal private property is? Making me a laughing stock for the amusement of your art-school friends is perfectly fine, right? Is that what you're telling me?'

'I didn't think you'd mind.'

'You didn't think I'd find out, more like.'

'How did you find out?' Lucas seemed confused.

'I'm on your mailing list, you muppet.'

'You are? I thought I took you off it. Shit.'

'Indeed. Now, what are you going to do about it? I want you to sort it out immediately.'

'But I'm in the middle of . . .' Lucas indicated the girl, who was sitting on the bed with her knees drawn up to her chin like a fearful child.

'I should probably be going anyway,' she said, unfolding herself and sprinting for the door. 'I can see myself out.'

'Lucy!' Lucas called after her. 'I'll call you.'

'Yeah. Whatever. That'd be great,' she said without looking back.

I continued to stand over Lucas with my hands on my hips, waiting for his response.

'I was nearly in there,' Lucas whined.

'She had a lucky escape. What are you going to do about that film? You've got to destroy it.'

'I can't destroy it. I made it for my coursework. Look, Ashleigh, I can understand why you're angry, but really . . . I thought it would cheer you up about that muppet of an ex-boyfriend. I thought you would find it funny.'

'Nothing about my relationship with Michael is funny,'

I wailed. Then I threw myself down on Lucas's beanbag and wept into my hands.

Lucas promised that he would sort the matter out, but of course it was too late. By the time Lucas had logged back on to YouTube, some two and a half thousand people had seen the clip. One of those sites that rounds up the best of the blogs tagged the Mini-Michael clip as the funniest YouTube video of the day. After that happened, there was no stopping the damn thing. It went viral. I soon lost count of the number of times the link to the clip reappeared in my in-box, forwarded by someone who had no idea (I prayed) what agony they were heaping on me. It was just a matter of time before Michael got to see the clip and guessed exactly who was behind the grimacing doll.

It was devastating. Any little shred of self-respect I had was ripped away. I told my brother that as far as I was concerned, he was dead to me.

41

'You have to talk to Lucas,' said Mum the following week. 'He's your brother. I can't stand this atmosphere around the house. You can't just keep ignoring him.'

Mum had no idea. As far as I was concerned, I never had to talk to my brother ever again. Lucas had sparked a life-long feud. It was perfectly possible that I could go for the rest of my days without addressing a single word in his direction. When I'd got back on my feet jobwise, which was more urgent than ever now, I would move out of Mum and Dad's, and once Lucas and I were no longer sharing a bath-room, I wouldn't ever have to see his face again. I no longer had a brother.

I could tell that Mum was very distressed. She hated the frosty atmosphere in what had been her happy family home. She hated the way that every time Lucas walked into a room, I would get up and walk straight out. But she couldn't seem to understand the depth of my brother's betrayal. There were people all over the world who knew how badly I had reacted to my break-up with Michael. I fell asleep at night to the sound of laughter in a hundred languages, as my Mini-Michael danced across computer screens in Texas, Taipei and Teignmouth. My friends had seen it. My former colleagues must have seen it too. The only way on earth that Michael hadn't seen it was if he had spent the past week holidaying in a closed order of monks. And there was fat chance of that while Miss Well-Sprung was around.

'I have no brother any more,' I insisted.

Though I have to admit that Lucas was making an enormous effort to patch things up. Since I wouldn't speak to him, he sent a hundred apologies by email, text and hand-drawn postcards covered in careful calligraphy, which he poked under my bedroom door. But my heart was frozen. I poked the postcards back under his door with the note 'Return to sender' scribbled above my name. I was going to keep up the big freeze for ever.

But then the unexpected happened. Or rather, the long expected happened. Ben the ancient spaniel went walkies for the very last time.

I was unfortunate enough to be the one to find him. It was a Sunday morning. For once I was first up. I knew that something was wrong as soon as I got to the top of the stairs. I looked down to see Ben's familiar brown body stretched out like a draught excluder along the bottom step. But all was not as normal. Ordinarily, the moment I set foot on the creaky board on the top step, Ben would lift his head and look up at me. Then he would thump his thick tail on the floor in greeting. That morning it didn't happen. It occurred to me for a second that perhaps Ben had sent me to Coventry on Lucas's behalf, but of course the stupid old dog wasn't that clever. Something was definitely wrong.

By the time I got to the fourth stair from the bottom, I was sure.

'Ben?' I whispered. 'Ben?' a little louder. 'Come on, boy. Time for breakfast. Get out of my way.'

He lay as still as the sheepskin rug beneath him. I crouched down on the step and peered at him. I dared not get closer, but I was close enough to see that there was no rise and fall of the barrel chest that always longed to be tickled. I stretched out a hand and gave him a poke in the side.

Nothing.

I put my hand to my mouth.

'Oh, Ben,' I sighed. 'Oh, no.'

I didn't wake Lucas. Fortunately, he had been out late the night before and would have slept through the '1812 Overture', played by a full orchestra at the end of his bed. With cannons. I got up Dad instead.

'I think Ben's dead,' I told him.

Dad's face crumpled like a tissue when he saw that I was right. Though Ben had often smelled like the wrong end of a donkey, he had been dear to everyone.

'What should we do?' Dad asked.

'I was hoping that you would know,' I told him.

'I've never touched a dead body before.'

'Not even a goldfish?'

'It was your mum who always flushed them down the loo.'

'Ben's not going to fit round the U-bend,' I said.

Together we wrapped the dog's corpse in a blanket and carried him into the conservatory, which was cooler than the rest of the house. Neither Dad nor I had any idea how long we had before Ben started to smell worse even than he had in life. Dad thought that perhaps we should put Ben into the chest freezer while we considered our next move. I told him that I thought Mum would file for divorce if he pulled that stunt. Mum confirmed my view when she came downstairs in her pink dressing gown.

'But what are we going to tell Lucas?' she asked, her eyes welling up with tears.

'We could tell him that Ben ran away,' said Dad. 'Like we did when next door's cat got his rabbit.'

'He was only eight. I don't think he'll fall for that this time.'

'I suppose we could just tell him the truth,' I suggested.

'But he's going to be so upset,' said Mum.

'The dog's dead whether we lie to him or not,' said Dad.

Throughout these discussions Lucas remained sound asleep. Breakfast was a quiet affair. Mum, Dad and I sat at the kitchen table with our backs to the conservatory, but at some point each of us was compelled to twist round and look at the dark bundle on the conservatory floor. It was such a sad shape. Mum was so overcome that she forgot to have a go at Dad about using the velvet throw from the back of the sofa as a shroud.

'Oh, Ben,' she cried, when she realised she had absent-mindedly left him a piece of crust that he wouldn't be begging for. 'How could you do this to us?

It was almost midday when Lucas eventually came downstairs. I could see Mum's bottom lip wobbling as she heard her son call out, 'Benny, boy. Where's my favourite Benny?'

But that morning there was no skitter of claws on the kitchen tiles as Ben raced to present himself for attention.

'I can't tell him,' she told me.

'I'm not doing it,' said Dad, who was wiping his eyes.

'I suppose I'll have to do it,' I said.

So that is how I ended the feud with my brother. I intercepted him at the kitchen door and took him into the living room. 'There's something you need to know,' I said. 'You should probably sit down.'

I could tell from his face that he knew what was coming. Not once in the lifetime they had spent together had Ben failed to greet Lucas at the bottom of the stairs of a morning. Lucas had not missed the implication.

'Ben's dead, isn't he?'

I nodded.

'Oh, Ashleigh!' Lucas sank on to the sofa and covered his face with his hands. His shoulders shook violently as he began to cry. I had expected him to be sad. I had not expected to see his actual heart breaking.

'It's OK,' I said. 'It's OK. I don't suppose he felt a thing. He was a happy dog. He had a happy ending. He had a good life.'

'He was my best friend!' Lucas sobbed.

The whole house went into mourning. Mum didn't open the curtains in the front room that day. Dad agreed that such a level of respect was appropriate. Ben wasn't just a pet. He had been part of our family. Lucas spent that afternoon sitting in the conservatory with Ben's body. He refused to eat. He just sat in one of the wicker armchairs with the squeaky toy that had been Ben's favourite. From time to time we heard a mournful wheeze and an 'eek' when Lucas squeezed the toy, as though he hoped the familiar sound might bring Ben back from dog heaven. While out in the garden, looking for some sage for Mum to add to that night's chicken dinner, I stepped on another of Ben's toys and was horribly moved by the pathetic sight of Ben's abandoned plaything. For the first time in months the tears that sprang to my eyes were about something other than bloody Michael Parker.

Lucas didn't join us for supper. Dad pushed away his plate half finished. As he turned from the table, he went to scrape what remained of his chicken into Ben's bowl. My mother choked on a sob.

'Move it,' she said to my father, as though the earthenware dish were a photograph of a beloved child.

At nine o'clock Lucas finally came into the kitchen and announced that he wanted a cup of tea. I made it. As he warmed his hands around it, I was struck by how young he looked. I could see the six-year-old who tormented me. I had to refrain from ruffling his hair.

'I feel so sad, sis,' he told me. 'Ben really was my best

friend. After you left home, he was all I had. He was like a brother to me.'

'I guess you'll have to make do with just having a sister now.'

I put my arm round his shoulders and he pulled me in for a hug.

'Are we friends again?' he asked me hopefully.

'We're better than that,' I said. 'We're siblings. You couldn't lose me if you tried.'

The following day I helped Lucas bury Ben in the back garden.

'Can't you do something to make him look his best first?' Mum asked. 'You must have learned that on your dog-grooming course?'

I told her that dog-grooming for funerals was a separate module her thousand pounds hadn't paid for.

Anyway, we marked Ben's grave with the squeaky rabbit, proper memorial pending. I knew it wouldn't be long before Mum got over her grief and wanted the rubber toy out of her flower bed.

When the burial was over, Lucas finally gave me what I took to be a heartfelt apology for the anguish he had caused me with his little film.

'It was funny, though,' he added.

I wanted to tell him that it wasn't, but I couldn't keep a smile from my lips. 'It was quite funny,' I admitted grudgingly. 'But you'll never do anything like that again, right? I just want to forget all about it.'

Fat chance.

42

The worst thing about Ben's death was that there was no longer any reason why Mrs Charlton could not bring her standard poodles, Roxy and Satin (aka Rocky and Satan), with her when she popped round for a cup of tea. And suddenly Mrs Charlton seemed to be popping over for a cup of tea all the time. She had recently set up a local branch of the Neighbourhood Watch and was trying to persuade Mum to act as treasurer.

Mum wasn't the only person Mrs Charlton was trying to persuade to work for free.

'Oh, it may be September but it's still so hot!' she sighed one afternoon. 'A real Indian summer. I don't know if Roxy and Satin will be able to cope with this for much longer. I had them trimmed in August,' she said to my mother, 'and that was supposed to be it for the year. On my pension . . .'

I saw the anguish in Mum's face and knew it was only a matter of time before she collared me. She caught me later that day as I tried to sneak from my bedroom to the kitchen for a cup of tea and perhaps a piece of toast.

'You've got to do something about those dogs,' she said, 'or I'll never hear the end of it.'

'I can't,' I said.

'Why not?'

'I haven't got my certificate.'

'Well, they're taking their bloody time with that,' Mum pointed out. (As far as she was concerned, I had finished the dog-grooming course six weeks earlier.) 'But I'm sure Mrs Charlton doesn't care whether you've got your certificate or not. All she wants is for someone to give those dogs a free trim before they expire from heat exhaustion.'

The pressure continued as I boiled the kettle and waited for the toast to burn.

'In any case,' said Mum, 'don't you think it would be a good idea to keep your hand in? As soon as your certificate comes through, you'll be able to start applying for jobs. Wasn't that the whole point?'

I couldn't argue with that.

'But I won't be insured,' I tried helplessly.

'Insured for what?' my mother asked. 'How wrong can a quick poodle trim go?'

'They don't want anything fancy,' said Mrs Charlton, as she led Rocky and Satan into my mum's pristine kitchen.

A good job, I thought. I said, 'I'll just give them a basic,' as I covered the floor with old newspaper. The only tools I had to hand were some kitchen scissors and a pair of beard clippers left over from the year Dad decided he might look distinguished with a goatee. Mother had quickly vetoed that and so the clippers had hardly been used.

I figured that all I had to do was set the clippers to a reasonable length and approach trimming the dogs as though I were giving some bloke a number two.

'But I'd rather you didn't watch,' I told Mrs Charlton.

'Why not?' she asked. 'The dogs like to know where I am.'

'I've found,' I said, 'when I've been practising on live dogs for my course, that they are actually better behaved and calmer with their owners out of sight. It helps me establish a new pack hierarchy,' I explained.

I had no idea what I was talking about, but Mrs Charlton seemed convinced. She allowed my mother to persuade her back into the conservatory with a newly opened packet of biscuits.

I was left with the dogs. Two standard poodles the size of small ponies, with tongues lolling out like great slices of ham. As I pondered which end of a poodle was safe to start on, Satan let out a tremendous fart that filled the room with a stench worse than nerve gas: then he sat down and refused to get back up. I would have to start with Rocky.

Distraction seemed like a good idea. I liberated a packet of prosciutto from the fridge. (I would later find out that Dad had been saving it for his Thursday-evening cordon bleu course.) I dangled a thin strip of the stuff in front of Rocky. As she wolfed it down, I clamped her body between my knees and made a start.

My plan to use the clippers got off to a fine enough start. I was astonished when I managed two very neat strips from Rocky's bottom to the top of her head. But that was all I had time to do before the dumb animal finished the prosciutto and realised that all was not well. She turned to nip me on the knee. Added to that, two stripes of poodle contained more hair than a year's worth of the average man's beard. The damn clippers were clogged up already.

I tossed Rocky another strip of prosciutto while I tried to unblock the clippers. That gave me less than ten seconds before she was at my other knee, trying to free herself from between my thighs. Satan, meanwhile, had belatedly decided it was time to come to his partner-in-life's assistance. While Rocky struggled and menaced my knees, Satan was worrying the bottom of my jeans and my ankles in equal measure.

'What's going on?' Mrs Charlton shouted.

'Everything is under control,' I said.

I threw the rest of the packet of prosciutto into the corner of the kitchen. Satan abandoned Rocky to her fate. I managed two sweeps of the clippers over Rocky's head, leaving her with something like a fluffy mohawk. I got in another line across her shoulders, leaving her with a huge bald cross on her back. Then Satan had finished the rest of the prosciutto and was after more. And failing prosciutto, or even Spam, Satan decided he would have to make do with my bottom.

'Ow!' I jumped into the air, releasing Rocky to join in with the attack. Before I could cry for help they had me on the floor, pulling at my clothes and growling like the hell hounds they were. Mrs Charlton and my mother came rushing into the kitchen.

'My babies!' cried Mrs Charlton.

'My baby!' cried Mum. I think that she meant me.

Lucas broke off from playing a war game to help the two women rescue me. Rocky and Satan were banished to the garden.

'They were just playing,' Mrs Charlton explained.

I was, thank goodness, largely unharmed, but there's nothing like the smell of drying dog-lick on your face . . .

And when it was established that I wasn't dying, the real trouble began.

'What has she done to Roxana!' Mrs Charlton exclaimed (Roxana being Roxy/Rocky's real name).

'She wouldn't stay still,' I protested.

'You have ruined my pedigree poodle!'

'I've only just finished my training. What did you expect?'

'I expected somebody half competent,' said Mrs Charlton to my mother. 'You're always going on about how talented your daughter is. This' – she pointed at Roxy, with her coat like a lawn cut by someone driving a ride-on mower under the influence – 'this is a bloody disgrace. She'll have to pay.'

'She will not. She was doing you a favour. If you weren't such a cheapskate, this wouldn't have happened. Always going on about what a poor pensioner you are while you're driving a brand-new Nissan.'

'That Nissan was a gift from my son, who is a good deal more talented and successful than yours.'

'Hang on,' said Lucas. 'Don't bring me into this.'

'You had better get out of my house,' shouted my mother. 'Before I call the police and have them come to take your dogs away. Savage, is what they are! They should be put down!'

Mrs Charlton gasped. Then she and her hell hounds were gone.

'Oh, darling,' said Mum, as she checked me for puncture wounds one more time. 'I am sorry. I shouldn't have made you try to groom those stupid beasts.'

'Ben wouldn't have let them anywhere near you,' Lucas chipped in.

'Can you forgive me?' Mum asked me. 'For making you risk your life like that?'

I nodded. 'Mum, of course I can. If you can forgive me for having lied about taking a dog-grooming course in the first place . . .'

It seemed that Mum could not. Forgive me for having lied about the dog-grooming course that is. There was much shouting in the house that afternoon. By lying about the course, said Mum, I may as well have robbed her. Did I have any idea how difficult it had been for her and my father to save that thousand pounds in the first place? And what had I spent it on?

'Drink,' I told her. 'Drinking to forget Michael.'

Well, I was hardly going to tell her I'd spent it on an old sock full of crap that I'd dropped down a drain in an attempt to win him back.

All day and all night my mother raved. She'd raised a thief and a drunkard. She'd lost the respect of an elderly neighbour in the process. She'd never be able to hold her head up again.

'Mrs Charlton doesn't have to know that Ashleigh didn't go on the course,' said Lucas.

'Don't you start,' my mother warned him. 'Two liars in my house! Whatever must I have done in a past life . . . ?'

The wailing started again when Dad came home, and again when Auntie Joyce came for tea the following day.

It was Auntie Joyce who actually came to my rescue.

'Well,' she said to my mother, without pausing in clicking her needles, 'you did say yourself that she went mental after that Michael left her. I think that's enough of an excuse. I was on a bottle of sherry a day right after Frank Farmer dumped me for Emily. We all have our different ways of trying to mend a broken heart. I'm sure Ashleigh feels stupid enough without being reminded. She'll make it up to you.'

Her aunt's wisdom seemed to calm my mother down. After Auntie Joyce left, Mum told me that she didn't want to talk about the incident any more. After the fire that forced my move back home, Mum had assured me that I didn't need to worry about repaying the loan. The only thing she had to say now was that the money would have to be repaid. And fast. I had to find a job.

43

About a week after Ben's death, I came back from the Jobcentre to find Mum and Lucas whispering in the kitchen. I wasn't in a fantastic mood. The woman in charge of signing on that day had been snooty and rude (for a change), suggesting that it was time I lowered my sights regarding my job search. When I told her that I wasn't ready to work in a fast-food restaurant, she told me that if that was my attitude, she would have to make a note on my file that I wasn't making much effort to find new employment. I wondered if she would make the same speech to the big guy in the queue behind me, who had a list of girls' names tattooed on his forearms (some of them crossed out). I got the feeling that the Jobcentre worker hated her job and the only enjoyment she got was picking on people who had better haircuts than she did.

Anyway, when I walked into the kitchen, Mum and Lucas sprang apart and smiled at me in a slightly forced way that suggested that I had been the topic of their conversation.

'Did you have a nice time at the Jobcentre?' Mum asked clumsily.

'Nice time? You've got to be joking. I got a lecture about not making much effort when I turned my nose up at a night shift at Greggs the baker. She said that it would be the ideal job for me, given my interest in cakes.'

'Interest in cakes? You could sue her for suggesting you're fat,' said Lucas.

I could tell that was supposed to be a joke, but I didn't reward him with anything approaching a smile.

'Tea?' suggested Mum.

I nodded.

Mum said that she would make it. That was something else that made me suspicious. Since the revelation about the dog-grooming course that wasn't, I had been making nine cups of tea out of ten in that house.

We all three of us sat down at the kitchen table. Mum had broken out a packet of chocolate HobNobs. Lucas grabbed three. He had never quite got past being the youngest and that feeling of having to defend his food from all-comers at all times, though I hadn't stolen a biscuit off him in a decade.

'So,' said Mum.

'So,' said Lucas.

'So?' said I. 'What is going on with you two today? You're looking shifty.'

Mum and Lucas shared a glance. Mum nodded at Lucas. Lucas looked frantically at Mum.

'You've got to tell her,' Mum told him.

'Tell me what?'

Mum smiled. Which meant that it must be good news. My first thought was that perhaps Lucas had bought a new puppy. Or, even better, was about to announce that he was moving out into a flat-share with his friends so that I could have his bigger room with its own en suite.

No such luck.

'I got an email,' he said. 'From some television people.'

Mum beamed. I stopped sipping my tea for a moment to better concentrate on what was coming next.

'They want to make an advert.'

'Really?' I said. 'With you?'

'Yes, with me,' said Lucas. 'And with your voodoo doll.'

'No.' I slammed my mug down on the table. 'No, Lucas. You promised. He promised' – I turned to Mum – 'that he would take that stupid clip down.'

'I did,' said Lucas. 'But you know how many people saw it before that happened. I couldn't get to every version of the clip that was out there.'

'Oh God,' I said. 'This is a disaster.'

'Oh, Ashleigh,' said Mum. 'You mustn't think like that. I think it's wonderful. These TV people have spotted the creative talent of both my children, after all. Lucas's film-making skills and your . . . your knitting.'

I glared at her. 'You're laughing at me,' I protested. 'Everyone is laughing at me.'

'But the money might be good,' said Mum. 'You were always telling me how expensive it is to make an advert. They want the rights to your doll. That's got to be worth some money. And . . .'

Mum didn't have to remind me that I owed money all over the place. To the bank. To my old landlord. To her. Most of all to her.

'Mum's right,' Lucas dared to pipe up. 'There is bound to be some money in this.'

'It depends on the product,' I told him.

'The product is Purple Phones,' said Lucas.

'Purple Phones?' I echoed in disbelief. Back in the day when I still had a job at Maximal Media, I had pitched for the Purple Phones account. I was fired before I found out whether or not they'd chosen to work with Maximal. 'Exactly who sent you that email?' I asked my little brother.

'A woman called Ellie,' he said. 'From your old firm.'

I snorted at the sound of her name. It was just too cruel. I had worked so hard to bag that Purple account and now my workplace nemesis was reaping the benefit. 'The bloody cow,' I said. 'This proves it. She sent that email to rub the fact that she's working with Purple Phones in my face.'

I stood up from the table. 'I'm going to ring her right now and tell her exactly what I think of this bullshit. First she steals my job and now this. She doesn't want to make an ad with you, Lucas. She's just doing this to humiliate me.'

'Don't jump to conclusions,' said Mum. 'Why would she do that? You gave her a chance at the beginning of her career. I'm sure she's genuinely interested in Lucas's work . . . and your voodoo doll,' she added hastily.

'Mum, you don't understand this woman at all. Making me look an idiot was Ellie Finch's hobby. I bet she's having a field day with this.'

'I think she's genuine,' said Lucas.

'Let's find out, shall we?'

I had already dialled my old office. A male voice I didn't recognise answered what had been Ellie's line.

'Is Ellie there?' I asked.

'Oh, yes,' said the stranger. 'She's in her office. I'll put you through.'

Her office! My office more like. While I was still at Maximal Media, Ellie didn't have an office. She had a desk in the corridor with the other assistants. I felt my jaw clench with tension as I listened to the hideous 'on hold' music that I had chosen from a very poor selection. Eventually, after much too long a wait, Ellie picked up.

'This is Ellie Finch,' she said.

'And this is Ashleigh Prince,' I said back.

'Oh, hi, Ashleigh! How are you?'

'Don't "Hi, Ashleigh" me,' I said. 'What the hell do you think you're doing, emailing my brother about that stupid voodoo-doll film?'

'Your brother?'

'Yes. Don't pretend you didn't know that. Well, it was a

very funny joke,' I snarled. 'We all laughed for at least thirty seconds. But I'm just calling to tell you to sod right off. Isn't it enough for you that you got my job, my desk and my clients, without pretending that you want to use Lucas's film of my voodoo doll for the Purple Phones campaign?'

'It's your voodoo doll?'

Ellie was continuing to feign ignorance. The absolute cow.

'Oh, Ellie, come on!'

'Seriously, Ashleigh, I had no idea it was anything to do with you at all. I hadn't even seen the film until yesterday morning, when the client sent me a link and said it was what they wanted for the new TV spot. So funny and poignant. Such a wonderful little character. It's exactly right for Purple.'

'Ellie,' I was still busy snarling, 'you are the biggest bitch I have ever met in my entire life. If you even had a heart, I suggest that you look into it right now and ask yourself exactly why you feel the need to torment me. Is it because your parents never loved you? Or were you simply born a total—' I used a word that I had only previously heard used by taxi drivers and slammed the phone down.

My mother and brother stared at me. They looked a little shocked. Even scared.

'I'm sorry,' I said, 'but she is.'

Before either of them could respond, my iPhone started ringing. It was the Maximal Media office number. I picked up the call and prepared to unleash another torrent of invective into Ellie's ear, but it was Barry who was on the other end of the line this time.

'Ashleigh—'

'Look,' I said, 'I'd like to say I'm sorry, but I won't. She's had that coming for a very, very long time.'

'That's as may be,' said Barry. 'It's between the two of you as far as I'm concerned. I'm just calling up to confirm that we really are interested in using the clip for Purple. And they'll pay,' he added. 'We'll look after you. I'll make certain of that.'

'I'm not interested,' I responded.

'Ashleigh,' said Barry, 'I need you to think about it. I'm sure you could use the cash. And I'm sure you know what a coup it is for us to have won the Purple account.'

'Which I pitched for.'

'Which you pitched for,' Barry conceded. 'Look,' he continued, 'I know that you probably feel you have very little reason to show Maximal any loyalty given the way that things ended over your presentation to Effortless Bathing . . .' I winced at the memory of that tiny penis projected on to a very big screen. '. . . but I hope you'll believe that over the years you were with us everyone at Maximal considered you to be a very important part of the team. A great colleague and a friend.'

'Don't make me laugh,' I said. 'Or cry.'

'Ashleigh . . .' Barry's voice became quiet and confidential '. . . I've got to tell you that this account means the difference between life and death to Maximal. We've had a bad year. If things don't pick up soon, then I'm going to have to start laying people off before Christmas. And you know what it's like out there right now.'

'Don't I ever.'

'You wouldn't wish that on anyone, I'm sure. Not even Ellie.' He had picked the wrong potential jobseeker to tug on my heartstrings. 'Or Clare.' He dropped his voice lower still. 'You know that if she lost her job, she'd have to sell her horses. Those horses are her life. Especially since her husband ran off with that dental nurse.'

'He did?' I had always thought Clare's husband seemed to have rather a lot of dental work.

'I don't know what Clare would do if she didn't have Ginger and Buttercup.'

I felt a pang of sympathy for Clare. She had always been nice enough to me and there was no doubt I could appreciate what she might be going through. A broken heart was not eased by unemployment.

Barry went one further. 'And in the current climate there's no guarantee she'd find another buyer, in any case. Horses all over the southern counties are ending up as dog food thanks to the credit crunch.'

'Oh, Barry,' I said. 'Please . . .'

'I'm just telling you the way it is . . . So I hope you won't dismiss out of hand this opportunity to help your former colleagues. You would be doing them a great service. I know that Ellie would be thrilled if you'd agree to the use of your creation. And I'd consider it a personal favour.'

When I relayed the conversation to Mum and Lucas, Lucas said that he would consider it a personal favour too.

'This could be my lucky break. You know how much I want to get into animation and how hard it is even to get a work-experience placement with a company like Aardman. Having a real ad on my showreel would set me apart.'

Mum agreed. 'You know that Lucas would do whatever he could to help you if the situation were reversed. And though I hate to say it, I could have used that thousand pounds I lent you for that dog-grooming course to help Lucas pay for his course materials.'

'All right, all right.'

But it was my humiliation that was up for sale here.

I told them that I would think about it overnight.

Lucas beamed as though he thought that construed my permission.

I had been bolshie in the kitchen, but in the privacy of my bedroom my resolve began to crumble. Without a doubt, Lucas's film of my voodoo doll had been one of the most embarrassing things to happen to me in my life, but perhaps here was a way to find a silver lining to the cloud. Every day since the Mini-Michael film first went viral, I had been waiting for a letter from Michael's lawyers, asking me to cease and desist from sticking pins in their client. But no such letter had come. If Michael hadn't bothered so far, then perhaps it would be OK. I could make Maximal Media promise that the doll would be given another name, like Mini-*Martin*. If Michael didn't care what I was doing, then maybe making some money out of the voodoo doll was the best that could happen. All the pain and humiliation I had been through would have produced something if not good, then bloody useful.

I needed the money. I needed to get out of my parents' house. I needed to pay Mum back for the course I hadn't taken before she guilted me to death.

At midnight I knocked on Lucas's bedroom door. He was still up, playing a computer game.

'OK,' I said. 'I'll agree to it. At least, I'll agree to further discussion as to what exactly Maximal are planning to do.'

Lucas jumped up from his seat and gave me a huge hug that lasted until he started to panic that his on-screen avatar had left some imaginary castle or other undefended.

44

So, two days later I found myself back in my old workplace, in the boardroom where so many of my worst nightmares had come true. Ellie stood at the head of the table, in the place I had occupied on the day of the Effortless Bathing debacle, and gave me and Lucas a presentation on Maximal Media's plans for Mini-Michael. I couldn't help laughing when she assured me that she would work hard to make sure that none of my original creative vision was lost.

'The integrity of your creation is of utmost importance,' she said.

'Ellie,' I laughed, 'get real. You're talking to me.'

The figure they offered us straight out of the box was impressive, but, having spent so much time on Ellie's side of the table, I knew it was in all probability only half of what they were prepared to spend. There were serious licensing possibilities at stake here. When I told them that Lucas and I would not be signing the deal they had offered so far, Lucas looked bereft. He thought I had just vetoed the entire project, but I assured him that haggling was part of the process. By the time Lucas and I had finished a pub lunch, we were looking at a deal twice as big as the original and a guarantee he would get to direct the animation. That clause was far more important to him than the money. Lucas ordered a bottle of champagne in celebration. While he got drunk, I drank just half a glass and prepared to go into battle over residuals.

Everything changed that early-September afternoon. Suddenly, after months of having to rely on my parents and benefits for everything, I was about to be an independent adult again. I left Maximal's office with a cheque for a grand in my hot little hands, with more to come later. It gave me great pleasure to go into the Jobcentre and tell my case manager that she would not be seeing me again anytime soon. When I explained that I had signed a deal with Purple Phones, her jaw almost hit the table. If I'd had a Big Mac to hand, I would have shoved it right into her open mouth.

At last I was able to leave home for a second time and get a new place of my own. When I announced my intention, Mum and Dad were delighted. Mum was rather less delighted when Lucas followed suit, but while I found myself a place a long way from my parents' house, back within Zone 2, thank goodness, Lucas found a studio flat just one bus-stop away, and when he moaned that there was no washing machine, Mum's face was covered by an enormous grin.

'I suppose that means you'll still be bringing your washing home to me.'

I can't tell you what a joy it was to have my own space again. Having to move back in with my parents had been a humbling experience, to say the least. Who expects the forward motion of their life to be brought to such an abrupt halt and then thrown into reverse? And who would have believed that it was a silly knitted voodoo doll that got my life moving forward again?

I was in my new place by the beginning of October, and since I had nothing to bring with me from my old flat, it truly was a fresh start. I could furnish my new home exactly as I wanted. As befitted my new life. The new me. I'd even had my hair dyed back to my natural colour to further represent the end of my period in ginger-tinged limbo.

As I relished the simple pleasures of being able to choose what was on the television and letting the washing-up pile up next to the sink until I felt like doing it, I told myself I was going to be much more careful with this second chance. No stupid man was going to entice me to throw what I had away. Things were going to be different from now on.

And indeed life got better and better. The Purple Phones ad was rushed out and became a huge success. The clients were delighted when it won an award at an annual advertising industry event. Maximal Media was saved by the sudden injection of cash. And how could I refuse when Purple decided it would be a good idea to try to rush out a cuddly-toy version of Mini-Michael for Christmas? I was more than happy to sign another contract that would pay off all my debts and allow me to buy my first car. At thirty-two! It was about time I upgraded from a bicycle.

As Christmas was approaching fast, I was especially excited about the presents I would buy for my family. Mum and Dad had always wanted to go on a cruise, and now that Ben was gone they no longer had an excuse not to. (I know that Ben had officially been Lucas's responsibility, but somehow the dog-sitting always fell to Mum and Dad.) I gathered together a pile of brochures and used my laptop to create a special voucher promising the holiday of a lifetime. I couldn't wait to see Mum's face.

Lucas was doing very well too. He had decided to take a sabbatical from college. It seemed silly not to when the Mini-Michael campaign had brought him to the attention of so many people who were willing to give him actual paid work right then, no matter that he hadn't finished his degree. Lucas was wisely capitalising on their interest while he had it. He knew a golden opportunity when he saw one.

Lucas wasn't the only one who had been offered a job. Having seen me at my steely best in the boardroom when we negotiated the Mini-Michael contract, Barry had asked me if I would like to go back to Maximal Media as a consultant. Having wallowed in the senior-products market for so long, the Purple campaign meant that Maximal Media was finally a force to be reckoned with in the advertising world. And that meant that Barry was suddenly courting clients who wouldn't be fobbed off with tinned-salmon sandwiches in the boardroom and the promise of Patricia Routledge. Ellie was leading the revolution, setting up meetings with prospective clients of the kind that Barry had hitherto only dreamed of. More mobile-phone companies, soft drinks, cars followed . . . Even record labels were calling up to see whether Maximal did pop promos as well as TV ads. At last the company had a client list befitting its funky name.

I agreed to go back into the office for two days a week as a consultant, earning for each eight-hour stint roughly what I used to earn in a month coming up with ever more outlandish creatures to become mascots for many household brands. Nobody seemed to mind that most of them started from a knitted tube. Handicrafts were very *credit crunch*, apparently. Apple even brought out a holder for their iPhone that looked like an old grey school sock. It retailed for twelve pounds a pop.

So suddenly I was no longer a clinically depressed stalker/arsonist. I was a trend-setting marketing guru with the kind of life that made me the envy of many a girl about town. I had an interesting job, a plush flat and a brand-new Fiat Panda. Even Ellie seemed to be happy to give me some respect. Now, that really was a result!

The only thing I didn't have was a best friend to share the good times.

45

Christmas drew nearer. News of my curious and unusual success had spread and from having no mates, I was now very popular indeed. My diary began to fill up with party invitations. There was even one from Helen, the friend who had introduced me to Michael and subsequently dropped me when Miss Well-Sprung came on the scene.

I hadn't spoken to Helen since she sent me an email after Becky's wedding, telling me, quite rightly, that I was a horrible person and she saw no reason why she and I would ever speak again. But now she was inviting me to her Christmas party. I toyed with the idea of telling her where to stick it. After all, even before the wedding-cake debacle Helen and her husband had chosen Michael over me. But another part of me wanted to rock up in my new car, wearing my new clothes and sporting a new haircut. It would be so much more impressive to people who knew how low I had sunk just six months earlier. 'But would Michael be there?' I asked. Helen assured me he wouldn't.

When I got to the party, Helen seemed genuinely pleased to see me. She threw her arms around me, and when she said, 'You look fantastic,' her voice seemed full of genuine pleasure rather than envy. There was no doubt I had hoped for envy. I was very surprised and gratified to learn that Helen's happiness for me felt better.

'We've missed you,' she said.

I dared to think that might be true.

Later, as she circled with a selection of Marks & Spencer canapés, Helen took me to one side and confessed, 'Well, you know that Kevin is looking for a new job and we wondered whether there might be any openings with you, or whether you just need someone to look after your personal accounts.'

'I haven't made a million,' I said, disappointing her and everyone within earshot, 'but I will talk to Barry on Kevin's behalf.'

'We'd really appreciate that. It's fairly urgent. There are rumours of big lay-offs at Wellington Burke.'

I wondered if Michael would be among them. It was hard not to wish it might be so, but I managed not to ask. That was quite a breakthrough for me.

I didn't feel like staying at Helen's party too much longer after that conversation, but I did catch up with some people I hadn't seen since Becky's wedding reception, all of whom seemed happy enough to see me considering I had been public enemy number one. I suspected that quite a few of them were actually grateful to me for having provided them with such a wonderful anecdote. Or perhaps they were eager for dirt. There must have been some darker reason behind my actions than being pissed off about being single . . .

'I did a terrible thing,' I said, apologising over and over. 'I will quite understand if Becky never speaks to me again.'

'Why don't you call her?' someone asked. 'You might be surprised.'

Deciding that I had got everything I could from Helen's party, I retrieved my coat and slipped out into the cold night. I pulled my iPhone out of my pocket. Becky's number was still in there in the contacts list. I could just call her. I brought her number up on the screen, but then I bottled out. I was feeling pretty good. I didn't think I could cope with an ear-bashing that night, and in any case I had another party to go to.

Lucas had made me promise that I would be at the Christmas party he was throwing in his flat. It was a proud moment for him. His first proper party in his own home. No need to worry about getting fag burns on Mum's sofa, though of course he was very worried about fag burns on his own sofa and made all his friends smoke outside.

He accepted my gift of a bottle of champagne gratefully.

'I'm going to hide it in my wardrobe,' he said. 'Don't want to waste it on this riff-raff.'

Lucas's party was heaving. If his neighbours hadn't been mainlining vodka shots in the kitchen, they would definitely have had cause for complaint.

'Is there any food?' I asked.

'There's Twiglets,' came Lucas's reply.

I found myself a corner of the sofa and talked about the Purple Phones campaign with a series of starstruck art students who saw Lucas as a hero for having got his work not just on YouTube but on cinema and television screens around the world. It seemed that Lucas had been kind enough to make sure they all knew that Mini-Martin, as he was now known, was my creation.

A girl with hair like a pair of thin black curtains wrapped her skinny fingers round my wrist and said, 'But before you got the advert . . . tell me, do you think the voodoo worked?'

I hesitated for a moment. The truth was, I didn't know. I knew nothing of Michael's life except for the fact that the firm he worked for might be laying people off. The girl with the Morticia Addams do looked disappointed when I told her. 'I don't think so. Though knitting is great for stress relief.'

'I think voodoo has real power,' she said. 'I think someone might have put a curse on me. That's why my last assignment was marked down.'

'I suppose that believing in something helps create a self-fulfilling prophecy,' I said, not liking where the conversation was going.

'But you seem to have the power,' said Morticia, 'to make things turn out right.'

I was grateful for a familiar face that suddenly appeared in the crowd.

It was only when I stood up to greet my 'friend' that I realised the friendly face I had fixed upon in fact belonged to Jack Green. Jack of the wet-T-shirt competition. Jack who had unleashed my inner cougar. By then it was too late. He returned my greeting with a wide smile.

'Hey, Ashleigh!'

'Look out,' said Lucas, noticing we'd seen each other. 'It's your toy boy.'

Jack was right in front of me now. He looked pretty cute in a soft grey-blue sweater and a pair of jeans that fitted him just so. His hair was a little longer than I remembered. Artfully ruffled. The colour of his jumper highlighted his rather nice eyes. By anyone's standards, Jack was a very cute-looking guy.

But he was so young. I put the fact that I had seen him naked right out of my mind. It would never happen again. I raised my Bacardi Breezer at him.

'Good to see you,' I said neutrally.

'And you. You look great,' he said. He hesitated before adding, 'I really like your dress.'

'Thanks. I like your jumper,' I responded in kind.

'It's new,' he said. 'I got a permanent job at last. First pay packet this week. Thought I'd treat myself.'

'It was a good buy.'

'It's pure cashmere, I think. Have a feel.'

He held out his sleeve to me. I rubbed the fabric between my thumb and forefinger. 'Yes, I'd say that's pure cashmere.'

'So,' he asked, 'how have you been doing?'

'All right.' I nodded. I became aware that Lucas and the girl he was talking to were watching us. I couldn't help but start to blush.

'I saw the ad you did with Lucas,' he said. 'I thought it was really funny.'

'Thanks.'

Over by the fireplace, Lucas was making an obscene gesture for my benefit.

'Is everything OK?' Jack noticed my attention was wandering.

I was angry with Lucas for taking the mickey, but I was suddenly equally angry with myself. This why I should never have a one-night stand, I told myself. Jack and I had nothing to talk about. And yet he had seen me in my underwear.

'I've got to go,' I said. 'Early start.'

'What? Really?'

'Yes.'

It wasn't entirely a lie. There was something I needed to do the following day and I would need to get going on it before breakfast.

'I hoped I might see you here,' he said. 'Have a chance to catch up.'

'Next year, perhaps?'

Jack looked a little disappointed, but even before I got to the door, I could see that he was surrounded by girls very eager for his attention. He was so good-looking. If he'd just been born a decade earlier . . .

46

With just a week left until Christmas, I still had lots of shopping to do. Previously, in a tradition that had started when we were teenagers, Becky and I would always do our Christmas shopping together. Prior to the wedding and my spectacular fall from grace, it had been just about the only tradition from her single life that Becky had clung to. She'd told me that she would always need my friendship because Henry just didn't *get* shopping for pleasure. It was simply impossible to get anything done with him in tow.

'He just clutters up the shops like an oversized Labrador in a Barbour jacket, and he has no opinion on anything!'

I could well imagine Henry's terrified face when Becky asked his view on a dress broadly identical to five she already owned. There were some questions you just shouldn't ask a man.

Becky and I always had such a good time together when we hit the stores. We'd make an event of it, having lunch somewhere really fabulous and finishing the day with a cocktail at the bar on the top floor of Harvey Nics. I was flooded with shame when I thought about those good times now.

Becky had been my best friend since childhood, and in truth she had never shirked that role. What I had taken to be insensitivity on her part after Michael dumped me was actually her way of trying to save me from myself with tough love. She'd tried to be kind, but nothing had worked.

And I had repaid her by icing a very nasty sentiment on her wedding cake. Her wedding cake!

I had behaved more despicably than the wicked fairy at Sleeping Beauty's christening.

Since the Purple Phones ad had put my life back on track, I'd been thinking more and more frequently that it was time I did something to make amends with my most important friend and ally, but I had let our estrangement go on for so long. A simple email or a phone call would not do after all this time. I suspected that even a handwritten letter might remain unopened. I would need to deliver this apology in person. And with a very special gift.

That was why I had to be up early after Lucas's party. I dug out the recipe I had used to make Becky's wedding cake and first thing in the morning I found myself in the queue at Waitrose with all the ingredients I would need to make another, slightly smaller version. I started cooking the moment I got home. I could hardly wait for the thing to rise. I paced the kitchen anxiously, willing the cake to be perfect. While I waited for the cake to be cool enough to start icing, I made a pair of tiny people out of marzipan. New models of Becky and Henry.

Decorating the cake went without a hitch. The icing was wonderfully flat. The little people had come out beautifully. But delivering the cake was a different proposition. How and when was I going to do that? I knew it had to be in person.

I called ahead to make sure that they were in, but I dialled 141 before calling to make sure my number didn't appear on the phone screen and I didn't say anything when Henry picked up the phone. I imagined him complaining to Becky that it was another nuisance call from British Gas, but I had what I wanted: the knowledge they were at home.

I parked my car at the end of the street. I assembled the

cake in the boot and almost lost the top two layers as I tried to lift it out by myself. I had to ask a passing hoodie to help me in the end.

When Henry opened the door, he looked somewhat shocked – as well he might be to see his wife's estranged friend, a wedding cake and a hoodie on his front step at eight in the evening.

'Is Becky in?' I called from behind the cake.

'Is that Ashleigh?'

'It is,' I said. 'And this is . . .'

'Clyde,' the hoodie made his own introductions.

'I'll get her,' said Henry.

I gave Clyde an apologetic smile. I had rather hoped that Henry would let us straight in so that we could put the cake down and Clyde could go back to doing whatever it was he had expected to be doing that evening. I imagined that helping me to deliver a wedding cake was rather cramping his style, but he said he didn't mind.

Becky came to the door. She had her hair wrapped in a towel turban and was wearing a dressing gown.

'Have I come at a bad time?' I asked.

'I don't think there will ever be a good time,' she told me. 'Not after what you did.'

'I've come to make amends for that. With this cake.'

'Nice touch.' She raised her eyebrows.

'Can I come in?' I asked. 'Only Clyde here is supposed to be on his way to meet his girlfriend.'

Becky frowned but gave in. Clyde dutifully wiped his feet as we shuffled into the hallway with the cake.

'Put it there,' said Becky, pointing at the table where Henry threw his bobble hat on his way in from work.

'Thanks, Clyde.' I went to find him a quid or something but he said it was Christmas and it was his pleasure and skipped away.

Becky still looked angry. When she wanted to, she could find an expression that would silence forty teenagers at once. No wonder Clyde didn't want to hang around.

'What is this supposed to be?'

Becky looked at the cake as though it were made out of dog mess and dusted with chalk.

'It's a new wedding cake,' I told her.

'I can see that.'

'I made it . . . I made it because I was wrong. And I'm glad about that. Take a proper look.'

Becky leaned in close. 'I dread to think what surprise you have in store for me this time.'

She need not have worried. Where I had iced 'I give it six months' on to the cake that I made for her wedding, I had written something that I hoped might go some way to making up for it.

'Here's to the next six months,' I had iced. 'And the next and the next and the next.'

'It refers to the fact that I was wrong about you not lasting six months.'

'I know what it refers to.'

I sensed no thaw but still I persisted. 'And to the fact that it's your six-month anniversary today.'

'Is it?' Becky looked surprised.

'Yes. Twelfth of December.'

'Oh my God,' said Becky. 'So it is. Twelfth of June. Twelfth of December! Henry!' she yelled back towards the kitchen. 'Do you realise that we've been married for six months today? What on earth are we doing staying in and having a Chinese takeaway? I can't believe you didn't remember!'

'You forgot too,' said Henry.

'Well, what do you expect!' said Becky. 'Some of us have been very busy at work this week.'

I took a step backwards. It seemed like there might be a

domestic. But when Henry dared poke his head into the corridor, Becky threw her arms round his neck and kissed him soundly.

'Happy six-month anniversary, sweetheart.'

Domestic averted.

'And to you, my little honey bunny.'

They started getting soppy, indulging in the kind of behaviour that might have prompted me to say, 'Get a room,' were I not still asking for forgiveness.

'I should go,' I said, when they still hadn't stopped kissing after what seemed like a full five minutes.

'No, don't.' Becky broke away from Henry at last. She put her hand on my arm and I saw that the softness that had come over her face while she embraced her husband stayed in place for me. 'Stay and have some Chinese with us. I'm sure Henry's over-ordered like he always does.'

'I never over-order,' said Henry.

'You always do,' his wife replied. 'But we'll get through it together. And then we can have some of this. Henry, look, Ashleigh has made us a cake for our six-month anniversary.'

'I've got some marzipan holly leaves in the back of my car,' I added. 'So you could change the decoration on the bottom tier and have it for Christmas too.'

'Brilliant idea,' said Becky. 'Because God knows I don't have time to cook and somehow we've ended up with all of Henry's family and mine coming here for Christmas lunch. They seem to think that it's our turn! As if being married has somehow magically imbued me with the ability to cook a three-course meal for twelve . . . Will you tell me how to do a turkey?'

I assured her that it was really very easy.

Henry carried the cake into the kitchen and found another plate, while Becky poured me a glass of champagne from a bottle left over from the wedding that had been in the fridge ever since. Then the guy from the Chinese takeaway arrived, carrying enough noodles to sink a junk. Becky was right. Henry had over-ordered, even now there were three of us to get through it.

After we'd toasted Henry and Becky's half-anniversary and broken into the cake, Henry tactfully left Becky and I alone in the kitchen again, claiming that he needed to get back to his computer.

'I think he's doing his Christmas shopping online,' Becky whispered. 'It'll never arrive in time.'

'He might be lucky,' I said.

'I'm just praying he found my wishlist at Net-à-Porter. He got me the most frightful bag-shaped dress you have ever seen from L.K.Bennett for my birthday. I told him that we'd have to have a family before I could start dressing like the mother of the bride.'

I laughed. Becky poured me some more champagne, and then she poured herself some more too, which made me raise my eyebrows in surprise. After all, the last time I'd really spent any time with her – not including her hen night – she'd been on the wedding-dress diet, which precluded all alcohol. All fun, if she was honest. Which she was.

'I can let it all hang out now I'm married,' she said, as she clocked the amusement on my face.

'I have missed you,' I told her.

'I have missed you too,' said Becky. 'I have thought about calling you up a hundred times but . . . Well, if I'm honest I decided there was no point. It was clear you just hated me. Why else would you have done what you did?'

'I think I might have been out of my mind,' I said. 'Looking back now, I really do think I wasn't quite in control of myself back then. I honestly thought that what I did was justified. I thought that everyone was laughing at me. I had to walk down the aisle in front of all those snooty women from the hen night. I'd just had a lecture from your mum. I didn't think anyone was taking me seriously. They were all belittling my pain. Now I know how hard everyone tried to support me by telling me I had to let Michael go.'

Becky nodded. 'You weren't the only one who was a bit unhinged. It wasn't until a month or so after the wedding that Henry pointed out to me just how crazed I'd been throughout all the preparations. A real Bridezilla. It was when we were lying in bed one Sunday morning, reading the papers like we used to when we first got together. Henry turned to me and said, "This is really wonderful. A Sunday all to ourselves again. No wedding fairs. No wedding planning. No bloody wedding diet. And at last I've got back the woman that I wanted to marry in the first place." Of course, I tore a few strips off him for implying that I'd been a nightmare, but I knew that he was right. I was so wrapped up in the whole thing I was even neglecting my fiancé.'

'It was a big event,' I reminded her.

'Yes. But not even having a wedding to plan should have kept me from being a better friend to you, instead of getting impatient and hurrying you on with your recovery so that I had one less thing to think about in the run-up to the wedding. We've been really silly, haven't we? Letting it go on for this long.'

I agreed.

'Let's promise never to fall out like that again. You and I have been friends since we were children. It doesn't matter what happens between us; nothing is so dreadful that our friendship won't be able to weather it.'

'I'll drink to that,' I said.

Becky stood up and held out her arms to me. 'Come here.' She gave me a hug.

After that we did something we hadn't done since we were in our early teens. We joined hands and chanted, 'Make friends, make friends, never, never break friends. If you do, you'll catch the flu and that will be the end of you!'

'Are you girls all right?' shouted Henry, hearing the noisy hilarity from the living room.

'Never better,' I said.

'Best friends for ever,' said Becky. 'And I don't mean that in a Paris Hilton kind of way.'

47

I slept really well that night. I think I had underestimated how much it bothered me to be estranged from my best friend. I had forgotten just how nice it was to spend time with someone who knew me that well. We soon slipped back into that comfortable way old friends have with one another. But it wasn't just reconciling with Becky that made me feel better that week.

The following day I was in Starbucks buying a special festive gingerbread latte for my elevenses when it struck me. The thought popped into my mind that Michael loved a gingerbread latte from Starbucks. But that wasn't the remarkable thing. The remarkable thing was that it was the first time I had thought about Michael that day, and it was eleven o'clock. He genuinely had not crossed my mind all morning.

It was like having practised yoga for years and discovering, all of a sudden, that you can go straight from up-dog to down-dog without having to rest your tummy on the floor like a basset hound. It was a small achievement but a significant one. The barista handed me my change. I dropped a pound into the tip jar and wished the barista a very merry Christmas indeed. I practically skipped out of the coffee shop, and, as I did so, I caught the eye of a very attractive man, who stepped to one side and held the door for me with a smile. When I looked back, he was very definitely checking me out! That hadn't happened in ages. In mourning for Michael I had become all but invisible to the opposite sex. Something must have shifted.

I was finally on the road to recovery. When I called Becky to let her know, she agreed.

'Thank God,' she added. 'And you see,' she said, referring to the chap who had held the door, 'now that door has finally closed, another one will open!'

Michael was on his way out of my head at last. It seemed like the best Christmas present ever.

That evening I went to Maximal Media's Christmas dinner, which was being held at a very swanky venue indeed. It was quite different from the previous year, when Barry took us all to the pub for lunch in anticipation of being hammered by the economic downturn that was preoccupying most of the world. Contrary to Barry's expectations the previous December, Maximal Media had sailed through the year. Its fabulous results were in no small part due to me, my brother and Mini-Michael. It was a fact that Barry recognised when he toasted us all.

'You know,' said Ellie, 'I don't think you'll believe it but I always looked up to you. I was in awe of your creativity.'

'There's no need to suck up to me now,' I told her.

'I'm not. I wouldn't have worked for you at all if I didn't think you were someone I could learn from.' I knew, coming from Ellie, that this was no small praise indeed. 'I'm glad you're back,' she said.

Then it was Christmas. From having dreaded every bank holiday, birthday or anniversary that loomed up on me that year, I could honestly say I was looking forward to it. My first Christmas without Michael. Bring it on!

Not only was it my first Christmas without Michael since he crashed into my life, that year for the first time ever I was going to host Christmas dinner at my house. My parents were astonished to get the invitation. Lucas asked if he could bring a new girlfriend. I told him I'd be delighted. I also invited Auntie Joyce and asked her to bring me some more wool so that I could help her out with her latest knitted-critter commission. She said that she would have loved to be there but she was having Christmas lunch with Frank Farmer, the feckless church caretaker who had two-timed her with her friend.

'Are you sure that's a good idea?' I asked.

'I'm only going along to torment him,' Auntie Joyce told me. 'I shall wear my best dress and refuse even to kiss him under the misletoe.'

'You go, girl,' I said.

Christmas Day was wonderful. I greeted my guests with bucks fizz and smoked-salmon canapés. I had even made some special canapés without soured cream for the new family dog, a big black spaniel who was the spitting image of dear Ben. Mum was determined, however, that this new dog, Bill, would not have Ben's weight problem. He was on a strict 'no-titbits' diet from the start. No matter that it was Christmas. No matter how sad his chocolate-brown eyes.

Lucas's new girlfriend, Chloe, was an instant hit, arriving as she did with a poinsettia for my mother and a bottle of champagne for me. As I peeled the Brussels sprouts, Mum sidled up to me and gave her verdict on her only son's new squeeze.

'No piercings,' she said. 'I'm happy with this one.'

Chloe gained even more kudos by popping her head round the kitchen door to ask if she could help in any way.

Lunch went brilliantly, with everyone asking for seconds. Mum told me that she had been thrilled to see how well I pulled it off, even if she did spend the whole day hovering by the kitchen door telling me that every ingredient I pulled out of the refrigerator would give my father heartburn.

The only slightly cringe-worthy moment was when Lucas revealed that he had met Chloe through Jack Green, who was Chloe's brother.

'You know Jack, don't you?' Chloe said brightly.

'Biblically,' my brother quipped. I was grateful that Mum and Dad were concentrating on the Queen's speech.

'He's mentioned you,' Chloe revealed then. 'In a good way.'

'Don't start,' I warned my brother, as I caught him pulling a face. But I would be lying if I said that my mind didn't wander to the memory of Jack's eyes. His broad chest in that fluffy cashmere jumper. And the six-pack that was hidden beneath.

Anyway, I finally got rid of my guests at half past eleven. The clearing up wasn't quite done, but I was just glad to have my flat to myself again. I pottered around the kitchen, collecting up corks and cracker parts in a bin bag. Any leftover chocolates or nuts went straight into my mouth. On the television, a choir of angel-faced children sang 'Silent Night'. I joined in when I could, feeling utterly full of the Christmas spirit. I'd had a Christmas just like I always dreamed I could. A happy family. A triumphant roast and vegetables that weren't remotely school dinnerish in appearance or flavour. And a game of Monopoly that didn't end in tears.

It could not have been a more perfect day. Except . . .

'Beep, beep, beep, beep, beep . . .' My iPhone required my attention. I looked at the screen. There were five messages: Christmas wishes from friends and former colleagues. Who knew that Ellie had such a big heart! And there . . . I almost missed it. A text message from Michael Parker.

48

'Merry Christmas, Ashleigh!' it said. 'Hope you are having a warm and wonderful Noel. Michael.'

I stared at those thirteen words in astonishment. I had not heard a thing from Michael since I received that fateful letter threatening lawyers, and yet here he was wishing me a Merry Christmas. It was clear too, from the fact that the text contained my name – my whole name – that it wasn't a text he had sent to everyone in his contacts list. Even the fact that he still had my number in his phone was a source of no little amazement to me.

I read the text again and again and again, until I knew it by heart. That didn't take long. But finding the meaning in those thirteen small words would take much longer. Why had he texted me? Out of politeness? Out of habit? Out of loneliness?

My heart thumped, betraying my excitement. I sat down on the sofa, discovering as I did so what had become of Bill the dog's squeaky chicken toy. I threw the chicken to the floor and sank back into the cushions. I held my iPhone in two hands and read Michael's message one more time. Then I looked at the message status to find out when exactly he had sent it. According to the message log, he had sent the text at around nine o'clock that evening, when I was busy trying to wrestle Mayfair and the utilities from the evil clutches of my younger brother.

I got a little thrill from the thought that I had not read

Michael's text until almost three hours after he sent it. It was quite a change from the days I spent glued to my iPhone just in case Michael should deign to send me so much as a question mark.

But what to do about it now?

I suppose I should have deleted that text. After everything he had put me through, Michael Parker should have been the very last person on my Christmas list. But it wasn't long before I convinced myself that to respond was the better thing to do. Christmas is, after all, a time for love and forgiveness. The big thing to do would be to send Michael my very best wishes in return. And perhaps fondest regards for a happy New Year too. Yes, if I responded like that, he would see me at my very best: as an adult, respecting social niceties and showing that I was capable of wishing the best even for my worst enemy.

It took me almost an hour to craft my response.

'Merry Christmas to you too. I hope you're well. x'

That 'x' alone took half an hour to decide upon. Was it too affectionate to add a kiss to the end of my message? After all, prior to this text, our last exchange had been on the subject of restraining orders. In the end, I decided to leave the kiss in. I signed off all my texts with a kiss. Even the ones I sent to my smelly little brother. It didn't mean anything significant. It was merely friendly. Surely Michael would understand that. If I left the kiss off, however, it might look as though I was making a point.

Still, when I pressed 'send', I felt as though I was jumping into the abyss. Not just jumping in but making a swan dive with a triple somersault into certain oblivion. As soon as I sent that text, I wanted to claw it back. And of course it was the little kiss that bothered me most. I was convinced that with that 'x' I had nudged the first domino in a train of dominoes that would end only when the final tile fell on to a nuclear button.

I was an idiot. I had just blown my cover. I had responded. In all probability, that was what Michael had wanted from me. Just a little sign that I still thought about him so that he could go back to resting in Miss Well-Sprung's cleavage, safe in the knowledge that somewhere out there I was forever hoping and pining, waiting for his call.

I opened the text-message window again. I decided I had to type a second message, explaining that I had only written back to him because it was Christmas and it seemed like the right thing to do given the time of year. I would tell him I did not expect or want to hear from him again. I was over him and moving on with my life, which, I might hasten to add, was pretty damn near perfect without him. That would put him straight.

Before I was able to get that second message out (and in retrospect, thank goodness I wasn't), the screen on my iPhone changed to let me know that another message was coming through to me. It was another message from the man who had broken my heart.

'So glad to hear from you,' it said. 'Been wondering how you are.'

Well, what was I supposed to make of that? He had responded to me within minutes. And in such a warm way! My mind whirred with the implications.

First off, the speed of his response suggested that he was alone. Unless he did have company but had nipped off to the loo to read my text and answer it. Regardless, the speed also suggested that he thought it was important to respond to me quickly. And that he said he had been wondering how I was suggested he actually cared.

'I'm fine,' I texted back. Then I chanced a question. 'How are you?'

'I'm OK,' he wrote. 'Christmas with the parents. You know what it's like.'

I didn't know what it was like, since Michael had never taken me to meet his mum and dad, but I responded, 'I can guess. I actually hosted Christmas at my place,' I added. 'For my whole family.'

'Lucky people,' said Michael's next text. 'You always were a fabulous cook.'

Wow. My heart beat a little faster. Was that a compliment?

I was about to text my thanks for the praise when I hesitated. Perhaps it was time for me to stop responding. While I was ahead. That way, if nothing more came of this unexpected exchange, I could at least have the satisfaction of knowing that Michael had sent a text that went unanswered. Not me. It was a small thing, but I knew that it would help me stay happy. God knows I needed all the help I could get. I had enough self-awareness to realise that this was a dangerous moment. If I was a love addict, then these texts were the equivalent of a row of vodka shots to a recovering alcoholic. I put the iPhone down on the coffee table and waited for my good sense to return.

There were all sorts of reasons why I shouldn't have been corresponding with Michael. I reminded myself that Michael had not deigned to contact me in months. But if this conversation was going to continue, the very least he could do was pick up his phone and actually call me.

I stared at my mobile, willing it to ring.

It did. But not with a call. Another text.

'It's been really nice to hear from you,' said Michael's SMS. 'Perhaps you'd like to get together in the new year. Catch up properly.'

He had suggested a meeting! I could not believe my eyes. I managed to wait a whole fifteen minutes, pacing the kitchen all the while, before I texted him back. 'Sure. That would be nice. Call me in January.'

And that was it for the night.

I turned off my iPhone to be sure.

49

On Boxing Day I went to Becky and Henry's house. They had entertained both sets of parents and assorted step-parents on Christmas Day and had thus declared that Boxing Day was going to be the very antithesis of that formal family celebration. They had invited only me and Henry's best friend, Julian, to spend the day with them, doing nothing but eating, drinking and watching DVDs. I turned up at midday with two bottles of champagne and my legendary trifle.

I had been bouncing off the walls with excitement all morning. I couldn't wait to tell Becky about my late-night Christmas surprise. As I waited for the appointed moment for me to leave for Becky's house, I had been through my text exchange with Michael at least a hundred times, close-reading both his texts and my own, wondering how he would have reacted to each of my messages, hoping that my final message to him had been just cool enough to ensure that he would do as I had asked and call me as soon as the new year began. If not before. Please let it be before.

The minute it was politely possible to drag Becky off for a moment of girl talk, I did so. Henry and Julian were occupied in trying to set up the PlayStation Julian had brought with him. (Henry wasn't allowed one of his own.)

'I suppose that means we're not going to get to watch my boxed set of *Lipstick Jungle*,' Becky sighed.

I didn't care. I didn't want to watch anything. I had much

more interesting things to do. I wanted to dissect my exchange with Michael with a third party. I needed a fresh opinion. I showed Becky the 'conversation' on the screen of my iPhone.

When she had finished reading, she looked up at me. Her eyebrows were knitted together in an expression that I recognised, though I hadn't seen it on Becky's face before. It was the expression my mother's face took on when she thought my brother or I were about to do something that worried her. Like take a sky-dive. Or inject heroin. Becky passed the iPhone back to me. She smiled wanly.

'It's incredible,' I chattered. 'I didn't think I'd ever hear from him again. But this must mean that he's been thinking of me. He must have broken up with Miss Well-Sprung, don't you think? He wouldn't have got in touch with me if they were still together. I'm pretty sure of that. Not on Christmas Day. He's not that kind of guy.'

How quickly I had forgotten exactly what kind of guy he really was.

Becky stopped me mid-flow by putting her hand on mine and pressing it gently towards the table so that I couldn't look at the screen of my iPhone, where Michael's words still flickered. She waited until my eyes were on hers and she was sure she had my full attention. It was a trick she must have used a thousand times on the children at her school.

'Ashleigh, please tell me that you're not going to take him up on his offer of meeting up.'

'But . . . why shouldn't I?'

'Where do you want me to start? You should not be seeing that man. You should not have been answering his texts. You should not even have been *reading* his texts. You should have deleted them unread. Michael broke your heart, Ashleigh, and you've spent the best part of a year acting like a headcase as a result. You lost your job: you lost your flat: you almost lost your best friend. And then he texts you and you agree to meet up with him. For goodness' sake, where's the sense in that?'

I murmured something about time and distance and closure and whatnot.

'You got closure. When he went off with that other girl. You were getting over it. Remember how happy you were last week? What offends me most,' she added, 'is that it's not as though he even called you. He didn't actually pick up the phone.'

'He must have picked up the phone,' I pointed out. 'He texted. You have to pick up the phone to text.'

'He texted! How much effort do you think that involved? Can't you see what's wrong about that? It's the most passive form of communication available. It took no effort what-soever and involved absolutely no risk. He didn't even bother to talk to you. He just sent you a text asking if you fancied meeting up and you agreed. If I had received a text like that, I wouldn't be in the least bit flattered. I would be less impressed than if he hadn't bothered to get in touch at all. At least his continued silence would have suggested consistency.'

'But he's reaching out,' I suggested.

'For heaven's sake!' Becky growled with disappointment. 'If he were really serious about making amends for being such a grade-one arsehole, he would have actually dialled your number and held the phone to the side of his head and talked to you. He would have risked hearing that you were angry with him. He would have taken the time to find out how you are and perhaps even to say sorry for having let you overlap with Miss Well-Sprung.'

'Perhaps he plans to say that when he sees me. Face to face.'

'If you see him,' said Becky, 'I will never speak to you again.'

'But I thought you said that nothing would ever stop us from speaking to each other again,' I reminded her.

Becky rolled her eyes. 'Don't do it,' she said in a whisper. 'For the sake of your mental health, Ashleigh. Please.'

Out of respect for Becky's opinion, I didn't mention Michael's texts for the rest of the day, but even while I got stuck into some game on the PlayStation, I still had one eye on my iPhone, which I had switched to silent out of politeness. Every five minutes or so I picked it up and shook it, to check that it was still working. Just in case someone was trying to get through.

But Michael didn't text me again. Not that day. Or the next. Or the next. Or at any time during the following week.

I saw in the new year at my brother's flat. I had expected it to be a fairly raucous affair, fuelled by Special Brew, but his new girlfriend was having quite the civilising effect on him. With Chloe in charge, the party food had been upgraded from Twiglets and Pringles to sausage rolls and fish goujons. All from Marks & Spencer.

I suppose I shouldn't have been surprised that Jack was there, seeing as Chloe was his sister. He was wearing another cuddly jumper. Navy blue this time.

'Is this one pure cashmere?' he asked me, holding out his sleeve for inspection.

'I think there might be a hint of silk in there,' I told him.

'How do girls know these things?' Jack was amazed.

I didn't tell him that the label was sticking out at the back of his neck.

Chloe, who was very much getting into the role of hostess, insisted on a game of Trivial Pursuit. An ironic game, Lucas pointed out quickly. In which we would have to drink every time we got an answer wrong.

Jack asked if he could be on my team. We got just one answer wrong. I was impressed by Jack's general knowledge.

'I loved to read as a kid,' he said. 'Still do.'

'But it does mean we're a long way off being as drunk as the others,' I pointed out.

'And you're especially pretty when you're tipsy,' said Jack.

'Winners have to finish whatever's in their glass in one go,' Lucas announced then. I'd already knocked back half a glass of chardonnay in a nervous reaction to Jack's compliment.

When the game was over, Jack stuck close beside me. He talked about his favourite books, all of which I felt I should have read, none of which I had. He told me about his gap year spent building a school in Rwanda.

'It just seemed important to give something back.'

He surprised me at every turn.

'Have you ever seen *La Bohème*?' he asked.

Had I hell . . . It was Jack's favourite opera. He had sung in a cathedral choir as a child. There was no doubt that my first impression of him had been very wrong indeed. As midnight drew near, however, I made an excuse to break off our conversation and headed for the bathroom. While the rest of the party counted down the last few seconds of the year, I was sitting on the edge of the bath, with my iPhone in my hand, willing that screen to illuminate with news from the person I really wanted to see in the new year with.

But midnight came and went and there was no message.

I couldn't quite believe it. I would have put money on getting a text from Michael on New Year's Eve. Wasn't it an obvious excuse for an SMS? Best wishes for the new year? I tried not to be disappointed when none came. Had I been a little more perceptive, I might have seen that it was annoying to think that, had Michael not sent me his Christmas wishes, I wouldn't even have expected to hear from him at New Year. I should have been angry with myself for having allowed that Christmas exchange to fill me with new expectations just waiting to be dashed. Those expectations had ruined my evening.

'What happened to you at midnight?' Jack asked when he found me. 'I was hoping for a kiss.'

I gave him a glancing peck on the cheek.

'Maybe I'll get a better one next year,' he said.

It wasn't until the 3rd of January that I finally got the text I had been waiting for. And what a text it was.

'Are you still up for getting together one evening?'

I waited ten minutes before texting back, 'Yes.'

'Great. How about next Wednesday night?' Michael wrote. 'I'll cook.'

'At your place?'

'Of course at my place. Do you remember where it is?'

'Has he mentioned Miss Well-Sprung yet?' Becky asked. 'At the very best I imagine he's texting you because she's realised what a no-hoper he is and she's dumped him.'

'He didn't mention her so I'm guessing that she has gone, yes,' I said.

'Don't guess,' said Becky. 'Ask. Most men are natural estate agents at heart. If you don't ask them what the problems are, they certainly won't volunteer them. Though I would put money on the reason behind Malevolent Michael's reappearance being that he isn't getting laid.'

I smiled.

'You shouldn't be so happy about it!' Becky lectured me. 'You don't want a man who only wants you because he's not having sex with anyone else. You want a man who wants to be with you above everybody. Not as a last resort.'

'Perhaps that's not what is going on. Perhaps he's dumped Miss Well-Sprung because he realises that it's me he wants to be with after all.'

'Don't you think that momentous epiphany might have been worth an actual phone call?'

'Perhaps he wants to tell me face to face.'

'In which case, don't you think he might have wanted to see you a little more urgently?'

'Everyone is busy between Christmas and New Year,' I suggested lamely.

Becky put her head in her hands. 'You shouldn't go,' she said, 'but I know that it doesn't matter what I say. You're going to meet up with him and you'll almost certainly offer him one more chance to break your heart while you're at it.'

'I won't,' I promised her.

'Whatever you do,' said Becky, 'make sure that he pays for dinner and you do not sleep with him. Make sure he takes you to a *really* nice restaurant and make sure you take a cab home, alone, straight after dessert. You can have the most expensive dessert on the menu because he's picking up the bill. But do not get drunk. Don't take the risk. No sex. Promise me, Ashleigh, that even if he begs you, you will not get naked with him. Even if he tears great clumps of his own hair out with frustration, you will not sleep with that man.'

'I promise,' I said. 'I will make sure he takes me some-where great, that he pays for dinner and that he doesn't get laid as a result.' Thank God I hadn't told her that Michael had already suggested his house as the venue for our long-awaited reunion. Becky would not be impressed by that. 'But you must understand why I have to do this. There are so many questions.'

'But there's really only one answer,' said Becky. 'He dumped you on Facebook. He didn't love you, Ashleigh. That truly is the bottom line.'

50

Despite the fact that Michael had suggested – and I had agreed – that we meet at his house, an option which required close to zero sartorial effort, I'm sure you won't be surprised that I spent the greater part of the following day in a beauty salon, prepping myself with the kind of care and attention I would ordinarily reserve for a black-tie event. Or, I imagined, for my own wedding.

'There's no need for you to get your bikini line done,' Becky reminded me when we spoke on the phone at lunchtime, 'because you're not sleeping with him, remember?'

'I remember,' I said. Though, of course, a bikini wax was the very first treatment I had subjected myself to that morning. I told myself that it had nothing whatsoever to do with meeting Michael. It was purely a matter of essential upkeep. I might decide to go swimming, for example. The fact that I hadn't been swimming in about eight years was neither here nor there. Why shouldn't I be grabbed by the urge to throw myself into the local lido and bob among the verucca plasters at any moment?

I was getting very good at making excuses for myself, even to myself, wasn't I?

Anyway, even though I say it myself, I looked the best I ever had as I walked out of that salon. My newly coiffed hair bounced and gleamed. My freshly exfoliated skin glowed as though I had just come back from a holiday in the Maldives. My nails were impeccably polished. I felt lighter and lovelier than a girl in a shampoo ad. If Michael was ever going to fall in love with me again (you'll note I was still assuming that he had been in love with me before), it would be that evening. I was in full bloom.

I arrived at Michael's apartment at eight o'clock on the dot. I was wearing a chic knitted dress and knee-high boots with impressive heels. I was working it. I had even received a whistle from the taxi driver who dropped me off outside River Heights.

Michael was wearing a pair of ratty old jeans and a sweatshirt.

'Oh,' he said, when he saw me and clocked that I had come empty-handed. 'I was rather hoping you might have picked up a bottle of wine from the off-licence on your way over. I haven't got anything in the flat.'

Was that it? Eight months since we had last seen each other. No big hug. No comment on how lovely I looked. Not even a 'So good to see you.'

'Wait there,' Michael said. He nipped back into the house to pick up a jacket. 'We've got to have something to drink.'

So we walked to the off-licence, which was somewhat difficult in my glamorous new boots. Still . . .

'I'm glad you could come over tonight,' he said as we walked. 'I'm snowed under at work so I wanted to be able to stay at my laptop until the very last minute.'

'Oh,' I said. And there was me thinking that his cooking for me was supposed to imply that he wanted to make an effort.

'How have you been?' he asked.

'I've been fine,' I said.

'You look well,' he commented. At last he had noticed.

'Thanks,' I said, fluffing my hair.

'Have you got nail varnish on?'

I looked at my nails as though I were surprised to find them so pink and pearly.

'You never wear nail varnish,' he said.

'These days I do,' I replied.

'Oh.' Michael widened his eyes. I felt a small ripple of pride. I had obviously wrong-footed him with my new well-groomed self. The fact that ninety-nine days out of a hundred I didn't look anything like this at all was not relevant. I had wanted Michael to think that I had raised my game since he chucked me and I allowed myself to think that he believed I had.

'Well, it looks nice,' he said. 'Ladylike.'

We were at the off-licence. He held the door open for me.

'Usual?' he said.

'OK.'

Our usual was a bottle of Montepulciano d'Abruzzo, the rough southern Italian red that went fantastically well with takeaway anything. That wine was cheap as chips but I took it as a good sign that he asked me if I wanted our 'usual' rather than push out the boat with something flashy and more expensive. It seemed nostalgic and that suggested to me that he had been remembering me with fondness, rather than as the mad cow he had threatened with legal action.

'Shall we go halves?' I asked, as he placed three bottles on the counter.

'No,' he said. 'Don't be silly. I'll pay.'

Sure, the wine was only £4.59 a bottle, but I took that as a good sign too. He was treating me.

Back at his place, we ordered takeaway from the local Indian, though he didn't order his usual.

'Watching my weight,' he said, patting his stomach.

He was a little paunchier than I remembered. He had always been paranoid about getting 'man boobs'. I must have spent a good five hours of my life reassuring Michael that he didn't have tits. Never would have. And since the break-up, I had spent a good deal more time fantasising that when I saw him again, I would tell him that I had been lying. He had a better cleavage than Eva Herzigova. But when he gave me the opportunity to tell him what a fat, middle-aged knacker he had become, I just told him, 'You don't need to worry about your weight. You look in great shape.'

'Well, I'm still going to the gym,' he said. 'Got to keep in shape.'

'I've been going too,' I responded. 'Pilates mostly.'

'I hear that's really good if you suffer from back pain.'

'It is,' I confirmed.

'I get terrible backache sitting at my desk all day,' he muttered.

'How's work?' I asked.

'Oh, you know,' said Michael. 'Work's work. Things have been busy because the government keeps changing the law to claw back some of the money they wasted bailing out the banks. It's making the firm a small fortune as we try to prevent them from robbing our clients.'

'Sounds exciting,' I said. Not really.

How odd that I had spent the last eight months having arguments with this man in my head and now we were having such a bland and pleasant conversation. I had waited for so long for the opportunity to tell him what an arsehole he had been and now I was listening sympathetically as he told me about some new bloke at work who seemed determined to kill all Michael's pet projects.

Meanwhile the first bottle of wine slowly disappeared. And then the second. And a little bit of a third.

By this point we were sitting side by side on the sofa. Michael had positioned himself there as we ate the Indian takeaway on his glass coffee table and came back to sit beside me again after clearing the leftovers away. Slowly we had moved closer and closer together so that from time to time our knees touched before one of us noticed and moved to preserve a physical gap. Now Michael reached out and gathered my hair in his hand, as though he were making a ponytail. He tugged at it gently, playfully. I pushed his hand away.

'I'm sorry,' he said. 'I just had the urge to touch it. Your hair looks great. It's so silky.'

'Thanks,' I said, managing to sit on the urge to say, 'I just had it done.'

'You always had great hair.'

'You're very kind.'

Thank God he hadn't seen me before my hairdresser fixed the brown mess.

'And I'd forgotten just how pretty your eyes are. Such a lovely colour. And such long eyelashes. Really beautiful.'

He looked deep into my eyes. I began to feel hot. In that moment I was every bit as nervous as I had been the very first time Michael and I went on a date, after I had stopped worrying what my friends would think if I dated an accountant and I started simply wanting him to kiss me. He moved a little closer. Was he going to kiss me now?

'Such a pretty mouth.'

He was.

The blood rushed to my face as Michael squashed his lips against mine. I didn't resist. I threw my arms round his neck and kissed him back with gusto. This was it! This was the moment I had been waiting for! He wanted me again.

It wasn't long before we had moved from the sofa to the bedroom, casting off our clothes as we went. Though even in the heat of passion I managed to cast an eye around the bedroom in search of anything that had changed. There were no new pictures. No photo of Miss Well-Sprung on the bedside table! The bed linen looked familiar. Even the Diptyque candle on the dressing table seemed to have remained burned to the same level. It was as though I had been away from Michael's bedroom for a couple of nights rather than eight long months.

The sex, too, was exactly as it had always been. We whipped through our repertoire with the efficiency that comes of years of practice. He smelled the same. He felt the same. He said the same things at the same moments. Everything was as it had been. As it should be.

I was elated.

Well, perhaps not quite so elated as I had expected to be, if I was entirely honest . . . There were even moments when I felt as though I was outside my body, watching the action on the bed with a dispassionate and underwhelmed eye. I got nowhere near having an orgasm.

'That was great,' Michael said, as we relaxed back on to the pillows.

'Yes,' I said. It wouldn't have been polite to disagree, but I was left feeling just a little unsatisfied. As I always had been, now I thought about it.

'I've just got to . . .' Michael nodded his head towards the bathroom '. . . clean my teeth. Make yourself comfortable.'

He obviously thought I was staying the night.

Was I?

While Michael cleaned his teeth, I took the opportunity to examine my surroundings more thoroughly. Sure, there were no new pictures, but now that I had a chance to breathe deeply, I noticed that the sheets didn't smell the same. Had he changed his washing powder? There was a distinct floral scent to my pillow. And on the bottom shelf of the bedside stand I noticed a half-used tube of handcream. Michael had definitely become more vain over the time that I'd known him, but had he really suddenly started taking care of his cuticles? I picked up the handcream. Calendula-scented. Not the kind of thing a man would buy at all.

Michael was taking a long time in the bathroom. I could hear the tap running. But over that . . . Was he talking to someone? I crossed over to the bathroom door on the pretence of looking for my knickers, which I'd discarded in that direction. With my cheek against the cool white wood, I tuned into Michael's voice over the sound of running water.

'Yeah, yeah,' he said. 'I miss you too. And of course I'll come and pick you up at the airport. I can't wait to see you. Of course I'm not still angry about that argument over Christmas. That's all in the past. Everything will be different when you come back from Rio. I promise it will. I love you.'

Rio? I love you? He was talking to Miss Well-Sprung of course.

51

When Michael ended his call, I sprinted back across the room and arranged myself on the bed exactly as I had been when he went to 'clean his teeth'. I heard him tweak the tap so that it wasn't flowing quite so quickly now that he didn't need to cover the sound of his conversation any more. And then he really did brush his teeth, with an electric toothbrush. It was another three minutes or so before he emerged from the bathroom looking fresh and perfectly innocent.

'That's a great view,' he said, regarding me naked against the pillows. I noticed he was still holding his BlackBerry. He waved it at me. 'I'm a slave to this thing,' he said. 'Can you believe someone from the office just called to ask me if I can be at a meeting at seven thirty tomorrow morning?'

I couldn't believe it. Did Michael say, 'I love you,' to all his colleagues?

Still, there was no further explanation. Michael got into bed beside me, placing the now silent BlackBerry on his bedside table with all due reverence. He snuggled into my side and kissed the back of my neck.

'Right, I've got to get some sleep,' he said. 'Early start tomorrow.'

'OK,' I agreed.

I wouldn't be able to sleep, of course. My mind was racing. There was so much that needed to be said to the little toad who snuggled against my side and was apparently intent on sleeping the sleep of the innocent, having bedded me and then assured his girlfriend that he would still make it to the airport to meet her flight. Perhaps I should have shaken him awake and told him there and then that I knew what was going on and he was a bigger shit than I had ever imagined if he thought that was an appropriate way to behave. Perhaps I should have just left, but instead I lay there, with his arm across my stomach, berating myself for being such an idiot. How could I have been so naïve to think that Michael Parker wanted me back?

After a while, with Michael deep in his dreams, his arm started to feel very heavy on me. I lifted it off my stomach and out of the way, carefully but not that carefully. Part of me wanted to wake him. But Michael was not disturbed at all. He remained asleep on his front. The only sign that he was alive was the occasional snore. Michael was one of very few people who snored while sleeping on his front as well as his back.

I hated him in that moment. Sure, I had said that I hated him a thousand times since he dumped me for Miss Well-Sprung, but I had never truly felt the proper weight of the emotion before. Whatever anger I felt for him prior to that night would always have dissolved at the sight of his smile. Now I knew I was experiencing something much stronger. Something that demanded revenge.

I had to take action. But what could I do?

I pulled my iPhone out of my handbag and logged on to Facebook. I could send Miss Well-Sprung a message to let her know who was sharing her boyfriend's bed, but that seemed a little tacky. Likewise, simply posting a photo of Michael's naked buttocks was too easy, and it would have the added disadvantage of alerting my friends to the fact that I had gone against all advice and ended up in bed with the worthless swine. The last thing I wanted was a lecture from Becky to add to the intense feelings of anger

I already had for myself. I had been taken in by Michael Parker. Again. No one could have been angrier with me than I was.

It was then that my eyes drifted to Michael's buttocks, exposed to the world as he threw off the sheets. (He always got too hot.) If only I could tattoo, 'Arsehole,' right above his. Well, I couldn't. But I could do the next best thing.

'Please let me have it with me,' I muttered to myself as I rootled through my handbag. Triumph! I had not one but two indelible marker pens, pinched from the Maximal Media office. I knew that they really were indelible because Ellie had written 'Idiot' on her assistant Jamie's forehead after he forwarded a confidential and deeply unflattering email to a client. The word had not come off with simple soap and water and Jamie had threatened to sue. Until he got a pay-rise.

So, with that kind of permanence in mind, I uncapped the black pen and got to work on Michael's bottom. I didn't have to press hard, though I doubted that Michael would have stirred if I had been using a tattoo gun. He was sleeping so soundly that after I had written my little message once, I went back over it a second and third time to make sure the letters were nice and thick. It looked great.

'I was here,' was what it said. Simple but effective.

52

The following morning I excelled myself. Despite having lain awake all night, I jumped out of bed looking eager to greet the day. It was clear that Michael still had no clue whatsoever that I had heard his late-night conversation with Miss Well-Sprung. When he stood up, I saw that my message to her was still perfectly intact and unsmudged on his buttocks. Magnificent. He leaned over and kissed me on the forehead.

'I'd have breakfast with you,' he said, 'but I've got that meeting at seven thirty.'

'I remember. Where is it?' I asked. 'Maybe you could give me a lift home on your way.'

I had a feeling he wouldn't want to.

'Actually,' he said, 'a client from Hamburg is flying into Heathrow and I said I would meet him there. We're going to have a quick cup of coffee before he catches a flight on to the States. I would drop you off, but I'm cutting it fine as it is and obviously he won't have a lot of time before he needs to check in again.'

I nodded understandingly. 'Do you have time for a shower?' I asked, all coy.

Michael was already putting on a shirt and spraying his unwashed body with aftershave.

'No time at all,' he said.

'Pity.' As I watched him pull on a pair of boxer shorts, which covered up my well-placed words, it was hard to keep the smile off my face. Michael had no idea, and by the time he did realise it would be much too late. I imagined Michael scooping Miss Well-Sprung into his arms and rushing back to his place for a quick one. I imagined her ripping off his trousers and finding my welcome-home message. If only I could have been a fly on the wall. Though I could already imagine Michael's excuses. Perhaps he would tell her that he had spent the previous night out with the lads. An impromptu stag do. Or that one of the wags in the office had done it while he was dozing face down on his desk after a busy day. At the same time, though, I knew that even if Miss Well-Sprung said she believed his lies, the seeds of doubt would have been sown. That was good enough for me.

'So, when will I see you again?' I asked. 'Are you around later this week?'

'Actually,' said Michael, 'I've got a busy few days coming up. I think it's best if we leave things a bit . . . er . . . fluid for now.' It was exactly the sort of thing I had expected him to say.

'That's fine by me,' I replied, knowing that even if we had arranged a date, by lunchtime that day he would definitely want to break it. 'In that case, I suppose I had better get dressed too. You'll want me to leave when you do, I'm sure.'

'That would be easiest.' Michael nodded, but he looked a little disconcerted, I thought. Perhaps he hadn't expected me to be quite so easy to get rid of. Perhaps somewhere deep inside he worried that I was only so chilled out because I had something up my sleeve. Well, it was too late for him to find out that actually I had something down the back of his boxers.

'I'll shower at home,' I said, pulling on my dress. Suddenly I just wanted to be out of there.

Michael didn't argue. He kissed me goodbye at the door. I walked out of the complex by myself, an entirely different woman from the one who had skulked around outside River Heights in the middle of the night, before dropping an old sock full of voodoo rubbish into the sewage system. If the doorman recognised me as that weirdo, he didn't show it. He put his fingers to his cap in a mock salute as he opened the door for me.

'Nice boots,' he said.

Those boots were turning out to be a great investment.

I strode off in the direction of the Embankment and enjoyed a short walk in the freezing January sunshine to clear my head before I jumped on a bus and headed home.

53

Sitting at my kitchen table, with my hands wrapped around a big mug of tea and life slowly returning to my frozen fingers, I thought back over the previous evening. I replayed the moment when Michael put his hands in my hair and, later, the moment when he kissed me. I remembered his face as he sat back to see whether I was going to object. At the time I had interpreted his expression as sweet, but now I realised that it had been smug. He was so certain that he had me again.

The odd thing was that that kiss *had* left me strangely unmoved. The butterflies and fireworks that had accompanied our actual first kiss were sadly absent this time round. Likewise, when we made love, I hadn't felt transported. There had definitely been a moment when I had wished that he would just hurry up and finish. I had been faintly irritated rather than filled with joy by his extravagant gyrations.

Was it possible that I had gone off Michael physically?

If anyone had asked me the day before with whom I had had the best sex of my life, I would have had to say that it was Michael. That morning, however, I was beginning to reconsider Jack. Maybe, with a bit of practice, he could have turned into a fantastic lover. Certainly, he wouldn't have had to pause halfway through because he was getting a stitch.

I laughed out loud. Never before had I compared Michael against another man and found him wanting. I really was becoming immune to Michael's charms. And then there was the small matter of Miss Well-Sprung. When I first met Michael, he had seemed to me like a man I could trust. He had seemed to be an honest, straightforward type of guy, but he had cheated on me with Miss Well-Sprung and now he had cheated on her with me. Clearly it was becoming a habit.

It was a disappointment to find out that I had been wrong about Michael's moral character, but at last I could appreciate that it was far better to have found out what he was really like without having got him to the altar first. Sometimes the failure of your wishes to come true is the best thing that can happen. Michael Parker was nothing special. I definitely deserved more, and, as a matter of fact, so did his new girlfriend . . .

It's said that the aftermath of the average break-up has five stages. Denial comes first. I certainly went through that one, turning up at Michael's office with flowers and an offer of marriage. Then there's bargaining. Some people promise God they'll reform their lives for a second chance with a loved one. I paid a thousand pounds for a ridiculous voodoo curse. After that comes anger. It's a shame I turned the power of that particular stage on Becky. Then there's depression. Who wouldn't be depressed about having to move back in with their parents at the age of thirty-two? Now I had come to the final stage: acceptance.

Michael Parker was not my Mr Right. That was all there was to it. It wasn't my fault. And even if he had cheated on me, the fact that we weren't actually destined to be with each other wasn't really his fault either. It was just the way things had worked out. I'd been sad, I'd been angry, I'd been mad as a box of frogs, and now I was ready to be happy again.

* * *

Later that day I received a text message. It was from Jack.

'Hope u don't mind. Yr brother gave me yr number. I really would like to take u out.'

I couldn't help but smile. Jack was persistent. You had to say that for him. And maybe his luck was about to change.

I texted back, 'OK. Why not? Give me a call and let's sort something out.'

Jack phoned back at once, full of ideas for my entertainment. I told him I'd see him that evening. I'd wear my boots. Perhaps my luck was beginning to change as well.

October 2009

Dear Reader,

I hope you enjoy reading *Getting Over Mr Right* as much as I enjoyed writing it. As I put the finishing touches to the manuscript, I can't help reflecting on some of the dating disasters that inspired me to create Ashleigh Prince and her Mr Wrong. Yep, I've kissed more than my fair share of frogs and toads . . .

However, I recently became engaged to my own Mr Right, the lovely Mark. After a wonderful whirlwind romance, gorgeous, kind, generous Mark proposed to me on a balcony at the Hotel Belles Rives in Juan-les-Pins. His proposal took me by surprise but I didn't have to think long before I answered. My entire body was shaking with excitement as I told him 'yes.' Four weeks on, I still can't stop smiling.

So at last it happened. At thirty-seven years old, I got my happy ending. Trust me, I'm not going to take it for granted. Not when I got here the hard way! Anyway, over the course of my two-decade-long sojourn in dating hell, here are the things I wish I'd caught on to several years ago. If you're struggling with a heartache of your own right now, maybe some of these thoughts will help you get to your own happy ending a little sooner.

1. What do you want out of life? Ask yourself what you really want and allow yourself to go for it. If you want to travel the world and have a boy in every port, you'll find plenty of chaps keen to oblige you. But if you want a happy ever after that involves a long-term relationship and maybe marriage and children, admit that to yourself and promise you'll only take steps in that direction, which means turning down that date with your married boss, pulling the plug on the Internet romance that never gets to a face-to-face meeting, or breaking up with the guy who will only spend a Saturday night with you if all the boys have got swine flu. Only date *available* men. It's the most effective way to save yourself trouble.

2. If commitment is important to you, then it follows that when a man says he doesn't want a commitment you have to believe him. Really, you must. If the man you adore has ever uttered the words 'I'm not ready,' don't even think about waiting until he is. If he says 'I need some space,' you must give him some. Don't bother trying to change his mind. It's a fact of life that the more you try to persuade the average man of the sense of something, the harder he will resist it. He's given you a clear indication of his state of mind. If you walk away you will minimise the damage to your self-esteem. Don't worry about quitting too soon. If he decides he does want to be committed to you after all, he will definitely pick up the phone.

3. Learn what commitment looks like. Romance is not the same as commitment. He may have taken you on a romantic mini-break but, trust me, he probably wasn't thinking how nice it would be to go

back to that hotel for your wedding reception. It's easy to do romance without commitment. Commitment is in agreeing to go to your grandmother's eightieth birthday party or in asking you to meet his parents. It's in checking the pressure in your tyres before you head off on a journey and in making you a Lemsip when you're ill. It's in making plans beyond next weekend. As a handy rule of thumb, if you're nervous about raising the subject of Christmas then you are on to a loser. One chap I dated on and off for two years let me know his plans for Christmas three days before the big event, when he dumped me. My fiancé and I were talking Christmas trees in August.

4. If you're dating someone you think of as a 'stopgap' while you wait to meet someone better, then for goodness' sake throw him back into the dating pool! You may be hogging someone else's Mr Right. And while you're dating Mr Almost There, your own Mr Right may be holding back from approaching you because he's too decent to steal another guy's girl.

5. Pick the nice guy. Hormones play funny tricks on us. When you're not swinging from the chandeliers ask yourself: if I hadn't picked him as a lover, would I have him as a friend? Is he nice to waiters? Does he rev his engine impatiently when an old lady is crossing the road? He may be impressive on paper, but am I impressed by the way he treats his mum? Kind, loving and honest beats rich, handsome and drives a Porsche every time. Though kind, loving, honest, handsome *and* rich is just dandy.

All that remains is for me to say thank you to Hodder and Stoughton – especially Carolyn Mays and Francesca Best – for giving me the chance to share another story. And thank you to Mark Carroll for making me very happy indeed.

Happy endings do exist. You just have to let them happen.

Chrissie
x